'A meticulously researched gothic [...]
ghosts and murderous [...]
evokes the [...] and
creative [...]

Praise for *T[...]*

'McDowell's confident writing boasts smart dialogue and a lyrical style throughout.' SCOTTISH REVIEW OF BOOKS

'The end comes together beautifully, drawing together the well-written strands of the story in a sweet shot of emotion.' THE HERALD

'A meticulously constructed novel.' SCOTLAND ON SUNDAY

'The storytelling in *The Picnic* trips effortlessly across the generations… a clear grasp of her characters' voices.' THE SCOTSMAN

Praise for *Between the Sheets*

'Formidably well read… controversial and provocative.' THE INDEPENDENT

'McDowell… has read deeply and questioningly. She raises important questions about how sexual choice relates to any writer's work.' FINANCIAL TIMES

'McDowell takes an original tack in her book.' SUNDAY TIMES

'A terrific study.' THE HERALD

'A exciting and provocative new book.' SCOTTISH REVIEW OF BOOKS

'A scholarly but fascinating look.' PUBLISHERS WEEKLY

'McDowell has culled incredibly juicy details.' NEW YORK TIMES BOOK REVIEW

ALSO BY LESLEY McDOWELL

FICTION
The Picnic

NON-FICTION
Between the Sheets:
The Literary Liaisons of
Nine 20th-Century Women Writers

Unfashioned Creatures

Lesley McDowell

Saraband

Published by Saraband
Suite 202, 98 Woodlands Road
Glasgow, G3 6HB, Scotland
www.saraband.net

ISBN: 9781908643391
ebook: 9781908643438

Printed in the EU on sustainably sourced paper.

Text design: Laura Jones
Cover design: Chloe van Grieken

1 3 5 7 9 10 8 6 4 2

"I have now renewed my acquaintance with the friend of my girlish days – she has been ill a long time, even disturbed in her reason..."

Mary Shelley, letter to Leigh Hunt
September 11th, 1823

In the quiet of this place, my thoughts echo loud enough to make me mad and I tell them again: my name is Alexander Balfour. Whatever else anyone knows, that is my name. The Infection of Madness *by Alexander Balfour.* Insanity and the Sympathetic Fallacy *by Alexander Balfour. Once upon a time the world knew of my work, knew who I was! My place among the greats. George Man Burrows. John Perceval. William Willis Moseley. William Browne. And Conolly, of course.*

Every man needs his nemesis. But I do not exaggerate when I say that for a briefer time than I expected, I was more famous than any of them. I don't expect gratitude from this new generation, or from the latest find that Vienna or Berlin throws up. They'll each wither one day, too. I am only an insignificant mind-doctor from an age long past, but it was not always so. Where they still remember Cullen, they might have remembered Alexander Balfour. They should have remembered me!

They will not raise monuments to me now. I apologize for the poor quality of my chairs, this bed, these hangings. They take little care of me here: the size of my lodgings! How do I fit my life's work in a room the size of a closet? But old men like me are only fit for jokes. I am... the same age as the century. I never thought to witness the legacy of my work.

Ha: my legacy. Stevenson's travesty outsold everything else, I heard. All that children's scribbler knew of insanity was the transformation of good into evil. Jekyll and Hyde, indeed. The Viennese prodigy will not have his battles to seek. The public will care no more for hysteria in women than they did a hundred years ago. But his 'sex' theories will draw lurid enough pictures. I cannot complain: he has only gone where we have led him. Without us, he would be nothing.

But in leading him so, what have we done? I never sought the dominance of the asylum. Instead, I watched my cities cede their rightful place in history. Witnessed how a study of the mind is no longer worth investing in. Instead, we forget the elites and mix with the masses, rejoice in the latest discovery that comes in the shape of a 'detective': I hear Conan Doyle is a rich man. My Edinburgh, the seat of genius, no longer exists: it is a playground merely. Who cares for science when a murderous madman is roaming the pages of a good book, or a nervous bride is stabbing her husband? They want juice and blood, the screaming hordes. Sensation is all, not feeling. Yet feeling is the basis of all human activity. Sensibility and sympathy. Hume's sympathy. Man's ability to feel for others.

But what would I know about sympathy, she would say, when I was only in it for myself? Perhaps she was right. How easy to gaze back at great figures, make seamless narratives of men born to be great. But men born to fail make for seamlessness, too; we simply care less to hear their stories. Like my own undoing, the loss of the immortality I was promised: what she promised me with her lies. Misled as Adam was by Eve – and as all men have been by all women, ever since.

Alexander Balfour,
London 1895

PART ONE

London & Gheel

1

Richmond, September 1823

I couldn't have known what it was. Not that first time. I wasn't to blame, although I believed then that I was, and for a long while afterwards. The wood smashed him down onto stone, not me. The chair tipped and my basin clattered to the floor. Blood bubbled from his burst tongue, his irises rolled and dough splattered yellow and thick on the stone slabs.

He made my girls scream out in terror. But when he tells me now that he still loves my frown, says 'Bella' with a confused tenderness, I think perhaps I don't blame him, either. Then I remember that first time: my girls' father, made monstrous. His arms thrashing against my newly-scrubbed kitchen floor; his legs bucking at the toppled chair. I might have moved with the heaviness of a woman three times my age but it wasn't from fear, or reluctance to help. I had to consider, slowly, that was all. *Aid or flight.* Then came my rush forwards, a sliding on the dough. I sent a footstool flying, which just missed Izzy as she stood rattling at the doorknob and crying out to leave. But I wouldn't let her go. A demon had my husband. It might take hold of all of us.

I know demons well enough. When I was growing up in Broughty Ferry, we thought about them every Sunday. Kail Kirk to fill our bellies. Cold church walls protected us from the sea outside on bright, fierce days. The sea lured men from the town and some never came back. Drink called to them, too, on a Saturday night, when the taverns bulged. The sea and the drink were demons both, and only prayer and abstinence could save us. When I was young, I thought they were enough.

But prayer and abstinence can't defeat the demon inside my husband. The demon I put there myself, with my unwifely thoughts of leaving. I was relieved, that day four years ago, to meet it at last. And relief made me clumsy, hurt my girls: I pushed Izzy too hard at her sister, and she fell. I was trying to clear the way, that's all, to still his head, but he flattened my fingers, twisting this way and that. If I could have made a fist out of my crushed hand, I'd have struck him, but Izzy's wails called me back. The demon is no match for my girls.

My sister's silver tea urn crashed down, and her copper pans. There was no point trying to save her wedding china, or the mortar and pestle she brought back proudly from Pisa. Tiny, bloody darts splintered in his cheeks, and my fingers flicked at his face because I didn't know what to do. I know now, though, how much time I wasted. Telling my girls to stay, to run and fetch help, to stay after all. I waited for my instinct for escape to show me the way out, but it let me down just as it had once before. I sat beside him instead, as still as he was restless, as though by my stillness I could force him to be quiet.

When at last he was, it was little thanks to any action of mine. The demon left as suddenly as it had entered him and the shaking stopped. I took a deep breath and laid my palm on his chest, felt for the heartbeat I knew I wouldn't find.

* * *

I was wrong that day. Expectation is an ambiguous thing. What was I hoping for, as I pressed my hand to him? Perhaps I'll ask Mary later. Mary, whom I love better than a sister, has told the whole world about monsters. She has written about a yellow-skinned, yellow-eyed creature galvanized by an unseen power into mimicking the movements of a human being. What makes a monster, though? For all her cleverness and all that I love in her, Mary has never witnessed what I have: the monster a man becomes when reason deserts him and he thrashes about, insensible, on a stone floor.

She did see, though, what I wanted all those years ago.

The first time I thought about leaving him came just before his first fit, but his heart did not stop that day, and there have been many more fits like it since, so I know my wicked thoughts aren't to blame. Just the same, something is nipping at my neck now. *Make up your mind, Bella!* A spot there makes my worry real and red, and I rub it with fingernails bitten down to the skin, while he sups at his tea. On this quiet September morning I'm thinking only about Mary's visit and what it means after all this time.

'My lecture for the Society...' he announces, looking up from papers that are forever strewn around our dining table. His voice is unusually high and sharp, and the change should alert me. But I take another sip myself and wait for him to continue. When he says nothing, I ask obediently, 'It's progressing well?'

It isn't progressing well: the creases on his forehead that have deepened over the last few days should tell me so, and the strange air about him. But I'm too distracted by my own thoughts. 'My lecture for the Society...' he repeats, and then it's too late and he's on the floor, kicking out and gasping.

I swoop down on to the carpet in my cheap workday dress like a voluptuous grey swan and bolster his head and shoulders. My hips and thighs grip his back as tea spatters on my skirt. I fix on them while he shakes and shudders against me, and all the time I think, *once we might have been happy.*

That thought could bring tears but I've frozen my heart, warm it only with facts. His fits are more frequent and lasting longer. Ten days since the last one. What will Conolly have to say to that when he sees him? Will he still insist that I care for him at home? *You won't escape him now, Bella,* whispers the voice in my head and I swear I hear laughter.

'There, now,' I say over and over until he calms at last and I can pour him some water. He grunts, his eyes still closed. The next part is always trickiest: I must get up, reach round his chest, clasp my hands together and pull him as gently as possible from the floor. But he's taller than me and heavy, for all he's so thin. 'Careful,' I say, as his arm pins down my shoulder and he stumbles. 'Don't pull, let me hold you.' But he doesn't hear me and as we shuffle out of the dining room together I ask myself for the hundredth time what we have done to deserve this.

I may ask, but I know the answer. Our wedding day wasn't the bright one I'd hoped for. Drear and dreich, the consistency of shame, our Glassite detractors said, but I wouldn't show them I cared. My sister's cold fingers had trembled at my neck, her white velvet ribbon knotted too tight, to be unpicked and redone once she'd gone. My mother's amber thistle brooch glittered on my collar, flame-shaped and just as fiery, making me suck the breath in between my teeth as I pinned it. I held my head high, though, and didn't waver once. Christy had never hit me before and the justice of it still spread hot and sharp across my cheek a day later. And if I'd spent my last night in my father's house alone in my room, full of thoughts of what I'd done and was about to do, then that was just as my sister had intended.

Our father made the peace between us as always, though, wanting the world only to get along. The gift of white ribbon was her apology to me: my gift was to wear it but I didn't apologize. Father had thought it best not to bring Robbie home for a ceremony without friends, and not held in our church. 'No need for your brother to see it,' he said, as though he was ashamed. And yet he loved David as much as I did. I had enough defiance to match his shame: what need did I have, I said to him, for family or friends or a faith that wouldn't accept our love for one another?

David was standing on the town hall steps that day, shorter for being round-shouldered, but clever and commanding in his black coat: that's how I like to remember him. People bowled away from him that day like loose beads from snapped thread, but he acknowledged neither their fear nor their lack of manners. From the carriage I watched, made happiest when the wind blew open his coat and revealed new trousers, tucked into new boots. He wasn't a man whose thoughts ran to fashion: my distinguished husband-to-be, whom they all called 'Devil', had made a special effort. So when I stepped down and his fingers gripped mine, I cleaved easily to what those little people feared. My prize, won against so many odds.

I was too warm indoors in my wool coat and gloves, though, and sweat tickled my spine and dampened my dark curls as we stood in front of a nervous town clerk and spoke our vows. But before the heat could claim me completely, we were outside in the rain once more and back at my father's for the toast; a party of four, half of us gleeful, half of us troubled. Christy, tearful and forgiving after too much sherry, hugged me on the doorstep tightly and extracted promises that we'd see her soon.

Even the rain, pattering on the trunks and our hats, couldn't make me regretful. I had no presents, no good wishes from friends, but I had what I wanted. Over the Tay to Newburgh that evening we travelled lightly, with few words between us, our happiness felt rather than spoken. And yet, when we arrived, and I stepped across the threshold of my new home to see the portrait of Margaret still hanging in the hallway, I wondered for the first time if I'd done the right thing in marrying my dead sister's husband.

2

Gheel, Antwerp, September 1823

The miniature of a dark-haired young woman that he carried with him everywhere wasn't, as many often supposed, a portrait of any sweetheart of his. Without it, Alexander Balfour wouldn't have forgotten his mother. But he might have lost sight of her, and with that, his reason for coming to Gheel in the first place.

He hadn't much longer to go in this backwater of a town now though, and he allowed himself a small, bitter smile at the thought. Not too many more of these dark, uneventful evenings in a forgotten corner of the world for him, *oh no!* A mosquito droned past his ear, the only sound to disturb the silence, and above its insistent buzz he sensed the rest of the town asleep without him, doors shut, shutters jammed. He knew, without much pity or regret if he were being honest, that his forthcoming absence would hardly touch the hearts of many of the inhabitants. Lack of friendship didn't bother him. But lack of success tormented him every night. His posting here was a failure and he'd only just averted a scandal into the bargain.

Alexander frowned at the smudged papers on his desk. Not that they were likely to comfort him. His rooms above the small, poorly-stocked country hat-shop were dark and bare but for these papers and desk, and a narrow bed, things that wouldn't miss him, either. The next man to rent this mean space wouldn't know what anguished hours were spent here, he thought, allowing the self-pity to which all Balfour men were prone, to swell and flood him. The loneliness of failure, of these rooms, of the unknown: despair had him reaching for his usual answer. This time, though, he'd used it up.

Yes, even the blackjack was empty. 'Nothing more to be given,' he murmured. Alone on this dark night, his loneliness was his own fault. Just the same, familiar flickers of resentment rose in his gut. He aimed the empty blackjack at the wall, hard, like a punch, but the leather only stroked the plaster the way a woman's touch might. *Nothing more to be given.*

Crichton gave him something, though; *he* never ran dry! Alexander's spirits lifted as always at the thought of him, the one true god who'd directed him here to this miserable town for a reason. The man taught by the great Cullen himself. Whose words kept his faith intact these last six months, fixed before his eyes every day. Literally, fixed; Balfour men were fond of the literal, something that often struck him when he wondered about his lack of success, as though that might be the reason for it. Nothing ever represented anything else for such men, not for his father, not for his uncle, not for him. They permitted no substitutions. So he was wrong for the art of his age, he'd realized that at least. Truth is beauty? No: Alexander Balfour wasn't what the poet wanted.

And so he continued to gaze lovingly every day at the words fixed to the shelf above his head:

'In order to conduct analysis with success, much depends on the previous knowledge of the person who conducts it. It is evidently required that he who undertakes to examine this branch of science in this way, should be acquainted with the human mind in its sane state, and that he should not only be capable of obstructing his own mind from himself... he should be able to go back to childhood and see how the mind is modelled by instruction.'

13

Analysis and childhood and instruction! The mind and the brain separate. How long Alexander had had the title in his head, he couldn't say. '*Childhood Origins of the Disordered Mind.*' The book he'd write one day that would make his name. He had enough ambition for that, certainly. He picked up the scrawled pages in front of him: what was it all for, if not for immortality? *The greatest of the mind-doctors.* It wasn't just the jenever, or his imminent departure from this place. He was on the edge of greatness, not an abyss.

His throat was too dry, though, and he sucked back gin-soaked saliva and swallowed. His stomach gurned – it'd been too long since he'd last eaten a good meal. He still thought inspiration could come from bodily starvation: not a romantic belief, he'd insisted more than once, but a provable one. Ah, now if he could just find such a proof for his other theories... he'd heard Flourens was in Paris and would demolish Gall's findings, all while he, Alexander, was diverted here in Gheel. Should he have gone to Paris, too? Gall said pride could drive a man insane; Combe that 'every man was open to Genius...'

Alexander coughed suddenly, the result of a chill he'd picked up – he was never good when the seasons changed. 'Keep fooling yourself with talk of greatness and statues – while Combe and Flourens and Spurzheim are making the kind of strides you aren't,' he muttered. Each name pricked at his soul as he stabbed at the marked papers on his desk. *Move faster*, he told himself. *Become stronger.*

But he was the weak son of a weak man. What had been his father's last words before he left for Gheel? 'Your mother would have been disappointed.' Alexander had been in his room packing the rest of his books, or the ones his brother hadn't destroyed, anyway. *Thomas.* The brother nobody mentioned now, who might never have been born.

'My mother has no more capacity for disappointment, in myself or any other body,' Alexander had replied eventually. His father had made to slam the door but it got caught, wedged by a chair Alexander had moved out of the way to get at some books on the floor, and the effect was lost. He'd smirked. *Just as weak men do.*

His father could only bluster. 'Don't speak of her like that! This is not what she wanted. What do you think you can achieve?' Bluster from a man with at least one mistress and a son he never spoke of. Yet he expected respect from their exchanges, not mutual dislike. Alexander could only shrug at the man he and his brother resembled so closely his elderly patients had often stopped them in the street to ask questions about their health. 'No more and no less than anyone else. Anyway, what does it matter to you?'

All his father had were complaints Alexander was used to by then. 'I've put money into your education, a great deal of money. You are to stay here!'

'Your expectations are nothing to do with me,' Alexander had replied, still calm. 'You'll go on here just the same, whether I do what you say or not.'

'You are the only one,' his father had said, finally. The sins of omission: Alexander wouldn't forgive him for those. So what if his father had managed to kick the horse muck off his boots? His weakness had only made him snivel and crawl and bow with the best of them. Alexander had forgotten how it had got him places: a wealthy patient list and a practice in a mad king's wife's square. But he'd only allowed himself to forget because it was the last thing he was after.

No: he was in this bare little room in Gheel waiting alone for an epiphany, not a practice. It hadn't come, after more than six months. He straightened up too fast and his knees protested. So he'd have what he knew he shouldn't and the pain in his legs would lift. He'd be more lucid then, too, more able to force the connection. What man could think with a dry throat, after all? He picked up his coat, which was too heavy for such a humid September night and would only make him suffer. Suffering was all he could think about as he stood swaying at the top of the stairs, before he dipped down into the darkness below.

3.

Richmond, September 1823

For the sake of my good girls who still love their father, whatever he's become, I take a kick at Hume and Locke before settling David on the bed. Papers are scattered everywhere. Our cottage is deceptive; for all it's so small, it must hold more paper than the library at Alexandria ever did, I always say, which makes him smile. *Used* to make him smile: he's forgotten how to laugh. The fits are robbing him of more than bodily control. The lump in my throat hardens.

'This mess, David,' I begin, but my voice tells lies about me, making me hoarse as though I've been crying. I pitch it higher. 'Parchments, manuscripts, letters, books, all lying about. Look – some are even as high as the fireplace, and that pile there almost touches the ceiling. There's hardly room for you in here, even the bed is covered in papers.' He grunts. He told me long ago to sleep with the girls in their room, and so they don't come in here any more, except last week, when Izzy cut some roses for him. 'Oh, look,' I say, sadly. The flowers, jammed into an old jug that's balanced on a book on the windowsill, are turning brown and pulpy. 'I'll need to throw these out.' Then Thomas Reid catches the edge of my toe as I turn, and I let out a squeal.

'Be careful!' he tries to snap at me, but his voice still slurs. 'Stop your complaining.'

'You've bruised yourself,' I nod, wincing and rubbing my foot.

'Where?'

'Just at your temple, there. Close to your eye.'

His long fingers quiver at the sore spot and I bat them away as gently as possible, dab around sooty smears that have rubbed off from the dining room floor. He sulks like the little boy he must have been once. 'S'only a bump,' he mumbles.

'Don't be silly. These can do more harm sometimes, you know that. Worse than a broken bone.'

But I forget how the slightest change in tone can upset him.

'Don't speak to me like that. I'm not some cretin!'

'David, I wasn't – you need to lie still...'

'Leave me alone!' he spits. 'Abandon me forever like I always knew you would. Whore! Slut! Where's my wife? What have you done with her? Give me back my wife!' Spittle hangs from his lips, his eyes bulge and he searches for a weapon as I try to dodge him, but I'm too slow and he grips me hard around the waist, stabs his thumb at my back. 'You know what I can do!'

I am the expert in his disease. No one knows the warning signs better. The torpor in his eyes just before the eyelids begin to flutter. The lolling of his head; the grey pallor of his skin. The bite-marks on the smooth little bar of wood I carry in my pocket are an eager pupil's good grades, but I didn't earn my marks today. How often it comes on him in the mornings! No one knows why, not the doctors who visit, not the medical pamphlets or chapters in David's books, not the articles in journals that almost make a kind of sense. Watching, not understanding, is all I can do.

Far too soon after we married, I found myself standing in the doorway of the windowless little box room my father occupied. He sighed as though he'd anticipated it all along. It was only to be expected, he said of my complaints. 'An older man's jealousy of his young wife, that's all. He'll get used to it. You have to remember there's thirty years between you, Bella.'

'I've already considered our difference in ages.' I sounded petulant, even to myself, and tried to be reasonable. 'Really, it's not that. He has ways I can't explain. He gets angry, for no reason.'

His fits hadn't begun in those early days of our marriage. My father, busy working at his ledger, would be going away to his new home in London in a few days' time, but I didn't know then how soon we were to follow him. It wasn't the best time to speak to him when he was working on his accounts, especially after all he'd lost, but he still had the kindly tone of a fair man. 'We're all angry occasionally, Bella. He's bound to get impatient with a growing family to keep now you have Izzy, and of course, times being what they are...'

'So you've heard nothing at all, seen nothing that seems strange to you, the whole time you've been here? You think he is as he should be?'

'David's a good man. There's no man I have known longer, or better.'

David *was* a good man. 'He's different now from what he was; he has moods, I don't understand them.'

My father continued to scratch at his ledger in the cold of his sunless room. 'Different from what you *think* he was, maybe,' he chuckled suddenly, his head still not raised. 'That's what marriage is for. To find out. You're young, you have a lot to learn.'

He's a compassionate man, and a good father. But he believes too many in the world are like him when they are not, and he should know this better.

'You know they call him "Devil" in Broughty Ferry,' I murmured. 'They're scared of him.'

My father looked up at that, his clear brow and even features tricked into a rare frown. 'Now don't you whisper like that,' he said. He looked worse than he sounded but I couldn't be surprised at his impatience. 'You of all people can't be cowed. You! My Bella – the best of the lot of them? No wonder he's suspicious if you don't speak up. *You* know better than to be scared.'

My father and my husband. They're not alike but they are in cahoots, I think, sometimes. 'I try, every day, I do. I try to talk to him but it's impossible. Sometimes...'

'What? Come now, my girl. You're a Baxter. We don't hide away. Tell him what's on your mind.'

I am not a coward. 'I've tried, but it's more than his work that keeps him from me. How can I make him hear me?'

'I told you: it's what marriage is about. Speak to him as a wife and an equal should. You weren't brought up to think otherwise. I didn't raise my girls to think they were lesser beings.'

'I don't mean he thinks I am lesser. He thinks *I am not there*. He doesn't *see me*.'

He turned back to his ledger, away from the spoilt little girl who longed too much to touch those grey curls, tug on the tweed coat draped across his shoulders. 'Don't let things fester between you,' he carried on. 'It's bad for your marriage, Bella, and bad for you.'

Was I mad to marry him?

But I only whispered those last words to myself as I slid out of his study. Diabolical is a word from the Greek: *diabolos*, meaning 'devil'. My father wouldn't recognize the diabolical in anyone. I am different: I know the diabolical when I see it.

I should have seen it this morning.

Recrimination lures me like those wicked sirens of the sea: how best to effect my punishment? What method to use this time? David releases me at last and lies back, exhausted. I pat the blanket across his chest as he closes his eyes, those pale, heavy lashes. A delicious guilt creeps along my spine. 'I'm not a man,' he sighs, opening his eyes again. 'I'm no husband to you. You don't want me. I can see it, I know.' He wheezes a little and I touch his shoulder.

19

'No more now, David. Excitement makes you worse. Please lie still. I can't get the rest of these clothes off you if you won't be still.'

'I'm sorry, Bella. Forgive me. You should leave me; take the girls. You'd do better without me.'

Does he read my mind? But I cannot send him away; and I cannot leave. The veins on the back of his papery white hands stand up thick and black, and I wonder, suddenly, if there's a name for what I'm thinking. Laodice. Clytemnestra. Agrippina. They chorus at me. *Why must you leave him? Why cannot he leave you?*

'What are you doing?' he starts up again. 'What's this?'

'Your hand is scratched, it looks bad. I need to bandage it...'

He protests but lies back all the same, and I pull out a pillow from underneath him. Uneven bones jut through his thin shirt. I wind calico carefully round his wrist and wonder if the philosophers are right, if pain is a feeling or a sensation. And which one I'll cause him. 'I have too much to do,' he grumbles. 'You'll have to write the paper up for me...'

'I don't have time to copy down everything you dictate for a week, David. The house needs me.'

He opens his eyes and stretches long fingers towards my waist, appealing now. 'Maybe I was lucky this time. Is it getting worse? Did it last longer than usual?'

I turn away, put the calico back on the dresser. 'No, not so long. But you know you shouldn't talk.'

'Did I hurt you, Bella? I didn't hurt you, did I?'

'No, no, not at all. I'm fine. Shhh. You have to rest now.'

'But I've got things to do.' He is struggling on his elbows now. 'Important things... my paper... my lecture for the Society...'

'Don't worry about your work. You must sleep. I'll look after everything.'

To my surprise, he gives in at this and shuts his eyes once more. For now, his shame and my own inability to offer anything more than a few soothing words and some liniment to rub his feet, nearly blue, prick something inside me at last. Not my heart. Not that. I lighten my pressure after a while and wait for him to smile, complain as usual that I tickle. But it's only when I stop and cover those long, white toes that look artful enough to hold a brush or a pen that I realize he is asleep.

I gather up the pillow, heavy and encouragingly thick, press it to my chest. *Would it not be a kindness?* Its pressure squeezes my heart as I bend over him; his faltering breath is warm against my cheek. *Would it not show love?* Trapped between our bodies, I release it slowly, push towards his neck, his chin, his lips. The eyelids flicker but David doesn't see as the pillow edges his cheek, and my hands prepare to press down, just as the bell downstairs chimes and I remember: Mary.

4.

Gheel, September 1823

No community was more godly than Gheel. At least, none that Alexander had ever known. Gheel's darkness differed from Edinburgh's or London's, the two cities that had been his homes until then. Antwerp wasn't built on the site of a dead volcano. It had no mounds to climb, no hollows to hide in, and lacked that sense of filth beneath its skirts, like the New Town or High Holborn, for all the baroque show of the Meir. There were enough alleyways to hint at decadence, but he was as likely to find a Madonna as a whore at the end of one. '*A fortified port merely, its best days behind it,*' he had written home to his friends. Alexander might have thought he was one of many passing through, but told himself he had more confidence than most, and more future. He'd take what the place had to offer him, and move on.

His was a jittery kind of confidence, though, too ready to strike back at unfamiliar shadows. Alexander distrusted what he didn't know, unless it wore a pretty dress and pouted at clever remarks. *We're all the same in that*, he thought, shrugging as he made his way across Gheel's cobbled square. Back in Edinburgh he'd always been sure some cut-throat would test him on his way back from the inns on Cockburn Street one night. He liked to imagine now, so many miles away, that he'd have more than welcomed the challenge to strike back, to crack knuckles on bone. His face might have had a sallow tinge and his shoulders hunched, signs of the scholar, but there was power in his deltoid and trapezius muscles. He'd lifted weights in the quiet of his study. And developed a mental toughness, too, that compensated for his lack of height or breadth. A welcome numbing of emotion that gave him the upper hand.

Squat lamps smeared black patches of the market square with oily rings of light and put him on edge this late evening for some reason, had him stumbling in the gloom. 'God damn for boots like these,' Alexander cursed, and belched, tasting bitterness on his tongue. 'And for sticking me in a place with no good cobblers.' He wanted a fight and had to remember that he'd never fought a single living soul with his fists before. 'Give me some dark body to let me prove myself,' he muttered, suddenly nostalgic for those dark Edinburgh streets, sick of shapes that never materialized. 'Is that too much to ask?' Apparently it was; nothing stirred.

He shivered in spite of the warm autumn night and his tweed jacket. Yes, a chill in his veins indeed. It had begun to rain, too, which made him too desperate for Wim's, and he stumbled and cursed again. He'd come to recognize most of the lunatics by sight within days of his arrival, so they were never what worried him, but alarm fingered his skin every time he passed St. Amand church. Gheel was ghostly in the places where the light didn't show and as the River Nete sucked its breath, he felt unnerved, ready for attack. The supernatural couldn't be coshed or charmed.

His morbid disposition, only. The impact of childhood events, he told himself. *Illusions, false perceptions made upon the senses, only*. The tavern closed at this hour but regulars were permitted one last drink or two. Wim also had the hall at the back, where dances were held on Saturday nights and fetes on Fridays. Alexander knew he'd miss these when he left, but it was another of Gheel's innovations that he planned to take with him.

Shutters smothered any light inside the nearby family homes as he approached the inn: the world was sleeping and solitariness stabbed at his empty belly, letting jenever and self-pity spasm into his throat. He shoved himself against the side of the hall, pushed at its stone wall with his fists. His hacking cough dredged up more phlegm that he spat into the gutter. *A pretty picture for a great mind-doctor!* Alexander heard his father's voice as he finished coughing up his guts, then he stood straight and counted the last few centimes in his pocket. Enough for beer or bread, not both. An easy choice for someone like him to make. Let his father make of that what he would.

The tavern door was unlit and he hammered at it three times before pushing it open. His loose sole caught on the step and he cursed again. This wasn't his night. Wim, stooped and wiry, looked up from draining glasses and nodded at him.

'*Bier?*'

'*Alstublieft. An jenever.*'

Alexander's poor Flemish, even after six months, meant he only ever exchanged the same few words. He'd change that, too: once he was in Montrose, he thought, he'd make the local inn a regular haunt and form friendships. Then he recognized young Stefan from the abattoir: his head had been shorn again. He wasn't one of Alexander's patients, but lice got everywhere. They didn't want them in their meat, too.

He shrugged off the tweed that once belonged to his father's brother, another doctor. So it ran in the family, this fascination with the sick and the injured, and he'd not escaped it. Warm, musty beer and a disapproving look from the saint on the wall were the only comfort he'd get for his inheritance tonight, he thought. He tipped his glass at her cracked face and decided to blame her instead. He'd heard of Gheel in his final year at university when a professor made a joke about the 'lunatic town', and had deplored the 'curse' of martyred maids upon modern medicine. Dimpna – patron saint of princesses, sleepwalkers, victims of incest and rape, runaways, the possessed, the epileptic, and of asylums and hospitals – was buried in the church there, where her father felled her in a single stroke, cutting off her head.

Not only Saint Dimpna: little shrines to the Virgin Mary signposted the country roads here, which had amused him at first. They took shelter in the hollows of house-fronts, reminding him he was in a Catholic country now, pricking the youthful atheism that his medical studies had only strengthened. The blue of the cloak bright enough to glow in the dark; the wet, red, open lips of the virgin. '*Just like a good whore,*' he'd written sneeringly to a friend soon after his arrival. But when he thought of all the dead mothers who passed on without any recognition from the world, he'd wondered what he was doing in Gheel. In a place founded on symbols.

Method, analysis, knowledge, examination, observation, instruction.

He'd muttered these words like a kind of catechism the day he arrived. The stinking, freezing coach had trundled over mud roads from the centre of Antwerp out to Gheel. *Science travels alone,* Alexander had thought pompously, but he feared he knew less than he should. About his new home he had some facts to hand: its four parishes, St. Amand, St. Dimpna, Holven and Elsum (he would be the 'overseer' of St. Amand); its twenty or so patients who lived in the town and the eight who would come under his direct supervision, along with the families who housed them. More deranged patients were housed on the outskirts, and the childless families who housed them earned the most. But neighbourly competition sparked their sense of duty, not money. *A family at Gheel is not considered respectable if lunatics are not entrusted to it...* His professors had criticized this particular exploitation of lunatics for money, but Alexander came to a different opinion during his stay.

The central asylum had been built in the thirteenth century to honour its patron saint, but only after Esquirol's visit was a new building hurriedly constructed to serve that purpose. A stronger system of inspecting patients before they were housed in the community was needed: those who were particularly distressed or difficult stayed there. In the rare case of worsening conditions, they could be readmitted. Alexander had no idea what to expect of such a building. Certainly not the comically low, red-brick, nondescript house that stood by the dusty road, its only distinguishing feature the tip of a flattish cupola that shone like the pate of a bald man in the sun.

He'd felt superior, and happy to add to the comedy of the scene. When the carriage stopped, he'd ignored the driver's hope for some coins. He was in a hurry: the pressure from his bladder, after an early breakfast that consisted solely of good strong beer, had threatened him with every bump and lurch the vehicle made. There was a chance he could relieve himself before anyone came out to greet him. But there wasn't a single corner or bush for him to shield himself. Bodily modesty had never been a great concern of his; at first it amused him that he might be caught pissing in public on his first day.

Even after everything that happened, he could still smile when he remembered that moment. Trying to unbutton his trousers with freezing fingers; pissing so much he had to jump out of the way of his own stream to avoid it hitting his boots. He'd buttoned up, gazed over fields of brown and yellow, and wondered how far the horizon stretched, if it could take him as far as Bonn and further. In the near distance, a cluster of red-brick houses stood further away, separate from the rest, and the sight sobered him at last.

There were no grand steps to the door of the asylum, no gargoyles or decoration of any kind, which Alexander liked. He hadn't been able to tell from the short letter detailing his appointment what kind of man its director, Dr Bulckers, was and so he'd surveyed the building for a clue. Even temper, straightforward, devoid of passion, except for his work: yes, he'd decided, he could work with a man like that.

How wrong he had been then, and about so many things. His first day had embarrassed him for all sorts of reasons. To be greeted at the door by a skeletal young girl instead of the man himself was bad enough. He worried, after all, that she'd witnessed what he'd done. 'My name is Alexander Balfour. Can you announce me to your Director?' But he spoke too loud, too fast, and tried again in French. *Je m'appelle Alexander Balfour. Je suis medicin. Ou est le directeur?* She'd responded in that language but not to his question.

'Mon petit livre est jolie, n'est-ce pas?' She held out a small, leather-bound book. He didn't know what she meant and tried a third time, more slowly this time, as if she were deaf. *'Monsieur Bulckers? Bul-ckers?'* She'd whipped her hand away, spun clumsily round on her tiptoes and danced back inside the building. He even heard her laughing.

That was the first time he had met Marie. *Every man had his nemesis.* But rarely did they come in the form of a laughing, mad girl who birled away so easily.

5.

Richmond, September 1823

I pause on the landing, feel for the little brown phial in my pocket, before I release it, shake a few drops on my tongue. I'm shaking when I open the door, though; guilt and hurry leave me breathless, a little too eager, too exposed. 'The stairs, I was upstairs.' My first words to Mary are meant to cover me, but I want help and in that moment I'm shy, too. I've forgotten much how my height over her makes me feel ungainly, the way it always did; protective yet gruff, like an abashed lover turning his hat in his hands.

How she always makes me feel: did Mary know it? Once, at home in Broughty Ferry on a breezy summer's day, we lay in the long grass behind my father's house and she leant her face in close, met my lips with her own, slightly parted, pressing lightly, and my lack of confusion surprised me more than the intimacy of her action. 'Just a practice,' she had smiled, giggled almost.

My flirtatious Mary. No: I haven't forgotten any of that. How could I? Other memories make me blush, too, and I'm conscious of my poor dress, and voice my regret before this slight, pale, too-stylish woman, who knows how to make me fearful of my own mind and who I'm struggling to recognize now, can even speak a word. There's delicacy in her pose but strength in her clasp of my hand. Strangeness in the new lines drawn on a face I once thought perfect. A history I haven't shared and cannot know, in the strain of her smile.

'I intended to change, of course.' I twitch in the light, unsure. 'But is it really you, Mary? Can it really be you?'

And then she speaks and I know, and a shiver runs through me that I swear must be visible. 'Isabella, of course it is me!' Mary's familiar soft voice is not without pain; her brow furrows as the noon sunlight behind her frames her black widow's weeds. I was always used to her in pale summer clothes but the darkness suits her strange new air, the experience that shows in her face. Strands of golden hair escape out under her hat. That has not changed: Mary is famous for her hair. She'll not keep it covered long, I think, and I blink and stare and stammer again, 'I was upstairs...'

'And I would hardly have recognized you, either!' There's a hint of reproach in my friend's voice – *my friend* – as though I've intended a disguise to fool her, and I'm about to swear my innocence when I see that she doesn't blame me at all. 'What has happened to you all this time, my dearest Bella? What has the world done to you?'

Her beauty is captivating; my beauty has gone, of that she has no need to remind me. But her tears are as real as she is, and they stain her white cheeks like misshapen roses.

'But no – I can see you are still *my beautiful Bella!* Yes, I see it still,' Mary steps into the hall and embraces me hard. 'How did we let them keep us apart?' Her arms may be thin but they're as strong as her hands – was she always so strong? – and she squeezes it out of me at last. 'My dearest, dearest friend. Mary!' I gasp. 'I've thought of you so often.'

It's true, and I'd hold her forever to make her understand. I wasn't repentant then, six years ago when she wrote to me, but I am now. I want to take back my chilly response to her request to meet that very last time. I want to take back my misplaced superiority and my promise to David. I want her help.

'I'll never allow it again,' is all I can say, but I know I'm false, for straightaway I remember and put my fingers to my lips. David should have been at the Society this morning but of course, he's still here. 'We mustn't disturb him,' I whisper.

'But he doesn't still object? Oh, Isabella, after all this time!' Mary's dismay might flood my little home: I pull her by her wrists into the parlour and shut the door.

'I haven't told him about your visit. He isn't at all well... I don't want to upset him.'

'Not even to write to me all those years – how could he have influenced you so?'

This beginning isn't what I want: only the past of our girlhoods should matter, not what has happened since. Mary glances round my shabby little parlour with a kindly but puzzled expression as if to say, *so this is where your superiority got you?* I pat the cushions on the chairs, pull the drapes back further to let in stronger light that only embarrasses the room more. 'I pretend it's really a palace,' I shrug and try to smile. 'I pretend all the time.'

Mary tilts her head in a coquettish way, like the girl of fifteen she once was and says, 'So then I can pretend, too!', and the breeze that has followed her in dries on my lips, and for that one moment we are indeed girls again.

She had been a tiny lone figure standing at the docks, looking like she might blow away in clothes too light for our east coast breeze, that first time I saw her. All her money had been stolen from her during the trip, she wept. My father was kind: Mary would need no money during her stay in our home. Her father had written and seen to everything, he assured her. That wasn't true: her father, Mr Godwin, wasn't a generous man and knowing the size of house my father had and the number of servants he kept, clearly felt comfortable contributing nothing at all for her stay. He didn't seem to know what a young girl might need, and not only in terms of money. My father didn't intend to reveal the man's true nature but he'd left the letter lying open downstairs. I saw no harm in reading what Mr Godwin had written, before I met his daughter.

'I do not desire that she should be treated with extraordinary attention, or that any one of your family should put themselves in the smallest degree out of their way on her account. I am anxious that she should be brought up (in this respect) like a philosopher, even like a cynic. It will add greatly to the strength and worth of her character.'

What kind of father wrote like that about his only daughter? What cold, self-sufficient little creature was he about to deposit with us? I'd read her mother's works and pored over their meaning many times, but for all his enthusiasm for serious study, I couldn't imagine my own father with his hugs and smiles and teases writing of me that way.

But my father's kind lie dried Mary's tears, and Christy's fussing with blankets and tea, though it was, in spite of the wind, one of the warmest days, made her smile and we soon uncovered her fondness for play, her sense of daring. She had sailed alone from Ramsgate, after all. I was only a few months older than her, yet in all my fifteen years I'd been no further than Edinburgh. I'd often wondered what it would be like to visit London, as Robert had done already a year ago. Christy was to be next: she would be the lucky one to accompany Mary back to Skinner Street in November. I was bored, and would soon be left alone at home.

Mary occupied Margaret's old room at the end of my landing. Christy was a floor above, and Robert's things were stored in the attic, next to the room lived in by Aggie, my old nurse and our housekeeper. Robert was away preparing for university in Edinburgh. My father had had some romantic notion of Mary and Robert becoming better acquainted but their paths didn't cross that first visit, and by the time they did, it was too late for him to catch her. So I had Mary all to myself, that first summer. Or so I'd believed.

But we all have a capacity for deception, of course, and I should have learned that sooner. Now she pulls the pin from her hat, revealing at last the thinness of her famous fair hair and I am truly sorry for what I did to her. My treacherous words to David that last year I saw her, just before she left again for the Continent with the new husband that everybody said looked remarkably like me, stab at me: 'It is quite a rave from beginning to end. You can have no conception of anything more mad-like. "Queen Mab" is sober sense compared to it...'

The poetry was as mad as its creator, David had said, and I agreed it must be. How foolish Mary must be to marry such a man, David had said, and I agreed she must be. But David still went to see him, and discussed his words with him. I could read the poems, he'd said, if not meet the madman himself, and I agreed this was right. Yet all the time, the madman was in my home, not Mary's; all the time, there was a demon in my husband's form that spoke to me as if it were a rational being.

This demon attaches the wrong meaning to words, digs down in directions I can't predict. '*While we stray we are allured by the charms of novelty. We wander from shrub to shrub and from tree to tree till we can no longer recover the beaten path which surrounds, without entering the forest,*' David wrote once. If I believe the mind is a forest, that David has only lost his way, perhaps I can forgive him.

But forgiveness is an elusive thing. Will Mary find it as elusive as I do?

'I'm so sorry you lost him,' I begin to say, but she knows what I really thought of her dead husband, of his morals and his work. My actions made it clear when I cut off all contact. Forgiveness makes her gracious, though.

'You would have loved him had you been permitted to meet him.' She passes her hand over her forehead as though the thought is suddenly too heavy for her to bear. 'I know it wasn't your fault, Isabella. But oh, he was truly the best of men.' She sighs heavily and it's apparent now how exhausted she is. 'Let me...' I start, but she interrupts, holds up a gloved hand.

'I've been through too much these last few years. I don't want to lose anyone else I love.'

'I've thought so often of this moment,' I say, sadly, 'even though it's caused me pain to imagine it. When I heard of your travels through Italy, of your arrangements with Claire and who knows how many others: David was right, I thought.'

I pause. I can't say any more. I can't say that when he told me what happened to her little boy, William, and her baby, Clara, I thought – me, with my wicked ways – that Mary had been punished for doing wrong. But what kind of God punishes a woman by killing her children? 'Misplaced faith is the worst of crimes,' I continue.

'Perhaps our husbands have taught us that, in their own ways,' she replies.

'Do you remember? When you stayed with us in Broughty Ferry?'

'I remember it gave me the freedom to imagine. The woodless mountains, or beneath the trees in your garden: so different from what I was used to. The space, the sky: how open it all was!'

But I don't want romantic thoughts of the landscape back home. 'I mean, when we were girls...?' I press on, will her to remember.

Ours was an unannounced visit to Barns o' Woodside, my sister's house, that day: I don't recall who first thought of it. We'd been trailing dark, cramped Dundee streets but Mary liked the haar that chased us those summer afternoons. It smudged out the sun and made us shiver in our thin dresses but it brought her closer to her mother, so far north. She liked to think of the woman who gave birth to her, and who once ran after an American adventurer, as a single traveller, journeying solo instead, intrepid and sure through fjords. Fjords that her mother saw, and that her daughter made a poor, man-made monster flee towards. And who would experience just such a haar as this.

We resisted the ribbons and brocades that caught our eye in the town: we couldn't arrive at Margaret and David's house with our arms full of parcels. *Subject to no jurisdiction under heaven but to Christ alone.*' Mary had her mother's book with her, at least: our excuse. I had nothing particular to offer but I braved the Tay all the same and felt my mistake as soon as we reached the shore. The long trail misled us twice, a sign that we should have turned back. But the oaks that hid the house were also my guide and eventually we stood by the pillared entrance. Mary pulled at the bell. He couldn't have expected us: the surprise would be ours.

When nobody opened the door, we picked our way through the trees to the scullery at the back but the kitchen door was locked. Mary was used to unusual goings-on in a family: the need to keep to oneself. She was always complaining how little time she had for herself at home, her stepmother wanting her for the shop, or Fanny needing help with their young step-brother. Her father tested them all on their reading, but she couldn't give it enough time. The battle between her father and her stepmother was easy, though: Mary was always on her father's side.

My family weren't like that. I knew who my mother and father were, and Christy's and Robbie's. Mary's father wasn't the same as Fanny's but her mother was. Her step-sister Claire and her brother Charles didn't know their father; but young William would. Mr Godwin cared for three children who weren't even his. We were lucky, Christy said, but I liked the sound of Mary's London home life, the sophisticated mix of untethered beings. My family shared nothing so scandalous as unacknowledged heritage.

I hoped to discover a secret, then, and peered through the kitchen window. The range was pristine as always, the dusty oak table was where it should have been, in the centre of the room. Bunches of rosemary and thyme hung from the ceiling; Margaret's new copper pots and pans glinted and dangled on their hooks. We couldn't force our way in because of neatness, I said to Mary. She pouted: already, she was good at that. She would get better. 'Let's leave a message for him. Let him know we were here,'

'With what? We've no paper, no ink, no charcoal, even.'

'Let's write it where *he* may find it – if he looks hard enough.'

Yes: a message for David. Not for my sister.

Mary raised a fist at me: the diamond ring, her mother's, glistened on the fourth finger of her right hand. Then she wiped the window with her sleeve. I covered my ears at the animal squeak of the glass but there was no blood, only the white of a jagged **MS** inscribed on the pane. She twisted the ring from her finger so that beneath her signature, I, too, could scratch my initials: **IB**.

'Now write *his* initials.'

'No, I can't.'

'Yes, you can. You have to do it. Below yours, just there, see? MS. IB. DB. The three of us, locked together. What a surprise he will get!'

What a surprise *we* would get, I thought, if he walked in now and caught us defacing his windowpane. But the birds in the trees were silent; without a breeze to disturb them, the leaves could be still and watch us, too. Mary pressed her body to my back and breathed on the pane over my shoulder, her arms tight around my waist. I shivered, then scratched one letter, and had just begun the second when something caught my eye and made me stop: a figure, walking through the hall, on the other side of the kitchen door. A large figure, womanish, skirted, a bun at the back of her head. Mary jumped back as I rapped on the window.

'What on earth are you doing?' She grabbed the ring from my finger.

'There's someone in there, I can see them,' I said. I hurried to the door, rattled the doorknob. 'Hello! Hello! It's Mary and Isabella, Margaret's sister! Please let us in.' Nothing. Margaret had a new nurse whose name I'd forgotten. I hammered again at the door.

'I can't see anyone,' Mary said, peering through the glass. 'Are you sure you saw somebody in the kitchen?'

'Not in the kitchen, walking past it.'

When I looked through the window again, though, the kitchen door was closed. It was impossible to see beyond it into the hall. 'That door was open when I looked in before,' I said. 'She must have shut it.'

'Who must have shut it? Margaret?'

'Of course not – I just told you, I saw someone in there. Why isn't she opening the door to us?'

I banged on the door again.

'It must be Margaret's nurse,' said Mary.

'So why isn't she answering the door?'

'Maybe she doesn't want us to disturb her.'

I didn't like to leave: I'd speak to David about the help he'd hired for my sister, how she had ignored me when there was no reason for it. I glanced back at the house as we walked away, to see if the woman would come to my sister's window, but no. By the time we arrived back in Broughty Ferry, it was very late and my father was annoyed with us. David was there, too, a happy coincidence. I interrupted his talk as soon as I saw him.

'But I dismissed the new nurse last week,' he said. 'That's why I'm here. I've taken Margaret to my mother's: I'm on my way home now. Your father kindly asked me to break my journey here.'

'The house will be empty when you get back – stay here, instead. Go back in the morning,' my father said.

'I've no fear of empty houses,' David shook his head.

'All the same, stop here, with us.'

No one was listening to me.

'I saw someone. In your house, walking past the kitchen.'

My father looked more amused than annoyed, now. David carried on with his meal: potatoes and leg of lamb, his favourite. Aggie adored him but would never exchange a word with him. Lamb was for special occasions.

'That's not possible,' he said at last, wiping lamb juice from his mouth: our best napkins were out, too, I could see. 'I dismissed the nurse two days ago. The house is completely empty. I locked up before I left: there was no one there today.'

'But there must have been. I saw her.'

I wouldn't be quiet, not even when Mary pulled at my sleeve. 'She must have closed the kitchen door, I saw her!'

No one would believe me, not even Mary, though Christy teased me about it for the rest of the summer. Margaret never returned to Newburgh. She died three weeks later, in the care of David's mother.

6.

Gheel, September 1823

Marie had been unremarkable to Alexander then: there was no hint of the beauty she'd become, just a few months later. He'd stood at the door reluctant to walk in without permission, but truthfully he was unsettled. The odd-looking girl had to be a patient, but he realized he had no clear idea of how to behave with one. He'd started to walk away.

'Doctor Balfour! You are here! I am Dr Bulckers!'

The shout pulled him back. A tall, grey-bearded man with heavy black eyebrows stood in the entranceway, gesturing to the skies as though Alexander had flown in on a comet. The contrast of his colouring was a gift to the student of physiognomy, Alexander had reflected, as he registered the thick red lips and hooded eyes. They told of an excessive disposition, a man whose conviviality wasn't to be trusted. He shielded his eyes with his hand, as if blinded by a too-bright light.

'Finally, sir. I hope I didn't frighten the girl...' But Bulckers interrupted him. 'That is Marie,' he said, with a dismissive wave Alexander found curious. 'You will meet her later. She will be transferred to your parish soon, so you will come to know her case well. But come in, come in!'

Alexander had thrust out his hand only to find it considerably smaller than his employer's: the other man's physical presence was belittling and he found himself behaving accordingly, flirting and flattering and stammering. *Like those foolish fiancées back in Edinburgh.* No – his recollection now was too harsh, inaccurate. He was never so contrite, nor so obsequious. He'd always relied on something he inherited from his father, aside from an interest in medicine: the ability to talk himself out of a bad situation, or into a good one. And that was a different thing from contrition. Alexander had got used to, as he grew up, a certain invisibility. Women had rarely noticed him for his looks: why should they? He was neither handsome nor ugly. And so he'd learned to make an effort to seduce, to rely on clever conversation, an excess of flattery. Hardly a unique strategy, he admitted that, but it never failed him. And he liked women who were as noticeable as he was invisible: striking-looking women with masculine features; attractive but not fashionably so, were best suited to his intentions. Who he really was: well, that was for Alexander Balfour to know, not the world at large. And certainly not any female.

Before he arrived in Gheel, he'd been engaged twice and each time to just such striking-looking young women, and both from wealthier homes than his. Neither found the flattery he showered upon them excessive or even strange, though he doubted with their looks that they'd encountered it much before. Rarity was often the secret of success.

On neither occasion did he see his promises through. He was chasing an altruism he didn't possess. He still believed he could appropriate it, though, but appropriation by marriage wasn't quite so simple. Neither of his fiancées had given him what he imagined they could. It was their failure, not his. And both women, as well as their families, had excused him the pain he caused them, blaming only themselves for his rejection of them. Thoughts of red-haired Esme Fleming who, Alexander had since heard, had become engaged to his friend, Arthur Hepburn, could prick his soul, but only when he was too soused to stand up straight. The comfort both she and her predecessor, Elspeth Stevenson, might have offered him could make him weep in the right circumstances. After the right amount of beer and jenever, of course. Neither woman, however, was the reason he quit Edinburgh when he did.

Alexander's flexible charm didn't disable the more combative Dr Bulckers so fast, which worried him at first. He was too overcome by the inside of the asylum building to be at his best. It wasn't the country house backed by meagre church funds that he'd expected.

'We are very proud of the asylum here, Dr Balfour,' Bulckers had responded, that pride gleaming in his face.

'It is a tribute to all that is new in our profession, sir,' Alexander said. 'You have every reason to feel so.' And he meant every crawling word. The white cupola shrouded white walls and lit up blazing white corridors and rooms. Light streamed in from long windows on either side; the floors, newly washed in carbolic and vinegar, glistened. 'I've never seen anything like it. No hospital at home values such cleanliness and light.'

Bulckers had beamed even more at that, and clasped Alexander's hand with a familiarity the younger man found bizarre, almost effeminate. 'It is our philosophy. Cleanliness and light. The Lord's philosophy!' He squeezed his new employee's fingers then raised them to his lips as if to kiss them, Alexander had thought with real alarm. So he'd flung his hands wildly about him in an expression of enthusiasm instead. 'And the patients' rooms? Are they as wonderful as this?'

'Their cells are exactly the same. High ceilings, painted white, cleaned twice every day.' 'This activity doesn't agitate them?' Alexander began to walk away, as if to inspect them.

Bulckers had laughed. 'On the contrary, Dr Balfour. They understand the routine very quickly! Routine is very important to our patients.'

But he wasn't to escape and discover alone as he desired: instead, Bulckers steered him into his study, as clear and bright as the rest of the building. The Director hesitated and frowned, beetle-black eyebrows trapped together. 'Now, Marie,' he said. 'You must not worry. I do not – how do you say it – throw you in at the deep end. She lives at present with me and my wife. She suffers from morbid delusions that have manifested themselves in tics, postules, a refusal to eat. The usual things.'

Alexander had nodded. He'd little real idea, but wanted to appear knowledgeable.

'But she improves. As they all do here, almost without exception. You will be part of our success, Dr Balfour!'

He was barely listening to him, but was nevertheless imbued with that sense of success from the start. He found Bulckers a seductive man, and the art of seduction was what he taught Alexander from that moment on. *A good mind-doctor needs to know how to seduce well.* Alexander had thought he was capable enough at the art but Bulckers was a master, combining authority with tenderness, the masculine with the feminine.

The two men had settled in leather armchairs that first day to toast Alexander's arrival. Twelve hours later, he spent the first day in his new post shivering in bed, the victim of a spring fever. Yes, he was a weak man. Yet it passed quickly enough. And every day after, he met with Bulckers in his study at the same hour, where they exchanged notes over a glass of Madeira. Alexander watched him with patients, studied his techniques, his play with power. One woman, unwashed, without a civil tongue in her head, refused to wear clothes the first weeks she was there. If she refused to eat, Bulckers would simply order her food to be taken away, and immediately she would fall on her plate. If she refused to get out of bed, he would tell her that she mustn't get out of bed all day, and in a second, she would rise and dress. He even asked her to tear the rest of her clothes to shreds: at that moment, she began to sew and make repairs to those dresses she'd damaged. All of this was conducted with the utmost charm as if he were at an assembly and charged with making the most beautiful woman fall in love with him. He never raised his voice, never threatened or whined or cajoled: every request was made with attention and care; love, even. The appearance of love: Alexander knew he could do that.

He saw Bulckers shrug only once, as though one particular patient's reaction was of no matter to him at all. That got her attention, just when she thought he wasn't watching. A clasp of her hands for good behaviour and raising them to his lips, then a withdrawal of affection for the bad: his treatment of patients was as physical as it was mental. 'Your father is very disappointed in you,' Alexander heard him say often, especially to young women. He meant, of course, himself.

It was a game. Never once did he ask about their child-hoods or why they felt compelled to behave the way they did. But who was Alexander to criticize him? Gheel worked. The few retreats that had sprung up in the wake of Tuke's success didn't house the mentally ill with the mentally healthy. The mixing of sane and insane had never been tested anywhere else but Gheel, a practice it had maintained from the sixteenth century. It was unique. A revolutionary kind of treatment, even though it had been practising its methods for centuries. Gheel 'cured' over sixty per cent of those placed in its care. Madness was curable: Gheel proved it.

Alexander returned his thoughts to the present: his beer glass was empty. Wim nodded as he tapped on the side of it for another and rubbed his temple before pushing back his long, dark red hair in a motion that recalled his mother to him, another of those little instances that were enough to spike him. He drained his second glass more quickly than he intended and was indicating a third just as the inn door crashed open. He and Stefan birled round, fists closed, but it was only his employer.

'God, man! Look at the state of you. Are you wanting to wake up the whole town?'

It wasn't beer or jenever that made Alexander forget whom he addressed. There was more to his tone than drunken

42

disrespect: a certain history between the two men. Bulckers stood panting in the doorway like an overweight washer-woman, his white shirt loose and open, and gave Alexander the sudden urge to laugh. That was, until the man's rush of words:

'It is Marie!'

He stepped close enough to see the tiny black whiskers on Bulckers' nose, the open pores like black pinpricks on his cheeks. The usual urge to meet skin with skin, repulsive as it was, made him picture his hand brushing against the bulbous cheek, red and wet. *Charles Bell: the difference between the sensory and the motor functions.*

'We've been over this before,' Alexander shrugged at last, and turned back disrespectfully to his beer. 'You've got what you wanted. There's nothing more to say.'

'But she has gone!'

7.

Richmond, September 1823

'What an age away it all is.' Mary picks up her hat, a stylish, beguiling thing of dark muslin and twirls it, brighter all of a sudden. 'I'll never be a girl again!' she says, as she puffs up her fine hair, lets it halo around her face.

'I know you don't mean that,' I smile back. She hands over the hat and its softness is a shock. It's long time since I've touched something so delicate. I set it on my head and pull a face, making us both laugh. 'You like it?' She claps her hands and I wince in case David hears. 'It was bought for me in Italy.' She leans forward, whispering, to humour me. 'A kind present from a friend after... you know.' Her face contracts but I only take advantage of her loss and use it for myself. I may be repentant but I know how shameless I am: David has made it clear often enough.

'His death, yes: I know what you mean – and it makes me think of them all the time – you must remember? How we used to frighten each other with so many tales? Do you remember the story of Grizell Jaffrey? It was our favourite.' But I'm speaking too quickly. Mary flutters only interest, not recognition, so I have to take a deep breath and go more slowly. Mary will want tea, like any guest, and I mustn't forget my manners, but I need an answer from her first. 'The witch who came back to haunt those who burned her at the stake? Remember?' Is there a physical way I can force Mary to recall the story? Panic nips at my breast, but needlessly: she remembers and the pain eases away.

'Yes! Yes, I do! Now, wasn't there something about a fisherman, too – the one who drowned in a storm in the Tay? He appeared to his wife one dark winter's night when she married someone else. Isn't that right?' Mary is excited by the memory now and she claps once more. I catch my breath at the noise: I'm waiting for a knock at the door. *Are they nearing now?* Yes: I feel them. They can hear us so we must be quiet; she mustn't clap like that again.

'Sometimes I think I must see them... "Hallucinations are the product of a diseased mind," the medical books say. Can they be right?'

Mary looks puzzled. 'I cannot know, but I remember strange happenings, when we stayed in Geneva...'

I cut her off; I don't care to hear about Geneva, her past with him. 'I've read about a gentleman who believes he's created a steam engine with his bare hands and is driven mad with despair and frustration every day as he watches it, useless and rusting outside his house, because no one will let him use it. And of a lady who swears her betrothed enters her bedroom every night to have relations with her, and her fear of getting a child by him makes her pull at her hair and tear at her limbs because her betrothed was killed in battle many years before. Such visions!' I rush my words so she may not stop me.

'Hallucinations, not visions,' Mary says, shaking her head. 'Visions are born of a religious mind.'

I'm surprised to hear this – her husband was a famous atheist. Has she taken up faith, after her losses? 'Blake says that when the sun rises he doesn't see a disc of fire shaped like a coin,' she continues. '"O no, no, I see an Innumerable company of the Heavenly host crying, 'Holy, Holy, Holy is the Lord God Almighty.'" And he doesn't question the sight. "I look thro' it and not with it.""

I sink to my knees suddenly, clasp at her skirts. 'I'm sorry for it all, Mary, truly I am sorry. I was wrong, I was misguided, and now everything is impossible and I cannot...'

'My Bella!' Her hands, soft now without their gloves, yet strong and sure, grip my buried head as I gasp a sob that disappears into the folds of her skirt. 'Let us be brave enough to be friends once more.' Her breath brushes my ear, settles on my hair. Her lips are as close to me as his must have been to her, once, and a husband's untimely death is on them. 'Let us grieve together what we have lost, what might have been,' she whispers. 'Let us help one another again.'

I can't be certain what, or who, was standing there by the window, I tell her. It wasn't long after we moved here to this poky cottage. The trace of the head, bowed down; the line of the low brow, the sun glimmering behind it. I called out, asked who the stranger was and what they wanted. Then it turned its face towards me and I recognized instantly the weak chin, the delicate nose. Those blue eyes, huge and staring. Watching me while I fed my baby.

I'd been unable to move at first that day. I gripped Kathy tighter, who started to wriggle, and only when she let go of my breast did I rush to the back door. But the earth under the window was undisturbed. There were no fingerprints on the window-sill. Nothing to confirm what – or whom – I'd seen.

Mary releases me, gazes silently for a long time before murmuring, 'Another poet says Fancy is "no other than a mode of Memory emancipated from the order of time and space". Imagination has will; Fancy has none. Imagination has reason; Fancy is a reflex action, that is all. A flick in the mind to the past, a blink in the light.'

'Was it my fancy, then?' I get up from the floor; I'm embarrassed, and regain confidence with my solid answer. 'Kathy has those same large, blue eyes: she did not get them from me.'

It was Margaret, of course: come back to watch over David and me with our girls. A revenant. Light as air, as breath, as cloud, as smoke. A wingless, colourless, sightless spirit back from the dead. Back to the living world she'd left behind, tracing the form she once was, to haunt me with the husband who was once hers.

My sister.

'David says I have the power to see more than most. You said so, too, do you remember? "You're a seer, Bella," you said. And I felt it: is feeling not knowing? Rousseau tells us feeling is the most important faculty of man. Without feeling, we are beasts. I see: I feel. So am I diseased or devout? Should I "look through it and not with it", as you say?'

Mary is silent. I persist. 'I know what our Glassite friends would say. But I lost the ability to be devout the moment I married my dead sister's husband.'

At last she speaks, slowly, that distant look still in her eyes. 'I waited for six days,' she says. 'I waited for six days and then we got in the carriage – Jane and I – and we went looking for them. Our husbands. The fish had eaten his face and hands. When I dreamt of him those days after – the nights I could sleep at all – he had no face.'

I cannot know how often her husband talked of ghosts. But I know how he died. That he insisted on sailing from Livorno to Lerici with his friend, Edward Williams, another man I never met. That he wouldn't wait for better weather, against all the advice he was given by better sailors than him. Mary's Shelley; always in a hurry as if he knew he had only a little time; always knowing better. The storm ate them up in minutes, and only spat them out a few days later. He was not quite thirty.

Mary continues, 'I have his heart. Others wanted it for themselves, can you believe that? But I have it. I keep it in the pages of *Alastor*. I keep it safe.' And unseen fingers prickle my spine, give me my chance to say it.

'Then you *can* help me. Because you understand it all. I knew you would! I couldn't leave him before, all those years ago, as I promised you I would. And I can't leave him now. There is only one other way.'

'Another way? What do you mean? Bella – here, you are so white, some tea...'

But Mary's concern isn't what I want. I'm aware of my heart beating fast, skipping and hitting my chest. 'I'd let him haunt me, if that was the price. I'd be glad of it.'

Mary shakes her head; wisps of hair float beside her and I want to grab them, stroke them still. 'You don't know what you mean.'

'I'd keep his heart beside me if I had to.' The excitement in my voice makes it tremble, and I can't look at her any more. 'Any penance, for my actions.'

Mary's skirt rustles as she gets to her feet, too, as though it's startled enough on its own account. 'You think I *wanted* this? That I'm glad of it?'

'No, no, you don't understand me – I want you to help me. Widowhood...'

And I'm gripping her hands in mine as tightly as I can, ignoring her squeal as I press on them, blind to the twisting of her face. The time has come at last. Yes, they are here now, in this room, with me and Mary. My chorus. Laodice. Clytemnestra. *Mariticide.* I recall the word at last and it has me rushing her with my intentions.

'He's so frail but he rules us all and I think, if I had help to end the suffering we all endure, me and my girls, end his suffering too, how much better it would be, but I cannot manage it alone, if you could help me... in my hands, you see, just before you came, I held a pillow, I put it to his face, I would have pressed down, you must help me do it.' And suddenly the room pitches black and I see myself tumble into darkness.

I'm not sure how Mary manages the tea while I lie unconscious on the parlour floor, but when I open my eyes and let the room take shape, she is cradling my head with one hand, and tipping the edge of a teacup towards my mouth with the other. I struggle to sit up, cling to her hand hard. My head dips inside itself; I picture my brain slopping in liquid, back and forth, banging into the sides of my skull.

'I'm going to be sick...' and my body spasms but nothing appears. 'Our grief,' I mumble, a trace of eagerness still there. 'We share a loss, as you said...'

But Mary stiffens beside me. 'You are so very tired, Isabella,' she says, and her voice sounds too far away for her to be so close. 'Are you not a great deal overwrought? David's illness, this house, you have so much on your mind, clearly...'

She coughs and the noise in my head stops. I will her to look me in the eyes, but she won't. She eases away from me instead. She thinks I've lost my reason. Is she right? Am I mad? Is David the sane one, after all; I, the mad wife he must calm and protect? Do I imagine it all? But then I remember: *I don't keep human hearts in the pages of books.* 'Have you been taking proper care of yourself?' Mary carries on, bustling over the tea. 'Perhaps there's someone you should see, consult with...?'

I feel the recoil as if it were the release from an embrace, lightly done and insignificant. But we both know what it means. *Mary!* And I've lost her, just as quickly as I found her again.

So I clear my throat and force a laugh that comes out high and sharp. 'It's been such a long, hot summer. I'm in the sun too much, I think, the vegetable garden. You know I can't take too much of it. And I imagine too much, you know how I am.'

Mary helps me to my feet, dusts down her skirts. I sit back in my chair and sip my tea like a good child. 'Did you know there's a play of my book on in town?' she says, brightly. 'Of course you must, the posters are everywhere! Here I am come home from Italy for quiet and rest, and am given none of it.' Her new celebrity makes her smile. I tell her I haven't been in town for weeks. 'Really? You've seen nothing at all?' She is even more delighted. 'Poor Isabella! Get David to take you when he's better. "Presumption", it's called. "Or: the Fate of Frankenstein". It's tolerable so I've given them my blessing, although they certainly presumed, I assure you. I won't have my poor doctor staggering about the London stage bellowing like a demented cow who's lost its calf. After all that's happened, I want some understanding of my work. Is that too much to ask?'

It's as though nothing has happened: I did not faint, I did not ask her to help me destroy my husband. But that ferocious rubbing of her cheek, the obsessive pulling at her eye with her little finger, those deep indents that run from her nose to the edges of her mouth, give her away. She may think me mad, but her own melancholy tells me more.

'I don't want to talk about their quarrel,' she says, suddenly. Were we talking of it? *'The station your rank and fortune gives you in society, the sphere which it entitles you to move in are such as I cannot in good conscience introduce my family into, as it could only tend to give them notions and habits of life wholly unsuited to my circumstances and the humility of their expectations.'* My father's pride ended his friendship with Mary's husband. He hadn't meant to cause offence with his letter. *'Shelley is certainly insane, he does everything he can to become notorious.'*

Mary is brisk, alert. 'You had every right to change your mind about coming with us to the Continent and stay with your husband instead. We only asked because your father told us what a difficult time you were having, and we felt we should do something. I've never thought less of you for your decision. Whatever David may have said about me and mine.'

She shakes a little more sugar into her tea. His influence hasn't lasted that long, I think, unkindly. Her abolitionist husband was famous for sweetening his tea with raisins.

'I bear him no grudges. And what about your girls, dear Izzy and little Kathy? Is everyone else well?'

Everyone else. But her kindness only makes me cruel: 'How is your father?' I ask, instead. The teacup is set down; she stands up and her stiff black skirts flitter around my small parlour like the wings of a trapped blackbird.

'Oh, he's enjoying his fame, of course he is. He can afford to – they got up a donation for him and now he's happy. He hasn't given a thought to me or how I'm going to manage with little Percy on my own. When I've always tried to help him, given him what I can, when I think of all he took from us... oh, is this David's?'

50

The few sheets of worn vellum she holds in her hands have been abandoned to gather dust in the bookcase. 'No. Yes. Well, it was – part of something he was working on. He – we – his illness is... he has a new post. Superintendent for the Press of the Society for the Diffusion of Useful Knowledge. It involves some practicalities, some writing, editing, a little commissioning. It focuses on new studies. You remember how well he likes anything new.'

Mary gives her full attention to the first page, then returns them all to the shelf. 'I'm compiling a volume of Shelley's best poetry,' she says. 'I've already invited Hunt to compose an introduction.'

'David's still working on revisions to his work.'

'Our husbands aren't rivals.'

'I know that.'

'So David is still publishing? I did ask some of our friends when I arrived, I think, but no one knew of any new work...'

'Mainly pamphlets for now. Small studies.'

It's as if I haven't spoken.

'And I am to write something for a magazine, something that will sell well and help provide a little income for me. Perhaps I should write about our ghosts! People love to read about a ghost.'

But she has tripped herself into difficult territory once again. She gives me – me! – a startled look.

'I don't know what I said before...' I begin a last attempt to bring her to me, but she shushes me with her hand. There's an abyss opening up before her and she wants only to escape it, and me, as quickly as she can.

8.

Gheel, September 1823

Alexander had never imagined to fall in love with a lunatic, if love was what it was. Love wasn't part of his disposition. He wasn't always understood on that point, especially by women. Hepburn liked to tease him about 'Crazy Janes' when he first announced his interest in mental disease back in Edinburgh. Respectable young women who would raise their skirts, caught up in the frenzy their weak, distressed minds made of them. 'The physician's bonus,' he called it, pun intended. Alexander gave what he said little regard. He was never interested in their bodies. It was in their minds that the real matter, so to speak, lay. What was between their legs was the same with any woman, sane or insane, respectable or ruined, as far as he was concerned.

And yet Marie wasn't crazy, even if he had called her a lunatic in his own mind. She was, he had to admit, possibly the sweetest-natured woman he'd ever met. When her skin cleared and her behaviour improved, she was almost unrecognisable as the girl who had greeted him on his first day so awkwardly. He'd see her in the asylum building every day: when she began working as a kind of secretary to Bulckers, he found himself looking forward to it. Teasing her about her pronunciation of the English words he taught her. Noticing how her innocent smile yet suggested something knowing. Alexander wanted that knowledge, where it came from. How it had caused her condition.

It began about four months after his arrival in Gheel. His loneliness, no doubt, had something to do with it. That failing of his, and a natural attraction for each other. And the lure of a relationship between a doctor and his patient: she venerated him, as she must, he reassured himself, but not *too* much. A little physical play, a flick at her shoulder perhaps, a gentle tug on a curl or two, was all it took. And there she was, sitting at the other side of Bulckers' desk, waiting for him. The Director had been called away on an emergency on the outskirts of town, leaving them alone. Alexander smiled at her, white, even teeth, his best feature.

'Last week I went to the baker...' he began, as he approached the desk.

'And I bought a loaf of bread!'

'Well done!'

'These are child words.'

'You are impatient.'

'Impatient?'

'You want to know too much too soon.'

She'd nodded and raised a defined black eyebrow, thick and curved. Her long face squared off at the chin, almost the way a man's would. It fascinated him: she would be beautiful without that masculine bone structure but it was also what drew him. Her black hair gleamed in the light; her clear skin glowed against the whiteness of the room and he imagined her rising up, agitated and ready in the glare of the sun, like a thoroughbred before the race. He moved closer and saw her flush smooth its way from the top of her bodice up over her white neck and throat, dappled with perspiration. He put his hand under her mane, which hung long and heavy and drew it aside to cup the back of her neck. She trembled but didn't move. When he bent and brushed the downy skin with his lips, still she didn't move.

Why did he want her? He'd pondered it often. He wasn't in love with her. But she attracted him, beyond her unusual looks. That base urge to touch flesh with flesh: to know her. What she was withholding.

The next time they met wasn't in the asylum building: Marie had fired stones at his shutters after dark whilst he was working and drinking and as usual, getting nowhere. He opened the cracked shutter with too much force and its hinges broke.

'Alexander! I must speak to you!'

He grappled with the broken shutter, not pleased to see her.

'Do you know what hour this is?' he hissed down at her. He wrenched the shutter from its last nail and hauled it inside his room.

'Alexander! Let me in!'

He reappeared at the window, a veritable Juliet. How she would pay for this. 'Go home, Marie. You can't come up here.'

'It is very important. Now. I must see you now. I will not leave here.'

She actually sat down on the dusty earth, right under his window.

'Climb up then, if you're so determined,' he muttered, but he had no choice. He stumbled on the stairs – too much jenever – and opened the door. She was breathless, babbling words he couldn't make out; her cloak had slipped from her shoulder, exposing white skin. An offering of flesh. It was the moment he should have turned back: when he could still tell her to leave. Then, what would happen, might not have. But he ushered her upstairs.

She perched on the edge of his bed, her back arched to show off her round little breasts as best she could. He shook the last few drops of jenever into a small wooden beaker and pushed it at her, wondering how to punish her for this liberty. He knelt close, crushing her hand until she squealed. But she smiled, too: she will enjoy this night, what she has come for, he thought. First though, he had to pretend.

'Has something happened?'

He didn't want her to change her mind, not now, and kissed her open palm, tucked her hand inside his shirt. She shivered.

'I am what you need.'

He'd heard these words from women before and was momentarily disappointed but, he reminded himself, she was a provincial. It was unfair of him to expect originality from her. Even so, he pushed her hand away.

'You are very pretty, Marie, but I...'

'No, that is not what I mean.'

He was tired, already, of this game: his drunkenness had moved to another stage and once again he wanted her gone. As he stood up she shot out her hand and grabbed his thigh.

'Marie! This won't do – you need to go.'

'You do not understand me. I can tell you things. What you want. Your "case notes", is that right? I want to be your first case.'

That stopped him as if she had thrown all her clothes on the floor. And that thought, and that image, changed his mind.

'To be my case... it is a very close relationship. Very intimate. I would ask you all sorts of private things,' he said, softly. She didn't understand 'relationship' or 'intimate', but his hand was at her neck, smoothing away the thick, dark hair, and he knew she understood that, at least. She kissed his mouth, her fingers pulled on his shirt, and he held them fast, before directing them down to his groin.

Marie told him many things that night, and on nights after that. She carried everywhere with her a broken china doll, whose nose was missing. A grotesque thing. But she had been given it as a baby by her grandmother and wouldn't let it go. He'd seen her stroke the doll's patch of hair tenderly and speak to it as if it were her own child. He wanted to get to the bottom of that: there was a story to be told there.

And so he began to ease it out of her. She could be capricious, withholding information until he fucked her. But then she would talk and talk, about the uncle who would sneak into her room at night when she was very young and get into bed with her; about her mother, who liked to whip her on the bare bottom in front of their household staff even when she was as old as twelve or thirteen. Tales to titillate him? Or the truth: caught somewhere between dolls and babies, a lascivious uncle and a sadistic mother. Marie liked symbols, so he teased out the story of the doll, suspecting what it represented so obviously. She took to making him small gifts to express her love, most of which he tossed in the fire when she was gone. One was a lace-trimmed handkerchief, embroidered with her initials intertwined with his. 'A wife's gift,' she said, once, and he'd let her pretend. They were by the Nete that afternoon, hidden by willow trees. 'The lace is from Bruges,' she'd said, as she drew the handkerchief across his brow. 'The thread is silk. I sold something to pay for this.'

She looked sly but he wouldn't play her game this time, he would not owe her. 'Sexual favours for a bit of lace?' he'd shrugged. 'You sell yourself too cheaply, my love: two pieces of lace, at least.' Love made women stupid. And it made men say things they shouldn't. When she began to cry at his remark – she'd sold a ring her grandmother gave her, it turned out – he patted her tears with the handkerchief. Then took her hand, directed it down, undid his trousers: she knew to clasp him firmly now. How she could pump at him until he was ready! He used her handkerchief after: he didn't believe in symbols, he meant nothing by the action. But she did: she cleaned the napkin and later presented it to him again. And again he used it for the same task.

Her extreme mood swings, her tears and temper when she couldn't get hold of him, he put down to her love for him. But one day he asked Bulckers about it, in a roundabout way. 'Cullen argued madness and melancholy were caused by an excessive congestion of blood to the brain,' he'd said. 'Do you believe it?'

'One must ask what brings about that congestion in the first place,' Bulckers answered patiently. 'Material causes, or the jealousy of an abandoned lover? The resentment of an ignored spouse? The passions have long represented, ever since the Ancients, one route to grasping the sources of madness.'

'Crichton emphasizes physical or corporeal causes....' Alexander brought up the name of his mentor only gingerly. 'Is pain a sensation, or an affectation or emotion?'

'The role of the cerebral cortex in pain is not clear.' Bulckers had taken a sip of his Madeira and shrugged. 'What matters is the self. What else is our work about? The questions that we ask ourselves: where is the self located? In the mind? The brain? The soul?'

What matters is the self... and what about his 'self'? That, and the impact of childhood on the adult mind, wouldn't leave him. Alexander knew better than most what stories there were to be told from childhood. Stories, lies, truths, what was the difference? The narrative itself was what counted. He had to be able to interview patients on his own and interrogate them about their childhoods.

But it wasn't until he'd lived in the town a few weeks that he realized Gheel's very structure prohibited the kind of disclosure he needed. Lunatics were encouraged to work hard for the families who housed them, but they weren't challenged about their backgrounds. Within each parish was separate accommodation for Walloon speakers and for Flemish speakers, for wealthy and poor. These unseen boundaries were universally obeyed throughout the town. Inhabitants and patients were free to come and go during the day between each section, but at night they separated. Those with nervous dispositions, or delusions, found that calm living quarters and regular physical work reduced their symptoms. No criminal cases, of course: homicidal maniacs could not be housed with the sane. But there was no interest in patients' background beyond establishing their religious persuasion, financial situation and social class.

No interest in where Marie had come from. And that was why he was standing there in the rain in the middle of the night, of course. Bulckers clamped his hands to his head. It was a dramatizing gesture Alexander deplored. His belly griped but he didn't hear it.

'Marie won't come to any harm,' he said, at last.

'But she is not allowed out at night. Why would the Lutyens let her go out?'

His fear was like overdone meat, Alexander thought, *and wasted on me*. He shrugged at his employer.

'So they haven't permitted it. Is she with friends? Somebody we don't know about?'

It was an afterthought, but Alexander was as capable of jealousy as any man. He wanted to believe, like the hero of any cheap romance, that he was the only one. Her sexual forwardness he'd linked in his case notes to the unwelcome attentions visited on her by her uncle, but surely only he knew about this man? Bulckers looked at him accusingly.

'A lover, do you mean?' he asked. *'Another one?'*

9.

Richmond, September 1823

'Where did you get that dress?'

My pallet of clean bed linen smacks off the wooden floor-boards. My arms, still curved, carry a phantom load.

'I've asked you a question! Where did you get that dress?'

He's been much worse in the days since Mary's visit, as though he's guessed the wickedness growing inside me that has my heart staggering back and forth like a drunk man. Solutions that once made me shudder have got wilder in my head, making a macabre kind of puzzle that should be unthinkable. Yes: *how can you think it at all?* But then my heart lurches again and I know I can. And his guessing only increases his descent into a place without reason. *I am making him madder.* 'But thoughts of blood and death and endings will do that,' I whisper as I creep about the cottage, trying to make myself invisible. *Mariticide.* I'll be keeping them company in the underworld, I think, and I wonder about their daughters.

My girls are safe, though, staying with my father. For now, I hardly know if it's evening or morning and I struggle to keep my eyes open. Candlelight blurs the dimensions of his room and the hot wax makes me dizzy, and depend upon my little phial even more.

'It's just a dress, David.' I wipe my brow and wish I'd left the linen he needs outside his door. I can't ask little Janey to take it up to him when she delivers it, and it would have made me feel servile not to have come into the room with his washing. I bend stiffly.

'It's a slut's dress, I tell you!' he shouts, slamming his fist on the desk. The unusual heat that's been promising us a storm finally whips white across the darkened midday sky, just before the world breaks open. He sits unaffected by nature's bad temper but I'm imagining trees crashing on top of us, tornadoes scooping us up and flinging us about the world like children's dolls, and my body twists for the door, to go to my father's and comfort my girls. But I trip on something at my feet and when I reach for the mantelpiece, my hand slips on some papers.

'You stupid, ignorant woman, watch what you're doing with those!' he shouts again. He's been here in this stale, sweating room for days. His ashen face says he's been wasting his time, too, that his work still isn't fruitful. I have a sudden urge to retch and count, slowly, to ten.

'The storm... I'm worried about the girls,' I murmur.

I don't see it. He picks up the first volume on his desk and fires it at my forehead so fast that I swerve too late and it clips my temple. Another gash of white, another roar in the sky and David shakes his head from side to side like a demented Elder, his white hair loose and tangled. The scene is comic and ghoulish all at once and I don't know whether to laugh or throw something at him myself. *Make it right. This is your fault. Quickly, make it right!*

'What do you want, David? It's late.' I don't recognize the whining tone, the impatience, the self-pity. It's not what I intend, it's wrong. Sweat slicks along the back of my neck; my hair is uncoiled and it tickles. I know how slatternly I look, I've been sewing and cleaning and cooking all morning. David knows it too, he knows about the wet under my arms. My sticking, gamey underclothes. My thighs soaking and hot.

So he's right, after all: I am filthy, sluttish. My dirty hair, my stained dress. I am wrong. Wicked. A witch of a woman who thinks only of evil deeds, and who lacks the nerve she needs to do them.

Busyness keeps evil thoughts at bay. I struck a good bargain with him, once, I remind myself. I believed I could be happy, living to make him happy. He didn't love the shade at all, he promised me, but the sun. The light was what he wanted. A melancholy word from me would make him unable to think or feel. And his affection made him my confidant: I told him everything. So should I tell him this, now? What I have planned for him, for us?

He's staring at me and I have to find the right words. 'My dress doesn't mean anything, David, you know that. And don't shout at me like that, either.'

How easy he finds it to hate me when he is this way. 'You wear it when you go walking at night,' he spits. 'Is that why you want me asleep in bed? So you can sneak out and go walking about the streets, picking up strangers, you filthy whore?' He dismisses me as though I'm worth nothing more of his time and goes back to rummaging about the papers on his desk. I hesitate: I have to try and make it right. *One last time. Give him one last chance!*

'David, it's my oldest dress. I'm only wearing it because everything else is packed away. It doesn't mean anything.' He grunts and mutters under his breath. 'You can't write in this bad light. Come, David. You're too tired for this. You should be in bed.'

It was Conolly, his medical friend from the Society, who happened on us by chance that day of his first fit. I was keeping David warm on the floor with a cushion and a soiled blanket rescued from the scullery, unwilling to move him until he was recovered enough to stand by himself. Kathy and Izzy watched from a corner, curious, no longer afraid. 'Describe exactly what happened,' Conolly said. He was excited about it. 'And in what order. Don't get a single thing wrong.'

Conolly always makes me smile. His innocent enthusiasm makes me think of small boys left alone in sweet shops. But I deferred to him and answered his questions as he took David's pulse, examined his tongue. Then he announced: 'Epilepsy.' Just like a child, with little idea of the impact of the word, he didn't think to break the news gently. 'Which means...?' My unnecessary question, full only of horror. 'A form of madness. The Ancients had it about right.'

Madness. Bethlem. Wretches in rags, chained to walls. Bleedings. Purges. 'I know what you're thinking, Isabella,' he said, as he stood up, brushing little pieces of china from his trousers. David's eyes were shut tight still but he was breathing regularly. 'But we have better remedies now. We can cure this.'

'How on earth can madness be cured?' But my rude challenge only brought out the authoritative in him.

'Madness is a lack of reason,' he chided me. 'To be amended by the very thing that's missing.' He talked like a medical tract but, in spite of his patronizing tone, I liked that he didn't mention God, or the Devil. 'In practice, it means plenty of exercise, fresh air, fresh fruit and vegetables. No alcohol of any kind.'

'I don't understand...'

'To help reason return to the mind. And reading is good for him, too, but not too much. Some say leave reading altogether, but I think not. It will remind him of the philosophies of good sense.'

'No bleeding? No asylum?'

'No asylum. David isn't a savage. He's an educated man. His mind is occasionally blighted by an attack on the brain. But we can control it. We can cure it.'

Conolly's confidence in his diagnosis made David enthusiastic, too. He recognized something in it, he said to me in the days that followed. And he trusted a common sense approach that was mirrored by his favourite philosophers. He read the relevant passage out to me: '*There are other powers, of which nature has only planted the seeds in our minds, but has left the rearing of them to human culture. It is by the proper culture of these, that we are capable of all those improvements in intellectuals, in taste, and in morals, which exalt and dignify human nature.'* This affliction disturbs the body, so fresh air and exercise will make it healthier, stronger, more able to resist the fits when they come, he explained. *Exalt and dignify the mind. He is not a savage.*

I wanted to believe Conolly. I wanted to trust the answer. Sensible reading to restore his reason, mend the parts of the mind that are damaged. But diet and exercise haven't made the difference I was promised. Only those like Conolly, who have not lived so close by madness, can make such a bold claim.

Yet I still follow his advice. Every day, a record of what David has to eat and drink. Today, porridge with salt followed by two plums for breakfast; soup made from Sunday's mutton and kidneys with mashed potato and broccoli for supper. Could that small amount of meat have made the difference? The mutton stock? The kidneys? Conolly said to avoid meat, but David insists on it.

I record his temper, too. His last upset: two days ago. No physical damage but angry words. No sense made. Time lasted: approximately forty minutes. A new medical volume also advises a journal of all irrational behaviour and all parts of diet to be kept. But what does any book really know? What does 'distemper' mean? Or 'distraction'? Or 'derangement'? I keep wanting to ask Conolly on his rare visits. He quotes at me, too: *'Mad Men put wrong Ideas together, and so make wrong Propositions, but argue and reason right from them; But Idiots make very few or no Propositions, but argue and reason scarce at all.'* Last month David accused me of stealing money from him; three days ago, he suspected me of meeting with other men behind his back. But according to the philosopher, it is a matter of adjustment, that's all. His anger, his paranoia, his fits, will all have been just, if his principles are correct and I am a thief, if I am an adulteress. But as I'm neither of those things, as he knows well when he's calm, he has simply drawn right conclusions from the wrong principles. All he has to do is adjust them, form the right principles once again.

How easy they make it sound. But I have my own strategies. I pull my fist out of my pocket slowly. In my open palm lies a tiny, plain gold cross attached to a gold chain. David blinks at this memento of my mother's that reminds him of his Glassite faith and the good standing he once had, not the cost to him of marrying me. His eyes have a misty look and for a moment I'm hopeful. Until he speaks. 'And what's that supposed to mean?'

His unusual reaction confuses me and has me stammering, something he also hates. 'It's… my, my mother's, David. You know it… you know what it means. You like it.'

'Two gold bars crossed with each other. It could mean anything. It *does* mean anything. Anything and nothing.'

'That's not true, it's a cross. Don't you see…'

'It's two gold bars, cheap gold, too! It's a shape, that's all. What does it mean? Nothing. It comes from nothing. Maybe it suits your weak slut's mind to make it mean a multitude of things – what d'you think, then, tell me? That its maker ran out of enough gold to make a brooch? That a craftsman suffered from a poor imagination? You see – anything and nothing!'

I don't understand. My dress is old and plain, it has lots of purposes, lots of meanings. I'm wearing it because I loathe it; because if I soil it a little more then I can throw it away at last. But the cross: it has only one meaning. Suddenly, he reaches out, sinks his fingers into my thigh.

'David, stop it, you're hurting me!'

'Every change that happens in nature has a cause!' I splay my hands on the desk to give me balance. He slams his fist down on my fingers and the pain carves a cry out of me. 'Can you deny the existence of the material world? Your weak slut's mind: I can see it! It is a thing of evil.' He grabs hold of my temples, presses his palms against my cheeks. 'Let me squeeze the evil out of you, let it be gone!' My head starts to throb, my eyes are closing. I can't move his hands, and I squirm but he shouts again, 'Let it be gone!'

I don't faint or fall; I shove him back into his chair and the effort makes me stumble, land on the floor. 'David, stop this, it's late,' I cry out.

'I know what it means, you can't hide it from me!'

He bellows at the window, slams his fist down hard on the desk before collapsing over it, wailing like a child. My fingers find a huge book beside me, heavy and sharp-edged. They grip it, trace the gold lettering, the brass etching that gilds the cover. I stand up then slide behind him. I see more clearly now, how it will go.

Bludgeon his head. Smash in his skull. Grab my girls and run away. Yes, let them find him here, believe intruders have done this murderous work.

I use both hands to raise the book high. Last words: it occurs to me I should offer him last words, but there's not enough time for that. I take a deep breath, hold the book above my head and take aim. He's still now, weeping quietly; his white hair is thin, his skull vulnerable and soft. It will be easy to crush his skull, it will end now.

10.

Gheel, September 1823

Bulckers had caught them embracing in his office. Marie's dress was open at her breast, Alexander's hands and mouth were where they shouldn't have been. Neither of them had heard his footsteps in the hallway. Alexander admitted responsibility immediately, but only to that single moment of passion. It was enough, though, for Bulckers to encourage him to look for a post elsewhere, and the appointment in Montrose that an associate of his father's had engineered for him, and that he had previously been reluctant to accept, suddenly seemed a much more attractive proposition. He'd returned to his rooms and penned his acceptance that day. Marie hadn't liked it: she was, alas, too much in love with him.

On this wet evening, though, Alexander very much doubted he was the only one she may have loved. She was forward, after all, and possibly not completely cured. He must suspect her of promiscuity.

'More than a couple of boys in the town have given her a look over once or twice,' he said, at last.

Bulckers knew Alexander was trying to provoke him. 'I had imagined – hoped even – that you might know,' he said, sadly. 'That you do not, suggests something much more serious. Something deliberate. We have to find her!'

'She had settled in at the Lutyens house. And they were happy with her. She was almost ready to go home to her family, you said so yourself.' The two men had argued about this, too. Alexander couldn't divulge what Marie had told him, and he couldn't take her away with him when he left for Montrose. But he wouldn't have her go back to her family.

'I was wrong, clearly.'

Bulckers had believed that being in the company of the Lutyens, a young couple with two small children, helped Marie believe in her own destiny as a wife and a mother. Alexander had found his reasoning simpleminded at the time and said so. It was the trigger for a second serious quarrel between them and showed the real professional divisions between them. None of it was Marie's fault, Alexander realized now: she was so willing, so grateful, so responsive to him, and he couldn't have failed to fall in love with that, just a little.

She wanted to be his wife, she said. As if he would have married a lunatic! But he still cared, even though their involvement with each other was at an end. Why else would he be out in the rain when he could be finishing his beer in a nice, warm inn?

'Has she taken anything with her?'

Bulckers shook his head.

'No, no, she has taken nothing!'

'Well, then she must have gone to meet someone and is planning to return. I don't think we need to panic yet.'

'No, no, you must help me, right this minute. I insist! She has been gone for over three hours! And... I will explain it. There was something. I did not believe it was important. But I will tell you.'

Alexander pulled his coat tighter against the rain.

'She did not want you to leave. She did not take the news well.'

'I know that myself.'

'Then perhaps she did not believe you. She begged me to keep you here, but I told her, in view of everything, of course I could not...'

Water trickled down the back of his neck. He was becoming bored with this. Bulckers and his old-woman concerns and Marie with her lovesick, wayward ways. He decided to be harsh with her when he found her: there would be none of the gentle goodbye he had planned. He wouldn't even fuck her, not even if she begged him.

'Very well. Where might she be? The church?'

'No, I have been there. Oh, I have taken risks with that girl! I should have paid more attention.'

This alerted him. 'What risks? What are you not telling me?'

But Bulckers was already crossing the square, Alexander following close now.

'I mean it, what are you not telling me?'

Beer from his breath sweetened in his nostrils. Marie wouldn't have gone far: she wanted them to hunt her. The shutter of a nearby house creaked open and watery candlelight rippled through the rain. He could hear voices.

'We've woken folk with our worry and we haven't time to organize a real search party,' he said. 'This something you're not telling me. Do I need to know it?' But he'd missed his chance. Bulckers was calm now and dismissed the question with an accusation that brought Esme Fleming to Alexander's mind: the angry, weak rebuttals he'd given to her charges: 'don't I see you all the time? When do you imagine I might have the time to court someone else?' Bulckers did the same now, making him feel powerless, suspicious: like a woman, being lied to. Alexander clamped his fingers in a fist and gritted his teeth. It was time he got away from the director and the games he played. He suggested they split up and Bulckers agreed.

'I'll go to the garden behind the infirmary. She liked dancing there, remember, that summer dance? Maybe it has some special connection for her.'

Bulckers said he would try the hall, as another flame was lit in another house and another shutter opened. *We're unsettling them all*, Alexander thought. *Even if they can't hear us, they know something is wrong.*

He hurried past the square and squeezed along the narrow path to the infirmary. It was drizzling now and overhanging branches fingered his hair, flicked water on his face. He wouldn't be searching for patients in the rain in Montrose, he'd make damn sure of that. Marie had gone off with a boy from the town, she was that kind of girl. She liked making a fool of him, punishing him for not marrying her, for leaving. He wanted only to stop playing this game, and his impatience made him call out her name, too loud. Keeping others in the town from alarm was no longer his priority.

He'd expected Marie to show herself when she heard his voice, so he was surprised when there was no response to his calling. He was outside the infirmary now, and moved out of the shadow of the building round to the side. Across the moist grass something caught his eye. Beyond the cultivated gardens that Marie liked so much was a large oak, planted over a hundred years ago by a grateful English patient, so he had been told. As he approached it, squelching across the wet grass, he could see that one of the oak's branches had broken, as if lightning had struck it. But there had been no storm. Yet the loose branch swayed there, hanging in the breeze, gently listing back and forth.

That was when he realized, of course, that there was no breeze that night. When he tried to run towards it, the waterlogged grass slowed him down and he stumbled. The memory of his stumbling, the wetness, the sound of nothing: it all appeared in his dreams for many nights after. The many nights after he found Marie had hanged herself. Trying to run, even when it was too late.

11.

Richmond, September 1823

I raise my hands still further and that's when I catch it: an odour I've never noticed before. Bitter, thick with lemon sharpness. Not the muskiness of old books or the sickly sweetness of dead flowers. The opposite of decrepitude. Lack of reason is an immature scent, primordial, I realize. It's sharp and sour like unripe fruit. Eat those and you'll be ill, I warn the girls all the time about the berries in the lane. Wait till they ripen. *Breathe it in, and you'll be ill with it, too.* His illness is a catching thing; and I'm catching it.

I lower my hands and the book tumbles to the floor. I clamp my hand over my mouth but it's too late: he's contaminated me. *The demon is inside you, too, and it's going to make you kill your husband.* Maybe not today, my voices tell me, but tomorrow perhaps, or the day after that. I'm not safe for him, or for anyone, not even for my beautiful girls. A great sob escapes me finally, all the tears I won't shed come at once and I sink under them, clasp at his feet. *Forgive me.* It is an elusive thing, forgiveness. But I have it in my hands now, as material as the ribbon I've pulled from my hair, and I'll wipe my tears with it, if he'll let me. I stand up slowly and put my arm across his shoulders. He is sleeping on his desk, and I bend forward, kiss the back of his head. 'Forgive me,' I whisper. *He will never let you go.*

I slip downstairs to the dining room. Something plummets inside me, like a paperweight on eiderdown, and I sit down and look about as if for the first time. The afternoon sunlight breaking through now the storm is past is cruel, and shows up filth not yet brushed from the mantelpiece or the windowsill. This is where we eat and I've done nothing to keep it clean. Teacups still lie on the table from supper, and the milk's sour smell carries the whiff of horseradish I've used to keep it fresh. I'm a good wife, I tell myself again: few could do more! I have nothing to be ashamed of.

So why this sobbing? Why this invisible little army of pinpricks stinging my shoulders, burning my neck and my cheeks? Isn't their whispering enough? *Once, you might have been bold. Yes, when you were first married, you might have been bold, then.* They're smarting the soles of my feet, forcing off my shoes. But burning can be beautiful, I think. Leaning back, I close my eyes. *But there was nothing to make you suspicious, then. Not even when Izzy came.* Now they tingle my back with a delicious fire, let loose little flames to lick around the base of my spine. *Just after your third anniversary, wasn't it?* I pull at my bodice, force my fist inside. *That's when you should have been bold! You almost were.*

And I'm almost ready to tear my dress from me when the burning stops as quickly as it began: I can chase them away if I want to. They're nothing, can do nothing more to me: something in my clothing I used to clean my dress, that's all. A reaction to something I've eaten, perhaps. I am different from my father. I can recognize the diabolical when I see it. Or feel it.

One of the few teacups on the table is cracked. I stand up, shakily, smooth the stained white cloth back over the table and pocket the damaged cup. The serrated edges of the small bread knife are not sharp, but still, when I pull them along the inside of my wrist, a nip at the vein dots blood. I lick the tiny cut, replace the knife.

You're a Baxter.

I shove the apron to my face: its fug of fish and eggs makes me cough, hesitate for a moment. I'm ashamed of what I'm about to do, but that won't stop me. I've been told too often how shameless I am.

You're a Baxter.

The little brown phial in my pocket: ten drops on the tongue, for whenever I am anxious, no more. I count ten once, then again, and it comes swiftly: that softness, then a clearing. Lines disappear, resume their place, happier this time, softer. I sigh and sit down.

'Mrs Booth! Mrs Booth! It is a matter of great urgency! You must let me in!'

The cry makes me start; a thumping on the front door follows, and I wait. A draught-horse heaves its load along the lane then soft, heavy bundles thud onto yellowing grass. I want them to leave me alone but something forces me out of the dining room at last, something beyond the insistent rapping at the door and when I reach it, I flatten my palm against it in penance. Or maybe a warding off of danger: *Do as you're bid and open the door!*

Our cottage faces north and ivy hangs over the doorway so the little fading light that gets in is blocked by a tall gentleman dressed head to toe in black. He's wearing a hat like a biretta that almost touches my skirt, he bows so low.

'Mrs Booth!' A long, white rat is sitting on the man's shoulder, nuzzling his ear. Why would a religious man require such a pet? 'What is it?' I say, my hand peaked at my forehead. My voice sounds strange and I almost expect him to notice and remark on it, even though we've never met before. But he has the confidence and self-regard of an orator, born to persuade. His 'Madam!' booms past, drowning out my voice.

'I've been sent to you, Madam, on a mission. A mission to save you! Please – may I come in?'

So they've sent him, after all: *well, I've been expecting it.* But he'll find it just as hard to cajole and convince me as they did all those years ago. Why would I listen to their arguments now? It's too late for me to reconsider, doesn't he know that? My church won't have me back, but he's not a Glassite. He must be from another order, but I don't ask which. I'm too distracted, watching fascinated as he slips off his biretta without unseating the rat, which twitches at his neck more closely.

'I don't understand... what do you want?' I say, playing for time. 'Are you selling something?' But I'm dazed with his presence, the help from my little phial, the shock of the morning and what I tried to do. I make a mistake, step back, and immediately he takes advantage of the space and slides into the hallway, trailing a scent of camphor.

'I've been sent by one who wishes to help you,' he sings as he passes. His is an unremarkable face but his voice is high-pitched and ethereal, and sparks laughter in me before tears burn my eyes for the second time today. He dips his head to enter the parlour, behaves as though he's been invited in. 'I have something to give you, Mrs Booth,' he croons, and bewitched, I follow him.

Our little parlour might be missing the china lamps and vases after David's first fit but the two easy chairs, the scratched mahogany side-table and small bookcase, and the small rural scene on the mantel above the hearth still fight for space. They all belong to Margaret, of course. It's demeaning to keep them, but I've no choice. I remember my apron, remove it quickly and bundle it up in my hands. I check my hair ribbon, too, forgetting that I've removed it, and wish my hands were less rosy. It's important he knows I'm still respectable, whatever they've told him.

'What can you have to give me? Has someone sent something?' He sits opposite, the poor sunlight giving his skin a sheen nevertheless. Perspiration glints on his face.

'I have indeed been sent – by a concerned party. And they want me to give you this.'

Only now do I notice the small wooden casket on his lap. 'I know what you endure,' his falsetto surrenders suddenly to a bass tone, sinister and low. Long, strong fingers drum along the top of the casket and he bares strong teeth in a wide, unreal smile.

'Do you know – what is inside it?' He offers the box but when I don't move to take it, pulls it away.

'I know,' he continues in the same tone, 'how you take him food and drink in bed every night until he is well again.' His fingers stray mesmerizingly to his collar, white and pristine, but don't soil it with contact. 'I know – how you make sure his books are by his bedside so that when he wakes he can gaze upon them and see his name written there: David Booth.'

He reaches down to the small brass buttons on his black waistcoat, plucks at one briefly, then flits away. 'I know – that sometimes when he wakes he is a little confused by his surroundings, does not recognize his girls at first. Am I right?'

How can he know such things about me and my husband?

'I know – that the first night after a fit you sleep on the floor beside his bed to give him the comfort of your company. And that you return to your own room a few days later.' His eyes are palest blue, fringed by black. 'Speaking eyes', my father calls them: Izzy has them, too. Offering up a soul out of innocence sometimes, or fear. But he's not afraid and he's not innocent. He leans in and whispers, as though he knows how much his voice dazzles. 'I know – that you have not shared a bed at night for a long time. He told you his working late would disturb you.' I open my mouth to speak, but he has more to say.

'I know – that you don't like to be alone. That is why you moved your girls into your room. I know about your irrational fears. Your fancies.'

'I know – what takes place behind closed doors. Between a husband and wife.'

'I see what others do not. That is why I am here to help you.'

'*I know what you mean to do!*'

The little brown phial: I'm afraid and need it now, but still he is speaking and I don't understand how he knows it all, when there's another knock at the front door and he stops. It's a soft tap, this time, light and feminine. 'It's Mary, she's come back!' I say, rising out of my chair. 'My oldest friend. I knew she would help me, after all!'

'Then please let her in,' he smiles at me again. 'I would be glad to meet her.'

I don't like him, but I don't want to leave him. He urges me again though, so I move, slow and heavy, across the floor. At the door I turn round.

But the stranger is gone.

12.

Gheel, September 1823

Alexander decided to leave the plaster of Paris skull on the window ledge. His many books, inked and cloth-eared, were still piled by the wooden bed-frame, yet to be packed and stored for later transportation. He began to pick them up and place them in the open wooden crate. His maps of the mind, drawn haphazardly and with little care, lay rolled on the bed. He'd already decided to carry those. His clothes, such as he possessed, had been forced into the single trunk in the middle of the floor. He was left, after this, to survey his few possessions with something like puzzlement, as if they didn't belong to him at all. Today, he was leaving. For Ostend, the package boat to Hull; then a coach to Edinburgh and Montrose.

Did I kill Marie? he asked himself again in the gloom of his rooms. Already though it was tickling the back of his brain: Marie, she'd be his first published paper. Without the melodramatic story of her last hours, of course. So he was answering his own question, then. For his responsibility was surely combined with her condition, her background, her treatment, her environment, each of which could be divided again, and then again once more. Not his fault.

She'd left a note, of course. She was a clever girl. It wasn't found on her body: she knew enough of his work to guess how it might be soiled when they cut her down. No: she'd posted it before she killed herself and Alexander received it the next day. Perhaps she didn't want to expose her private thoughts to the world. He didn't inform Bulckers or divulge a single word of it to anyone, telling himself its contents were only what one might have expected. A great deal about sacrifice and betrayal. The romantic sort of note one might have expected from a love-sick young girl. Well, she wasn't in her right mind.

He knew Bulckers was glad to be rid of him, and he was glad to be going now, too. What his employer had kept back from him had also been excised from Marie's notes: that she'd tried to kill herself once before, after giving birth to an illegitimate child that was subsequently taken from her. Alexander had no idea why Bulckers chose not to divulge that information: he considered it a serious professional misjudgement and one for which he would never forgive the man. That Marie had failed to tell him herself he found strangely more understandable. He had suspected the grotesque doll she carried everywhere signified a baby, but he'd guessed nothing about a previous suicide attempt.

And so: the tragedy of her death could not be his fault. He'd learned his lessons here: closeness to patients gave him the information he needed, but it compromised him, too. He hadn't yet found out how to achieve one without the other but he would – at Montrose.

Poor Marie! She had taught him a great deal. She would have met a good man, even had a good life, perhaps. She hadn't needed to cry over him.

'Ah well,' he sighed out loud. He wiped the dust off the skull and, having second thoughts, slipped it into his knapsack. Failure stank and this room was clogged with it, the dust motes that hung in the air were full of it. He'd cleared away most of the evidence of his drinking habits but he knew that his sins had seeped into the walls somehow and would only incriminate him further as soon as he was gone, so that all the townsfolk would soon know the truth of his corruption. He hadn't saved Marie. He was to blame, after all: he'd corrupted her when he could have saved her.

The tears that pricked his eyes did so because only a few minutes had passed since he'd finished the last of the jenever. So he would be leaving drunk? That was easy enough for him, always had been. At university, Alexander had been the ideal student. He could study after a night of carousing because he simply carried on drinking more the next day. He'd attended not a single lecture in a sober state. And yet his work was always admired. Lennox accused him of having a doppelgänger sit in his place; Hepburn said his father must have better contacts than Alexander let them believe.

But they didn't really care, and neither did he. Instead, they had laughed, during late nights drinking in taverns off the High Street, about the 'butcher boys' and 'sawbones' who hadn't the means to obtain a degree, those sons of farmers and the poorer merchants who would be apprenticed out to work on His Majesty's ships, or maybe one of the better metropolitan hospitals, if they were lucky, once they were qualified to do so. For men like them, it was a very different matter. They kept their hands clean.

It was time for him to go. He'd carry his trunk and knapsack downstairs one last time and wait for the coach that would take him through Antwerp and on to Ostend. His time in Gheel was over. He needed to wash it clean of him. Montrose wouldn't contain it all, the losses and the fears, if he didn't put it behind him.

Forgive me, Marie.

But the feeling was fading already. He was sober now: the tears wouldn't come, he knew he was at the end of it.

Give me another chance.

Alexander didn't know of whom he was asking forgiveness. There was no one to hear him: no one to grant it. And he didn't see why he should need it. Already he was shrugging off the notion of his corrupting influence on Marie. It was nothing to do with him. It wasn't his fault, after all. He did his best to help her.

He leant down, away from the lies that lingered, suspended above him in the thick, clammy air and that might just choke him if he didn't hurry. He pulled at the handle of the trunk and heaved it down the stairs. Yes, it was time for him to leave this place, and all that had occurred here, far behind. Something better awaited him elsewhere. And who knew, a better woman, too, perhaps? He smiled at the thought of it.

13.

Richmond, September 1823

The breeze breathes autumn: the storm that smashed the heat three days ago littered my garden with leaves and branches that still lie strewn across our path. But we are leaving, my girls and I. We are heading home: to the land I come from. It's all arranged: a short holiday for a tired wife and her girls, he understands that; has even, to my surprise, welcomed my request with something like eagerness. Perhaps even he knows I'm not safe for him. Perhaps he's pleased to have this break from me, as I am from him. I call to my girls to button up their coats and give their papa a last kiss goodbye. Like a good wife.

I've hardly slept. The stranger's visit: did I conjure it? *What I wanted to do. The book, heavy in my hands.* Shame has stayed with me ever since, and now, three whole days later, my cheeks still burn at the thoughts I've had, the lies I've told throughout my life. *In sickness and in health.* My hands are roughened with the cooking and cleaning I do myself. *As long as you both shall live.* My hair, once thick and shiny, has become thin and dull. In the autumn sunlight, I might forget the woman I am now, the woman I was never meant to be. My heart fills, holds close to my chest, as if to stop any beauty there from fleeing. But why should I want any of it back? Beauty only makes us passive women: Mary's mother said so. *'The world cannot be seen by an unmoved spectator, we must mix*

in the throng, and feel as men feel before we can judge of their feelings.'
To be active is more important. *'Marriage will never be sacred till women, by being brought up by men, are prepared to be their companions rather than their mistresses.'*

But I've been no companion. Scott's bride of Lammermoor, who killed her husband on her wedding night, was turned mad by what was facing her. So they snigger: as so many women might do, given half the chance, they say. We women aren't meant to like it, what lies ahead of us in the marriage bed. But the story is not only about a crazy bride. That would be too minor a tale. It's about the struggle of good against evil. The inescapability of the past. A predetermined future. Not about a mad woman on her wedding night at all. A story told to Scott by his great-aunt Margaret Smith, who was murdered by a female servant in a fit of insanity, they take care to mention.

What did David marry me for? Because I could talk to him about the separation of the mind and the soul? Did that make him want me? Did he want a better companion, one enlightened enough to suit him? Like Mary, whom he could not have. I'm too fond of my books, Aggie always said so. It means I am still, even now after the birth of two girls, pleased to be told I am pretty. David did, that wintry day in the garden, when the ground was covered early with snow. Mary was gone; I was almost seventeen. We talked about Blake and the nakedness of the human soul. An erotic subject, couched in cold words. Trying too hard to tempt him.

'It's an openness to God, and that's a rational position.' I was being arch, showing off. He smiled at my conceit. Mary might have gone, but she left something of her daring behind for me.

'An artistic position, not a rational one, Bella. We often assume one cannot be commensurate with the other and Mr Blake merely took advantage of this prejudice. He marketed himself well. A stunt, merely.' I raised my chin to show my mouth to its best advantage, and blew the cold air smoky with my breath. 'I don't think Mr and Mrs Blake appeared naked in the garden just to make people talk.'

'Then you think too highly of either of them.' That flush on his cheeks. His hair was still coal black then. His eyelashes were pale, though, and made grey clouds of his eyes. I loved to warm his face with my wicked words, see if I could make him stumble with his. A wilful sixteen-year-old, a most dangerous age: I must watch for it with Izzy and Kathy. Yet I struggled to keep the subject going. When he reached out to brush that leaf from my hair, it was to quieten or distract me, but I caught his hand as he grazed my fringe. The only knowledge that matters is the knowledge of what you can do to someone, and how to effect it. And so I pouted. 'My hair is part of nature, too.'

He looked over my head. 'Your hair is beautiful. I wouldn't spoil it with any decoration, natural or otherwise.' His voice was hoarse and I wouldn't let go of his hand. I took it to my breast instead, inserted his fingers inside my cape. My surprise that he didn't pull away undermined me. Knowledge can be too much, sometimes. 'How beautiful you are. The most beautiful...' And so words made him fall. I was worse than Eve: I was helping him betray the memory of my sister. We both knew what we were doing.

And now I must wonder what it was about *him* that *I* loved. He once belonged to Margaret. He once wanted Mary. What did it mean to be as Mary's step-sister, Claire is, now: a governess in Russia? The courage or the desperation to *mix in the throng*. The world he showed me beyond Broughty Ferry when circumstances forced us to London were not romantic stories. I think of David, lecturing me about ethics and language, preaching the importance of the Sacrament and the congregational system on which our Glassite church was founded. The accumulation of property was a sin, but I knew it already. Did I believe I could uncover some romance in him? His dalliance with Mary, yes: I thought there was desire in his soul.

A pretty tale, then. And as empty as it is pretty. But I was shameless. When the early days of our marriage made it so. The heat of his mouth against my neck. The bristles on his chin that tickled my throat. A palm, pressing on my breast. Fingers that worked once to loosen the buttons on my bodice. His lips tracing down to the faint curve of my small, flattish breasts and his tongue licking at my nipple. What he did to me when we were alone in bed, once upon a time: when the points of my hips jutted out to spike him as he lay on top of me; when he wondered at the babyish dip of my back, the white smoothness of my thighs. How he touched me as if a woman's body was new to him. And every time I wondered if this was how he touched my sister; if I cleaved to him the way Margaret did, once. What made me open to him more. Made me whisper wanton things that were never in my head, and he'd turn me over, slap my behind hard. I'd be his mistress, not his wife, and that thought made me worse, made me reach for him with words I never knew. Later he'd be soft to me again, and we'd curl together and the madness would leave me.

In the mornings after such nights – *did they happen or did I dream them?* – David ignored me, twisted himself out of our bed as though I was something dirty, diseased. I learned that I wasn't supposed to enjoy those nights. A good wife would fear them; only a mad, bad wife could want them. My husband was disgusted with me for it. Whether for the enjoyment I displayed, or for the badness or madness that motivated it, I never knew. He was disgusted, too, that *he* enjoyed those nights. And that I knew he did.

So soon after we married, the man who delighted, once, in touching me, was equally delighted to have a reason to sleep apart from me. When night came and he couldn't control himself with me; after Kathy he slept apart from me. I'm not a child any longer. Was that what he loved about me?

I've no one to tell. I think to myself every day that this is the way of all marriages, and sometimes it's easy to imagine he's right to conduct himself as he does. I was born wicked, as our faith has it. But my original sin is peculiar to me. I've never worked hard enough to get rid of it. The Devil's in me, too. So we are mad, both of us, my husband and I.

But I am the whorish one: the slut who enticed him with talk of nakedness. Who knows what real depravity is. We must stay away from each other. He never knew of my girlish nights with Mary: sneaking into her bed and huddling together in the cold and dark, 'practising', as she would say, as we warmed ourselves under the covers. Our night-robes curling up between our legs, her hot breath on my ear, fingers at my breast: all of this was long before David touched me. Yes: before David, I was shameless, I tend to forget that. I cannot blame him for everything.

I shiver as a few pale pink rose petals flutter loose from the overgrown branches that knock against the cottage window. I shield my face and the faint purple trace of a bruise on my temple, turn away from his proffered arm. The air is smoky and the dust churned up from the road makes me cough: it's time we were gone. Hundreds of jobs are still to be done, I tell him. The latch on his bedroom window is rusty and broken; the path to the front door has to be weeded. I can't turn round and face him. 'We won't be long,' I murmur. 'Only a few weeks.'

'Don't forget the letter.' Soft words; his beard grazing lightly. A cool kiss, brief, to mark the shame of my leaving. His treacherous wife.

'Of course I won't.' His hand is fast around my wrist; I strain for Kathy's plump fingers with my free hand because my box, with all my personal things, is under my arm. His jealousy would prise it open, but he hasn't noticed it. 'Take care, David,' I turn and whisper, press one last kiss to his cheek. 'And don't worry about us.' I strike a lighter tone. 'You'll be happy with a house free of us all at last.'

He tells Izzy and Kathy to behave at their aunt's as he lifts them into the carriage, then abandons his cheerful tone to hiss in my ear, 'Don't forget the letter! In person, you must deliver it in person.'

I nod again: it's intended for the manager of a hospital in Montrose, a kind of asylum, he told me this morning. He patted my shoulder when he saw my alarm. I only want your opinion of the place, he said. A radical establishment. A rest for men of genius. I must see it for myself, and report back to him of conditions inside, its inmates, or patients. If they're the right co-habitants for him; if it's somewhere that will benefit him. I tried to argue that I'd scarcely recognize such a place, but hadn't the strength to oppose what he seems to have set his mind upon. More of a retreat than a hospital: yes, perhaps it will help him. Perhaps these last few days have brought him to a point and there's room for hope, after all. But I can't follow far down that path. He isn't the only one who needs counsel and rest. Perhaps there will even be someone I can confide in, someone who will make me safe for my girls.

'I won't let you down,' I say with a conviction I want to feel. 'I promise you. I'll write and tell you as soon as I've been there. You can trust me.'

He raises my bad hand to his cheek and I wince. My gloves cover what he doesn't remember. 'You're a good girl, Isabella.' Then he whispers: 'Have you seen Margaret? What does she say?'

He asks about her every day. I thought at first he meant my vision but now I wonder if he even knows she is dead, if my husband has lost that much of his reason. But I've no more time and tell him no, I haven't seen her. He loses the eager, sly look from his face and shrugs. 'No matter. Don't forget the letter, Isabella.'

'I have it safe. Please don't worry. I'll deliver it.'

'In person, it must be in person,' he reminds me again. Once I'm seated beside my girls, my box safely on my lap and his letter tucked inside my coat pocket, I lean out of the carriage window, strangely sad to be leaving the squat little dwelling that's been my home for so long.

But already David has disappeared inside the cottage and closed the door behind him, and I have a sudden glimpse of flight from a bloody scene indoors, of a smashed skull on a bedroom floor, a glimpse that delights the blackness in my soul. It knows what I still wish for. It whispers, *another chance*, and taunts me as I grip my box and smile at my girls. Taunts me all the way to Ramsgate and beyond, as I wonder if I will ever see my husband again, if I will ever come back.

PART TWO

Broughty Ferry and Montrose

1.

Montrose, early October 1823

He eased himself slowly from the carriage, his limbs stiff and resisting after the long journey. Remnants of stale bread and discoloured meat made their way up from his gut after bilious days on the road, had him retching at the roadside. The east coast wind tore at his coat-tails, and he cursed bad food and a rude welcome into the bargain. But when Alexander could finally look around him, the edges of the town had given way to what he wanted.

'Ah, Venice of the North!' He didn't mean a sneering tone; he saw little to deter him from his plans. 'Aye, and it is,' the driver frowned, as if only a fool would question the logic of it. He nodded across thick green fields. 'I can take you nearer the place.' Alexander shook his head. 'I want the walk,' and the coachman shrugged, ordered his horses to move on. *Athens for Edinburgh, Venice for Montrose.* 'Scotland, the new civilized world!' he smirked, as he stood alone in the quiet of the road. 'Ancient and Renaissance in one!' But he wasn't displeased.

He might have been thinner and weaker from lack of decent nourishment, and the fever that had delayed his journey, laying him low in a tavern for days. His tweed coat hung off his shoulders and his shirt was loose-fitting now and flapping, but as he tasted salt on his lips Alexander thought only about the fullness of his future. He flexed his arms, stretched out lean fingers. 'A surgeon's hands,' Hepburn had teased him once, back in Edinburgh. He took off his hat and ran these same sensitive fingers through what was left of his dark red curls after a barber on the way had seen fit to hack at them, and for too many coins. But at least the beard he'd been growing since Gheel was full. 'There's more than one Alexander Balfour,' he murmured, as he surveyed the stretch of land around him. And one of them would be left behind.

Such conclusions didn't arrive, though, without a little anxiety beforehand – should he have gone back to Edinburgh after all? Tried for a position in Groningen or Leiden? He'd taunted himself with the different options, let them spike his new-found assurance as the coach jolted along. But none of those places provided him with the opportunities he wanted.

Time was moving on: late afternoon already. He was impatient to make his entrance; he'd ordered his trunk and packages to be sent to an inn on Apple Wynd so he felt free of his burdens. The October light was strong and the unseasonably warm air had travelled with him through the days all the way from the Continent as he crossed Ferry Road, in spite of the wind that had him clutching his hat. He knew better than most that there was no time like the present. No one could accuse him of putting things off.

Buttoning his coat, Alexander took a last look about him then made for the fields ahead. The asylum might have been far in the distance but he could still see a new, plain, homely building, the kind he'd liked so much in Gheel. *No symbolism here!* The hospital matched the period of other new terraces in the town, but the coach had passed enough narrow wynds and dark little closes to remind him of old Edinburgh, too. He wouldn't be stuck at the margins as he'd feared he might. He'd come back to the centre. *Where men of genius need to be.*

The absence of his new employer, William Browne, aided his sense of possession as he approached, his boots kicking up earth and grass from dry fields. His delay had meant he'd missed Browne, who had already departed for Paris for almost two months. His new deputy would be in charge from the very beginning. Alexander had been assured, though, that everything ran 'like clockwork'. They expected him to slip in, then, and stay quiet.

He laughed to himself as he walked on, enjoying a few late brambles on the way, whistling against the wind while he pictured time alone with individual patients, case notes building as stories were revealed like layers of underclothing. *Souls stripped bare.* Nothing would spook him here as it had in Gheel.

Nor as it had in Edinburgh before that, what had set him off so fast and so surely for a backward town on the Continent. The memory of a lone man stepping out of the night to stop him on his way back to his lodgings just off the Canongate could still haunt his dreams from time to time. Not a rogue to steal from him, or batter him to the ground, but another kind of man altogether, with a special proposition for a medical student like him. The coarse Irish burr of his voice had left Alexander stumbling over cobbles that night back to the light of the streetlamps, away from the darker corners of medicine. He hadn't been disillusioned by something many suspected took place. But might his ambition been tempted to benefit from it? 'Mind-doctors: grave-robbers of a different kind,' someone had said laughing, just before he left for Gheel, and the city was full of talk. Alexander didn't see the joke.

He did now that he felt safe. Montrose: too pretty for vice but not for madness, he thought as he made his approach. Black smoke swirled high from one of the asylum's four solid chimneys and he pictured the fine fire laid ready in the parlour for him, where he'd sit with a drink in his hand and time to impress himself on the place. 'Too comfortable already,' he smiled at his own excitement. 'You'll get lazy. And complacent.' *Balfour men.* He'd defy that heritage here, he'd work and learn and work some more and, in time, publish those books that would make his name and gain the acclaim of his peers. *The greatest of the mind-doctors.* Perhaps, yes – a little complacent, then. But so what if he was? This was a fine building in front of him: he could afford to be.

Too hot from his hurry and panting now, Alexander forced himself to slow down and unbuttoned his tweed coat and loosened his neck-tie. A warmer day than he'd thought, hopefully the sign of a milder winter to come, made him picture fresh air and exercise over the next few months. Some local hunting, perhaps. He'd be as fit as his patients; what was good for them was good for him. Such cheering thoughts as he neared his new home; he should have known better. He'd remember the innocence of that walk much later, when events kept him from sleep and led him to a bottle. A journey that belonged to a different Alexander.

Because when he stretched his neck free of his tie altogether and looked up again, he saw that the blot of black staining the blue sky wasn't from a chimney at all. None of the chimneys seemed to be in use.

His legs were surprisingly heavy as he tried to run, doing their best to hold him back: his body defying what his mind wanted, but the mind won every time. So he ignored the mix of nausea and bile rising in his throat at something too familiar and horrible, traced the plume to its source. Someone had smashed an upper window in the attic, and the smoke pouring out was fast getting thicker and blacker.

Alexander had to stop for a moment and catch his breath. He shielded his eyes with his hand and saw, or imagined that he saw, flames licking the edge of the attic window frame, sending wooden flecks birling into the air. 'Fire!' he called out. The front steps of the asylum were shallow and easy for him to take three at a time. 'Is anyone here?' he shouted into a silent, deserted hallway. 'Fire!'

But he was the trigger, after all. Thanks to him, chaos ensued. Women of all shapes and sizes, yet made uniform by the plain grey dresses and white caps they each wore, poured from rooms, down the central staircase, across the hallway, as though they'd been hiding behind doorways in expectation of alarm.

Inmates. They shrieked and yelled as he expected, and paid him not the slightest bit of notice, but gushed from the building into the gardens outside, their escape made easier by sheer volume. He'd pictured isolated cases, not this mass of hysteria; another Alexander, disgusted with throng, might have turned tail and run after them, kept running until his breath gave out. But he was new-fashioned, now. A different creature.

He pushed past them all and made for the stairway as a woman called for calm, and he gave quick thanks for her assistance. With no clear idea of where he was going, though, and nobody to direct him, he'd to trust he hadn't miscalculated: the smoke was about four windows along the third floor on the left. The smoky gloom of the attic corridor was ghostly and he stopped, momentarily unsure a living person was the cause of the danger.

'I'm not here!' A girl's voice was shrill and absurd, but reassuring nonetheless. 'Nobody can find me!' she shrieked and began to sing. The irony was scarcely lost on him as he followed her crazed voice from room to room, feeling his way through the dark and smoke to immense heat and a final locked door. 'Let me in!' he shouted as he put his shoulder to it and heaved. 'Let me help you! Unlock the door!'

He'd passed a heavy, antique chair further down the corridor, and he dragged it now to the door, and summoned, with more effort than he expected, all his upper body strength to raise it to his chest and fling it forward. The door cracked enough to release a blast of thick grey smoke and he fell on his shoulder, groaning and rolling back. The girl in the corner burst out laughing as if he were a special show sent just to entertain her.

Fire had claimed the window frame by now and the ceiling above it, too; they had only seconds. The girl jerked as Alexander reached for her and pieces of ash fell scalding on his cheek. She sank her teeth into the back of his hand. 'God save me but I'd leave you here!' he yelled as he hauled her bony body over the floor, just before burning beams from the ceiling cracked and landed where only seconds before they'd wrestled together. Rough hands pulled them both through the doorway as boots scrambled past, water sloshing down on their heads. The girl sobbed in his arms, and he took off his tweed to wrap it round her shoulders. The bite-mark on his hand stood out amidst the black of the soot.

'Dear God, Euphemia!' The same strong female voice, which had called for calm before, belonged to a woman in uniform, middle-aged, with a heavily lined but fond face made unnecessarily severe by the cap she wore. His throat, clogged with fire and pain, cut off air to his lungs and he struggled not to panic. 'What have you done?' The matron's capable arms smothered her charge as he spat up smoky phlegm, hard and fiery as coal.

'She's a patient, I take it?' Too late, he wiped his nipping eyes with sooty fingers and they streamed, making him cough again. The girl's orange-gold hair was singed black at the edges. Tears made pink tracks down her face.

'We never thought she'd have an accident like this.'

'It wasn't an accident.' Alexander's tongue was sticky; he tried to lick his lips. 'She locked the door. She set it on fire. I heard her laughing.'

'Oh, Euphemia,' the woman moaned into the girl's hair. 'They'll not let you stay now, will they? They'll not let you stay.'

Alexander tried to stand, but his legs shook too badly. 'I'm Alexander Balfour,' he started to say, 'Dr Browne's assistant...'

'Oh, good God.' The woman reached for him but his trust was shaken. 'I thought you were a visitor. Dr Balfour, what a thing for you to see.' She tried again; this time he shook her hand, as soot-stained as his from the girl's blackened hair, and he winced at her grip. She introduced herself as Agnes Munro, head of the women's staff. She didn't expect him till later, she said, the parlour wasn't ready for him, but his focus was on the girl who'd now pulled away from the matron and sat hunched, as if hurt and apologetic. But she was smiling under her thick, red hair.

'Put her to bed and have her watched.' He was too exhausted for prattle.

'Of course, Dr Balfour. But you've saved her life – did you hear that, Euphemia? The new doctor has saved your life!'

The girl was a lunatic and a dangerous one – he'd have her sent home faster than she could blink after this, he thought. Browne had clearly underestimated her. He coughed up another ball of black bile and spat at the floor, agitating Mrs Munro further. 'Follow me to the parlour, you can rest there while I see to Euphemia. Do you think another physician should be called for?'

'I'm fine, it's only a little smoke inhalation,' he said, but she interrupted him.

'Oh no, I meant for Euphemia – you're in no fit state to examine her. Should I send for someone else, to make sure she isn't hurt?'

He wanted to tell her to send for a cart to take her far away and dump her in the biggest midden they could find, but said nothing. His need for whisky was more urgent than his need for water, and he urged Mrs Munro on in the direction of the parlour. The ground floor was still in chaos, but two young female assistants were making the beginnings of some kind of order. He thought for a moment he might be sick, and leant against the corridor wall. His own form of madness was in coming here, entering this business – he closed his eyes. 'It'll be the shock,' Mrs Munro said gently at his shoulder.

Ten minutes later, he sat alone in a sparse parlour, a useless mug of water in his shaking hand. His breath, fast and shallow, made his heart skip hard once, twice, again, as he remembered the heat, the urgency, the fear as flames rose up and smoke began to choke him – remembered it from long ago. And thought now how the past and the present together slammed up against one another, as if their separation was a thing of no consequence; and he thought of the young man who'd once saved his mother from the flames, and who had just performed the feat again for another deranged woman. And he thought, too, of how he despised them.

2.

Broughty Ferry, early October 1823

'Tell us another story!' my daughters shout, all the way from Richmond. The sky thickens as we head north and the breeze picks up, so I stitch a little extra muslin into the lining of their dresses, sew tales into their hearts. They don't remember this first home: London is their home, just like Mary's was, but it's not the smoky, busy, noisy place she endured, teeming with folk from every corner of the world. My daughters' city is quiet, lush and warm. So will they be as open to the skies and the breeze here as she once was? Will they need it as much as she did?

I'm still waiting for my head to clear though, and my need for the little brown phial to ease. I thought a new kind of air and coolness would do it, but there's a formality to returning that keeps me tightly wound. Expectations to be met and rules to be followed. Things that cover what lies beneath. But I know I've done what's right, so I place my head on the pillow, close my eyes and smile, even though we pitch and roll with the waves. We're good sailors, me and my girls. We could walk on water, I swear it, and be condemned for witches because we'd never drown. For all I distrust it and hate it, the sea has never made me sick.

I thought the River Tay was the sea when I was young, I tell my girls. *Another story.* I smile and begin, clutching my shawl around my shoulders as shouts go up and ropes bang against wood. Another bright morning, and my girls have biscuits and an apple each. 'Something else about when you were growing up,' Izzy says and snuggles closer while Kathy, ever-independent, sits straight and focused. It's calmer than usual, and we've all had a good night's sleep.

'Have I told you how Uncle Robert and Aunt Christy would drag me from my books?' I say, and they shake their heads, even though they know I have. 'Your grandfather would buy them for me when he made a visit into town, and I'd sign them with my own name: "Isabella Baxter: *do not steal*".'

I pause. '"You're nothing but an old bookworm," Robbie would say to me. He's got the same black curls and pale blue eyes my mother had. I take after grandfather, and so do you, Izzy, we both have dark hair and dark eyes.' Kathy says nothing. 'But you have his smile,' I say to her, and pinch her cheek, gently. 'And then Robbie would shout, "And no one will want to marry you."'

'But Daddy married you,' Izzy protests.

'Yes, but I didn't know that then. And I didn't care if no one wanted to marry me. I was going to be Lady Jane Grey. "Then they'll cut of your head!" Robbie would say.'

I'd picture myself blindfolded and fumbling for the block, asking for help to find it. The delicious feel of the axe, tested against my neck before the steel of its first blow. Injustice crunching my bones, ripping muscle; the slop of my blood on the ground. I had a bloodthirsty nature, Aggie would tell me, as if I didn't know it myself.

'And stick it on a pike!' Kathy shouts. So she has it, too.

'Aggie would always tell me not to mind, you know. How kind she always was to me. "Come on with us," she'd say.' And I look past my girls for a moment over the blue water. Aggie feared for the disappointments a life without the drama I thirsted after could cast up, so I'd pretend she was right and let the sand ruin my boots and the water leak into my brain, and count the hours until I could come home to my books.

'And then what?' asks Izzy.

'Well, I've told you before. Grandfather's old house was high on a hill, and we'd see the sea lie so inviting far below. How it sparkled silver in the sunlight.' I knew that was just a trick it liked to play, though. I'd trip over pebbles with the others and pretend not to notice what I knew and the others didn't: that the sea wasn't evil, no matter what they said in church. It was never so *exciting* a thing as evil. Only a check on the exciting life to be led beyond Broughty Ferry. A great ignorant mass of water hemmed us in and it had no right to do so.

'And that's when I found the wedding ring buried beneath the pebbles one day,' I say. My girls' eyes widen. They haven't heard this before. It was dark gold, with an inscription, and slipped onto my finger, a perfect fit, much to Robbie's disgust.

'Where is the ring now? Have you still got it?' asks Kathy.

'Oh no, Aggie made me give it to her. But I was clever, I watched her bury it back under the pebbles where I could come and get it later if I wanted.'

'Ach, some poor lass's lost it,' Aggie had said. 'She micht come back and find yon again.' But I knew it wasn't lost. An angry bride had torn it from her finger and smothered it under stone. Throwing it into the water would have been pointless, she'd have known that. The sea would have spat it back at her.

It wasn't only the sea and the way it kept me from the world. Aggie told me about womanish glaistigs and caoineags who lived by waterfalls and burns. The stream at the bottom of our garden sounded like an old woman's spiteful gossip: Aggie said they drowned a witch in it, in the old days. But the sea was worse, its waves sucking round our ankles, spitting spray in our faces. Pulling and pushing, to show how big it was.

There were wrecks, too, pulled down where it was dark and cold and lonely. I couldn't tell my mother. We had to whisper in her room, where the curtains were always drawn and it smelt of camphor. My mother was brave, our father told us all the time. I couldn't tell my brave mother I didn't like the sea.

Water is meant to be good: Peter was a fisherman. The good folk of Broughty Ferry fear the sea because they respect it, but it's a bully everyone pretends to like out of fear.

And now it's my girls who will learn, just as I learned from Aggie. I can choose to tell them what to expect: tell them why nothing in their homeland will be the way it sounds. About 'love-feasts' and 'Kail Kirk' and 'the King of Martyrs' and 'holy kisses'. They'll think, as I once did, that it's about love. That it sounds romantic, when it's the soiled slime of cabbage soup and the stagnant whiff of repeated pages.

Or will I spare them?

* * *

'Ye have to wear it,' Aggie had said. 'It's your best.' The dresses of the youngest daughter are always the most worn, even when there's money to spare. Margaret's clothes were new, then Christy was given the best of whatever she'd grown out of. I had the best of whatever Christy managed not to ruin beyond repair. By the time her dresses reached me they'd been mended and altered so many times they were hardly the 'best' of anything.

I had different colouring, too: dark where my sisters were fair, the pale shades that suited them only drained and dulled me. My mother never noticed what little my clothes did for my appearance: she was already thinking of higher things, and that other place. Her eyes would glaze over me when Aggie brought me downstairs, ready, looking beyond me.

'You look very bonny, but not *too* bonny,' was what Aggie would always say. 'Dinna want folk sayin' ye're no better than ye should be, now. Dinna want ye gettin' noticed for the wrang reasons.' I could only wonder what those wrong reasons might be, as she fixed a small bow to my little tartan tam-o'-shanter. I'd taken a long time that particular day. None of my school friends ever had to spend a whole day in church. Aggie's fingers were strong but they were calloused and clumsy and I winced as the hairpin jabbed my skull. 'Ston' still, ye wee besom.'

She was angry with my playing for time. I still can't explain my moods that year, my sense of frustration that went beyond a need to travel far beyond the sea. I'd so much to be grateful for, Aggie would remind me all the time. 'Think of all yon lassies who've nothin'!' she would say.

'I need my gloves,' I sulked. It was too warm to wear them.

'Whaur did ye huv them last?' We scowled at one another, our faces close. I saw the blue film circle the brown iris of Aggie's eyes, the lids bare of lashes to shield her watery glare.

'I don't remember.'

Aggie shook her head. 'Then ye'll hae tae dae withoot them.'

It was what I wanted but it gave me no satisfaction and my face crumpled.

'Now, then, we'll hae none o' that,' she said, impatiently. 'Whaur's yer Bible?'

My coat pocket. I pretended about that, too.

'Then ye'll hae tae go withoot that an a'. Deary me, what are they gaun tae say aboot ye, at kirk?'

'I don't care. I don't feel well. I feel sick. I want to stay here with you.'

As Aggie spun me round to face the door, the much-repaired right seam on my dress gave way once again. My horrible Sunday clothes. So I was late for church, and angry. My father and mother ignored my arrival: my mother, already transported, her lips parted, eyes half-closed, murmured along with the preacher. Margaret held her hand, sat close. Christy and Robbie fidgeted either side of me. My right foot was ticklish inside my boot and unreachable. I sat, rigid as a monument, counting till ten, twenty, a hundred. My nails gouged the flesh of my palms as the itch at my ankle spread to my toes. I stared down as if my look could stop the burning and ripped the inside of my lip with my teeth. But martyrs aren't allowed in our church. My pain was meaningless.

And at that moment something spread from my heart through my chest to gather at my throat: I couldn't breathe or swallow for the Devil stopping up my mouth with his fistful of words, choking me: You will never be saved. *You will never be saved.* Original sin condemned us all, but never to be free? Was there nothing I could do? I wanted to spit them out, the Devil and his words: why else was I here, if not for salvation? You will never be saved, he forced the words through tears that spurted, and at last I coughed him up, all his hatred and sin and death, but it wasn't enough.

I began to tremble and when Christy put her hand on my forehead she pulled back as if she'd been burned. I had a fever: we disturbed the kirk that day, my family and I, as my father lifted me up and carried me outside, called for assistance from a passing farmer and his cart. I remember nothing of the days after, just those words that seemed to point out the path I'd chosen. For what can those who will never be saved do? They can do as they please. But I never believed the Devil's voice or I would have left David the first time. I didn't believe I couldn't be saved.

* * *

Do I believe I can be saved now? The question makes me pull my girls closer. Disillusionment suits a land of high blue sky, as high as it is narrow, enlightened as it is intolerant, I think, as we sail towards Dundee.

But the stiff east coast breeze freezes us all into rationality: my girls no longer cry out for a story. I'm sure the wind will chase away my fancies that have only gotten so much worse lately. It's hard to be carried away by passions when you're rubbing your hands together from the cold all the time. We blow on our fingers, comb the salt from our hair, tuck our scarves into our dresses and stuff paper into our boots at night, until one day I call out, 'We are here!' and the Tay pulls us along like a child with a toy on a string, bumping us carelessly, snatching every so often and tipping us up.

And still we don't falter, my girls and I. We wave at the dockside though no one there can possibly make us out: my sister might be that speck so far away, welcoming us from the edge of the world, too small to save us should the river change its mind and throw us away instead, tired of its plaything. But I say nevertheless, 'I think I see her, waving over there: *look!*' and they scream, 'Aunt Christy!' as we lurch and swing towards her.

3.

Montrose, early October 1823

Alexander scraped his chair away from the parlour fire over the stone floor to the door as fast as he could. A foolish reaction that made him swear softly through cracked lips. Just some sparks that had flown out near the edges of his coat. But enough to get him moving. *Coward.* He felt sick. Where in hell's name was the damn whisky? Anything medicinal, even. Just to stop the trembling in his hands and the hot, shallow breaths in his chest. When would that damn woman come back and see to him? He tried to get out of the chair but his legs wouldn't let him. He swore again – he wasn't this weak.

Crichton, he thought, suddenly. And just when he most wanted the past to mean nothing; when he'd been planning his future on his walk over the fields. Alexander struggled to his feet and caught sight of the clay pitcher high on the mantel. He opened it and took a sniff. Brandy! It'd do. He tossed his water onto the stone floor and tipped a good measure into his cup. How it burned his throat more, and his belly, too. But it eased his breathing and cleared his mind. His father wasn't right. History didn't repeat itself, not if you didn't let it. It was a story whose ending could be changed. As long as you knew the beginning.

As long as you knew the beginning. He gulped back as much of the brandy as he could stand, let tears nip his stinging eyes. He wiped his nose with the back of his sooty sleeve, and became aware for the first time of what he must look like. His face would be black with it, too. He'd forgotten that from before, how he'd looked afterwards.

'From before' was a story whose ending he'd have changed. But knowing the beginning of the story didn't make any difference.

He had a sudden fear that Crichton might be wrong after all, and took another gulp. *In the end is my beginning.* If the mentor he'd never met but only read could appear now in front of him and occupy the seat opposite, what would Alexander choose to tell him? A right way to begin. And a wrong way. *Analysis.* Yes: the choice was his and he could flex his muscles as he made it. For the choice of any patient waiting to be analysed was one that made for an unusual dilemma, no matter how rich or how poor, how illiterate or how well-educated he or she may be. The choice – or the dilemma – was always, would always be, how much power to give away.

Crichton wanted his fellow practitioners to give up their power in order to reclaim it, Alexander had always understood that. The choice to lie, or tell the truth. He might then have chosen the summer of 1813, say. How much power lies there, he wondered. The brandy bubbled up in his gut and he belched, suddenly weaker. Giving up what he scarcely felt he had at all – Crichton had to be trusted in his theories or he, Alexander, would have less than nothing.

So to begin again – this time, with two boys of Scottish parentage who were both, it might be assumed, under the age of fourteen. Perhaps their home was on the north side of the Thames. Their father, a member of the College of Physicians in Holborn.

He leaned forward towards the very fire he'd been so fearful of just moments before. Closer: closer. Choices brought him closer. And so: another one! Winter, maybe five years later then. A single, older son, this time: a student in Edinburgh. Home: north and south. Father: nobody.

Then again, he thought, leaning back for a moment, perhaps he'd choose neither. Alexander, mindful of the noise outside the parlour, reminded himself: he was a hero now. He had saved the life of that foolish girl, the matron had said so. He could face this easily. And so he closed his eyes to picture it better: a district densely packed even before the viaduct. Or perhaps he'd choose cobbled closes with each ancient tenement floor piled high, in a rickety fashion. No: he knew what he wanted. A father in a rare good mood, walking his sons all the way to the river to gaze across at open fields. Young boys pretending they could see across the water to France, playing gruesome games about guillotines and aristocrats.

Memories are merely stories we convince ourselves are real, he had told himself before. Those two boys might have been on their way home that summer ten years ago. The younger one may have carried a basket of mussels, the older a bag of plums he wasn't meant to dip into but couldn't resist when his father wasn't looking. Maybe they were happy after a golden day by the river; maybe their father was unusually merry after a visit to a quiet tavern.

Alexander paused and opened his eyes. *And maybe they never existed.* Like the medical student home from a city of rock and smoke, sitting awkwardly at a breakfast table while his mother sang dreamily, her night-dress open and loose. Perhaps he had never existed, either.

But trading on the 'ifs' and 'whatevers' where Crichton's urging led him, a story could only ever be a story; he knew he could reveal its lack of power to himself, show its submission to the mind that controlled it. Yes: he'd follow those young boys to the front door of what might have been their apartments in Holborn. Cramped looking, perhaps, but vast to two boys. And through three floors of narrow, high-ceilinged rooms, with a tiny maids' quarters at the top and a place for the cook in the basement.

Through a front door that was unusually ajar that day. Outside, that younger boy would hear the cries of the French watchmakers and the Italian traders, sounds that never seemed strange to him. So the unusual never worried him. Perhaps that's what made him slower to follow his brother, the one he followed in so many things, that day. And perhaps it was the adored elder of the two who called out for his mother first; perhaps he was the one who ran ahead to the drawing room. Trellis wallpaper might line the hallway, ensuring that the younger boy would, for the rest of his life, loathe patterned walls.

Or would it? Did this boy of twelve really run in to see portraits wrenched from the walls? Ornaments smashed, their broken pieces ground in to the rugs? Plum drapes gashed and every chair upturned, some missing a leg? That the same dagger that ripped through the drapes had gouged tabletops and cushions, too?

Did he really ask his older brother, 'Vagabonds, d'you think, Thomas? Pirates and thieves! Who else could have done this? Have they robbed us?'

Perhaps the older boy really did ignore him and call out for their mother.

Was he afraid? The boy didn't want to think of his mother in the hands of thieves and kidnappers, not with her unsettling kind of beauty, her distractedness. Her too-high colour in the cheeks, the too bright-ness of her eyes, the transparency of her skin. Like a tubercular victim's final hours, he would think when he was older and knew about such things, when she seemed to rally and loved ones believed the worst was over.

Perhaps the later story was better, after all. Switch, then. To a young man who had seen worse than a woman in a state of undress; who was now a man of the world; who would soon lose a brother. The mother's suggestion was ominous: 'Why don't I come and stay with you at university?' she had surely murmured, a dreamy look in her eyes. 'We could find nice rooms somewhere and I could cook and keep house for you, my lovely boy.' She'd reached out, hadn't she, and pushed back a dark red curl from his forehead, slid her hand around his chin. When he'd returned, after spending the morning trailing the streets, he'd doubted the sight: but there she was, still sitting in the same place at the table, and in the same nightclothes.

'There you are,' she'd said, as though he'd been absent only a second or two. 'When will we leave? Your father won't miss me.' She wasn't joking as he'd hoped, for she held him by the wrist. 'You must take me with you. *Please!*'

Yes: we couldn't always believe what our eyes told us. So Alexander turned away from this particular vision and back to one of the worried young boys instead, running on through a house of more distress, more furniture torn and portraits slashed. Their father would have surely caught them up by now, to pant beer in their faces. He wouldn't have been quick enough to prevent them witnessing though, as he flung open the bedroom door, the sight of their mother lying naked on her bed, her arms ripped and bleeding.

No: we couldn't always believe what our eyes told us.

How could those young boys know it wasn't her first attempt? Or that the letters scattered beside her, written by an unnamed woman to her husband, had triggered this particular mental collapse? But when she was at last ready to receive her sons, and they returned her smiles, they knew exactly why she couldn't embrace them, why her arms were bandaged all the way to her elbows. That much, at least, they knew.

But where it began would always remain a mystery to them. Only endings can truly be known, Alexander decided, and he felt a cool blade run along his spine in protest as though the ghost of Crichton himself had taken up arms against his blasphemy. *Endings, not beginnings? Are you mad?* He'd have to shut him out: the old genius was misleading him, no wonder he'd not cracked the code in Gheel! Endings, yes, he knew those all right. When he'd spent that day studying in the room his father grandly called the library, relieved to escape his mother. Then smelling smoke and running to his mother's room, where he found her heaping books into a pile that she lit with tapers. Grabbing her just as her flimsy nightclothes caught aflame and flinging her to the ground, rolling her over and over. The blackness of the smoke; its stench on his hands and clothes.

The same stench he could smell now.

Locke would have all humanity a mass of experience; Gall would place an overactive memory in the frontal lobes. 'Witness that high forehead: "cranial prominence". Ha! Let them cut it out and separate it,' Alexander said out loud to the deserted room. If Flourens could remove the entire cerebrum, then the cerebellum, and finally, a part of the medulla, without a cessation of respiration, then a man wouldn't die without his memory. No: on the contrary, he could breathe more easily without it.

Would this son have cut out the part of his mother's brain that had so troubled her, if it left her breathing still? Yes, he might have been mad or brave enough to try, had he known enough in time. But how could she have spoken, told anyone what was going on inside her head? For not knowing the right thing to do, Alexander never forgave – what? Not any god. The world? Himself? His father?

His father believed that if a family had money, sick relatives were well looked after in asylums. He ignored the latest testimonies of punishments in such places for minor offences like a lack of punctuality, or a refusal to take prescribed medicines. Such treatment was for the impoverished mad, not the rich, he said. Only poor men had their brains bludgeoned by cruel staff members, or were rendered immobile by repeated beatings. Only the poor were tortured and badgered by those meant to care for them. Not women from wealthy homes. Or sons, for that matter.

And so, across the river from where two young boys played once, their mother was held in the brand new purpose-built hospital where her eldest son would one day also be an inmate. The dungeons and watching galleries, the high, barred windows and hard floors, the stench and dirt and darkness, the chains and hooks and belts, the paralysing medicines and the impatient, underpaid physicians – they only found out about those later, but by then she was dead of typhus, shortly after the authorities confirmed that they had no infectious patients.

But Thomas – he was still alive. And he was still there.

4.

Broughty Ferry, early October 1823

My sister and my daughters have taken to each other with no effort at all. Christy won't hear of my leaving so soon and the urgency of David's letter itches my skin. She fastens a chain round my daughter's plump, pink neck. Her strong and hardy garden looks like it could knock my lush, lazy borders back in Richmond down in a fight, and I'm suddenly sorry for it.

'All that smog. Even in the summer you have it! And the dirt, I don't know how you bear it. It can't be good for the girls.' Her voice is shrill; the lines on her cheeks run deep. *Never the prettiest of the Baxter girls*: words I overheard once prick at my memory. My throat tightens at hopes not realized. *You can't have them.*

'The girls like it very well.' I say. 'We're hardly in the city streets. Richmond is very pretty countryside.'

Christy's doubtful look ages her, forces her chin down. 'However pretty, however far from the worst streets, it's still an unhealthy place, Bella.' She tucks a grey curl under her cap. The eldest female member of our family; the oldest living female Baxter.

'I can't think how you'd know anyway, given that you haven't been there these ten years past.' But I've never invited her to visit and Christy forgets that, or is too kind to say. *You will never have them.* She sets Kathy on her lap and strokes her hair. Kathy's eyes close in the sun.

'And what I remember of Mary's father's household shocks me when I think of it now. The dreadful mess of it. And that poor sister of hers left to do everything.' But Fanny's long dead now and by her own hand: Mary got the man her older sister wanted. What sisters can do to one another.

'And that bookshop his wife had!' Christy continues. Gossip is more solid and comforting than ghostly, unborn children, I think. 'She worked her fingers to the bone keeping that bookshop going. And the people who came in. All sorts. You didn't know what to expect from one day to the next.'

'It's hard to believe you're the same person who once came down to London as a girl, and stayed there for a whole summer,' I say, reaching out for Kathy. *Came.* 'You loved it at the time. You didn't want to go home. I remember. You told me.' *Go.*

But she squeezes her thin lips together as if my words could infect her. There were peasant women in France, Mary said, after the war, who stood outside their ruined cottages with their arms folded and their mouths tight. She and Claire didn't dare ask them for help even though they'd lost their mule and eaten nothing for two days; even Shelley's charm couldn't make them smile. They were still the enemy, this little party from England. Did these women look as Christy looks now? At an enemy, here to take what little she has left?

'I didn't love it at all,' she says at last. 'What a thing to say! I was happy to come home. I never wanted to be away in the first place. I only went to please our father.'

'You know that's not true. You begged father to let you go there once Mary went home.' My arms are still empty.

Christy shakes her head and I think, *how much we are changed and in so short a time.* 'And she's another one,' she begins again. 'Back from Italy, I hear.'

I decide to try not to care about any of it, yawn at Kathy who smiles and copies me. But she is the mirror of her father, not me.

'Yes, she is. She came to visit.'

Christy tuts. 'She's a wicked woman.'

You were jealous of us.

'Oh, for heaven's sake, Christy. I don't think even you believe that.'

'Yes, I do. Her whole family is wicked, no wonder she's ended up as she has: a penniless widow with a little boy, and still disowned by her husband's family, from what I understand. And what's that sister of hers doing?'

'Claire is a governess in Russia for a very respectable family. There's nothing for her to be ashamed of.'

'Russia! It's hardly a respectable place. I've read about the lives of these governesses abroad. Only the other week in the newspaper there was a story about one poor woman, starved and turned out to die in the streets. And that's when their employers are not after them for all sorts of sordid things.'

'Stop it, Christy.'

'It's true: I read of it. And how does Mary decide to support that little boy of hers now? By writing more *novels*. What kind of novels, exactly? More of that sinful rubbish.'

I have to stand up. My hands can't undo the knot: I pull off my hat and wince as it catches on my hair. 'It's hard to believe you're our father's daughter,' I say. 'You're getting fearful and foolish in your old age, sister. Fearful of what the neighbours think, and foolish about what constitutes real thought.' *Surely that's enough? Don't you want me gone now?* Christy rises clumsily and Kathy almost tumbles to the ground. *Stay here with my girls: it doesn't mean you will have them.* 'You always were conservative – Mary said so, too. What was it you and Fanny argued with her once? That women had a right to be domestic? My father's education was wasted on you! All you want is to be respectable.'

I should laugh at that: I want to be respectable, too, after all I've done.

'There's nothing wrong with being respectable,' Christy's feelings fan across her cheeks. 'After you and David married – well, how easy do you think it was for us here?'

112

'They were our friends. They shouldn't have turned their backs on you,' I say. 'If they'd been true friends...'

'Don't speak about my friends.' Christy gathers up the cushions from her chair. A cloud hides the sun. 'They did what they thought was right. And it's taken me all this time to make it up to them. To show them...'

Kathy's looking up at me. It's not for her to hear. 'So why did you let us come back, then? If we're such a source of shame for you?' Christy pulls her shawl needlessly about her shoulders. If I go back indoors with her I will suffocate, or smother her. 'It's much more wicked to turn your back on your own family,' I say.

But when she faces me, she is gentle, appealing. 'I think you should come back here, Bella. You and David and the girls. Yes, you shocked people. But London's an evil place. See what it's done to you. You look as though you haven't had a decent meal in years, there's no colour in your cheeks. I hardly recognized you when you arrived. That place is sucking the life out of you.'

I falter at her concern, which makes me peaceful until evening and the change occurs again. My sister leaves her mending, and we are quiet all the way to evening, when the arguments begin again. My sister leaves her mending to ask if I have written to my husband yet; I only shrug in reply. She doesn't understand him – but then, neither do I, and perhaps this should bring us closer. I want the closeness that Christy and I have never shared but it's too late; Christy thinks literary people shouldn't have children and what am I to do with that?

A candle close to my face makes me blink. So fresh air and good food have made little difference. Her warm parlour doesn't stop me fingering the little phial in my pocket.

'Is there anyone you can consult?' she says, after a long silence between us. My girls are asleep in bed; I should feel freer now, but I don't. 'A local doctor?' Christy won't be put off. 'I wouldn't normally advocate it but I'm concerned: you're wasting away in front of me.' First Mary, now Christy. What

113

belief they place in doctors: my husband, too, now, and the letter I've still not delivered burns in my pocket. *Stop wasting time here. Stop arguing with your sister. Anyone would think you didn't want to save your husband...* I pat my skull with my fingers, those bumps under my thin dark hair, what they can tell me.

'You always did love to exaggerate,' I sigh at last.

'No, I don't. That was always *you*. You were the actress in the family.' My strength evaporates: the phial, I need some. 'You're jumpy and touchy,' she continues relentlessly. 'Oh, what have I said now? For heaven's sake, Bella, don't cry.'

The ancient napkin at my cheek is almost threadbare: a birthday present she has kept all these years. 'I am well. Coming back is difficult, that's all. What I'm doing here...'

'You're visiting your family, what is there to be so upset about? You see, this proves what I'm saying, you're not well.'

I sniff a little. 'I've heard of a good place that provides rest for those who need it,' I say. 'In Montrose. David suggested it: a kind of retreat. In fact,' my fingertips tingle, 'I'm going to make the journey to see it for myself.' *Put me with the mad folk. Let me rest with my own kind.*

'But I can't accompany you...'

'I'll go alone: you can keep the girls while I'm gone...'

That light in her eyes is like a knock at the door, and then I realize that both are real, and start up. 'Who can it be at this time of night?' Christy tuts and I sneak the phial out of my pocket as soon as she is gone. Twenty drops this morning: twenty now. My hand shakes: more drops than I intend slip down my throat. I'll take less tomorrow: avoid it in the morning, wait until the afternoon.

A cough and a breeze and Christy, coy and blushing in the doorway, holds a heavy wooden box in her hands. Her voice is raised in wonder. 'A visit from the new minister already! He only arrived yesterday. He wouldn't come in, when I told him you were here, of course, but he said he would call again.'

A new minister? From our church?

114

Christy makes a dismissive motion. 'Of course – I haven't told you.' She places the box on her chair. *What are you hiding?*

'I have become a member – of the official church.'

The candlelight is fading: she is a dark hulk standing in the corner and her voice is muffled.

'When did this happen? Have you told our father?'

'He knows everything about it.'

'And he's happy?'

Her profile blurs in the dimness: her words echo low, as if she is far away. 'He trusts me.'

I can only make out her mouth, moving fast in the gloom, explaining something I don't understand. Christy, the most conscientious one, who fasted even after we had come home to good food. 'Is that not my box?' I say, but my vision is hazy – *too many drops!* So when Christy opens it to reveal the same book that lies inside my box upstairs, the one John Conolly purchased for me only a few months ago, all I can do is finger the faded gold print on the worn black leather that I recognize because I've touched it before. *A Treatise on Insanity* by Philippe Pinel.

And that's when I know, too, that Christy has been going through my belongings. She means to play a trick on me. 'I have to go to bed,' I announce, strong as I can.

'Goodnight, Isabella,' I hear behind me, but it doesn't matter what she is saying because I'm struck still by the sight ahead of me at the foot of the stairs. A young woman is standing there. Her hair is paler than mine, more watery somehow. Her dress, too, is grey muslin just like mine, but more transparent, waving as if caught in a breeze. She has her back to me but when she begins to turn round, her profile depicts exactly what I see in my glass every day. The same chin, the same eyes, the same nose and forehead; they're all mine. I stand there, looking at the ghost of myself until I cannot bear the sight any longer and I close my eyes, smell the lavender that Izzy picked for me earlier and that my ghost is carrying in her hands, and my legs give way and I sink down to the comfort and safety of stone.

I struggle to wake this morning: strange dreams have disturbed my sleep and my head hammers when I open my eyes. I must face Christy though, and I splash water on my face, button my dress with trembling fingers and grip the banister as I tread carefully on the stairs. The dining room door is open, she thrusts the letter she's reading under her table mat. *Too late: I saw you!*

'Bella!' Her guilt makes her start, rush to my side. 'You should have stayed in bed after fainting like that.' *So you can cover your tracks.* My legs are shaking. 'You'll take a full breakfast this morning: you haven't been eating enough, that's what caused it. What kind of sister am I? You weighed no more than a bag of feathers when I carried you upstairs...' *You cannot fool me.* My girls squeal in the garden: I squint through the window, blurs of colours by the bushes. The wooden box is on the mantel.

'Is my book still inside it?' *How long are you going to pretend?* How like Margaret she is, even with her frowns.

'What do you mean?' She busies herself, gathering up plates, brushing crumbs into her hand. 'It's your box, you should know what's inside it.'

'But that isn't my box,' I say. 'It's the new minister's.'

'What new minister?'

This pretence will have to stop. The new minister is doubtless the intended recipient of her letter. Full of complaints and recriminations about her bad sister, the one who shamed her.

'The one who called last night.'

'For heaven's sake, Isabella. Why would a minister come here?'

'I heard you speak with him. *I heard you!*'

Must I strike her to make her own it? What she will have said to him, what he wanted here last night... and then I see it. They mean a conspiracy between them. They'll have me put away, both of them, then Christy will be free to keep my girls for herself. I see it in her eyes.

'No minister called here last night,' she says, sharply. 'I don't know what you're talking about, Bella, but I think you better eat something. You look worse today than you did yesterday and I don't like the way you're behaving.'

I mutter something about fetching a hair ribbon from my room. It's a ruse: instead, I go out into the passage and wait on the stairs a few minutes. *To catch her in the act*: sure enough, when I slip back into the dining room, she starts up.

'For heaven's sake, must you creep up on me? And what are you doing, coming in the front door?'

'I've just been upstairs, as you well know. I haven't come in the front door. I haven't been outside at all.'

She will not trick me.

'Yes, you were – I saw you go out to the garden just a minute ago, Bella...'

My girls: make sure my girls are safe.

I rush out to the garden and there, at the far end by the bramble bushes, my eldest daughter is talking to a dark-haired figure who has her back to me. She wears my dress, at my height, and bends down to my daughter and brushes her hair from her face, just as I would. I turn away to face the house, my hand over my mouth to stop the scream that threatens to break out, just as Izzy's hand touches mine and I look down to see her standing beside me.

It's time for me to leave. Christy's home is not the sanctuary I need. I need another kind of refuge altogether. *Asylum.*

5.

Montrose, October 1823

'And how are you finding us now, Dr Balfour? Not as mad as you'd expected?' Only a fortnight since Alexander's arrival in town, and the predictable jokes had begun already. Mr Stewart's remark had been made often now, and in the same tone. In the small, dimly lit assembly hall Alexander reflected on provincialism and liveliness and wondered whether there was a link between the two. Perhaps the self-satisfied Stewart would appreciate *that* remark; but then he'd have to shout above the noise of the dance, and at that moment he realized he couldn't be bothered, not even to see his host redden and stammer at the insult. So he smiled instead and gave a shallow bow.

'Indeed not, sir.'

The older man groped his belly as though he'd hidden a delicious pie somewhere about him, and his wig slipped a little to the side, hinting at baldness. He wheezed with disappointment suddenly, wine-laden breath in Alexander's face, and laid a heavy fat hand, bare but for a single ring, on Alexander's arm. Alexander understood the compliment but this physical intimacy was too much. The man's pale coat and shirt; his white necktie and gold buttons; his shiny, fashionable boots, were all meant for a younger man, and one with charm.

'I wasn't about to be one of the benefactors to a madhouse,' he confided, his mouth close to Alexander's ear. Alexander leaned away. 'But it's been quiet enough there, I hear.' Stewart pulled away, too, and raised his voice. 'Apart from your own escapade, that is.'

Alexander was famous now, of course. *The hero of the hour, indeed*, once word got out that he'd saved the life of a sixteen-year-old inmate, Euphemia Ross. Once he'd had a chance to recover over the few days that followed he'd decided not to get rid of her, after all. Instead, she'd become his first patient. His first case, to talk as fully and freely as she wished.

But Euphemia was conniving and liked to prolong their sessions by dodging his questions. He remembered how only the previous night she had appeared at his door, the dim light catching the outline of young, full breasts hanging heavy inside the thin nightdress.

'I'm going to call Mrs Munro, so that she may take you back to your room,' he'd said. *I won't be caught this time.*

'But I want to tell you something,' she'd persisted.

'Are you being truthful? You know I only want to hear the truth.'

She'd nodded and he'd led her over to the covered divan by the draped window, meant for his comfort, not hers. 'Put this blanket around you, I don't want you getting cold.' He held it out to her and she came close, pressed her breasts against his fist. Her eyes were brown, unusually for redheads, made small by pale eyelashes, and they blinked in a pointed face like some wayward elf, he thought, suddenly. With the body of a street woman. But he had to use her in the right way.

'It's important,' she'd said, more sure this time. 'What you want to know about me. Why I'm here.'

'But I know that already,' he'd settled himself on a chair beside her, at the back of her head. 'What else do you have to tell me?'

'I can't talk while you're so far away,' she pleaded. 'Come closer.'

Yes; she had a fairy-face, they'd have called it in the country. Wide-apart eyes and a pointed chin that might have had her burned at the stake in a crueller, more ignorant time, if the crops had failed or a baby had died. He moved his chair. 'There you are. I could hardly be any closer now, could I?'

The blanket rose with her breathing, her fingers tickled her white neck and she pushed her hair back from her face. He knew those movements and what they meant.

'Begin, Euphemia. Talk to me.'

'I have a confession to make first. Will you hear it?' she whispered and sighed again. 'I want to make another fire.'

He should have expected this and was annoyed that he hadn't. 'You did that at home once and now you've done it here. Where do you think it will take you now?'

'There are fires in hell,' she said, distractedly.

Religious mania? He scribbled on the paper block. Childhood dreams?

'Tell me about fire when you were a child,' he said. 'Tell me what you remember about fire.'

Euphemia stifled what sounded like a giggle again. 'The blacksmith had a fire. He chased my brother and me,' she said. 'But we told and he was punished.'

The self. What she imagined and what she remembered. He was starting to wonder if childhood was simply an act of the imagination. He knew what the poets would say. But they couldn't be right. Crichton was right, wasn't he? The act of recollecting one's childhood: he had done it for himself, and he wasn't making anything up. Was he?

'Why did he chase you?'

'He wanted to marry me. He caught me and made me.'

'Made you what, Euphemia?'

'He made me shake and shout.'

'How old were you?'

'Ten.'

The year she had her first fit. Was she confusing several events in her mind? He couldn't be sure.

'What else, Euphemia? Did the blacksmith frighten you?'

'He made my brother shake and shout, too.'

But her brother didn't suffer from fits, Alexander knew that.

'I have to trust you,' he said, as soothingly as possible. 'Your brother doesn't start fires. Where were you when this happened, can you remember? Was it a bright day or a wet one? Were you on your way somewhere?'

'It was bright and I was coming back from church,' she said, dreamily. Was she telling him the truth or a story? 'And I saw it.'

'Saw what?'

'I see things all the time. I'm good at seeing things. People forget I'm there, and that's when I see them.'

He'd made notes, dispirited and unsure, through the night, rousing her with wine when she felt too sleepy to continue, sure that at any moment the breakthrough would occur and he'd understand what she meant. Or at least be able to separate out lies from fact, story from reality. It was only when daylight began to filter through the pale drapes, though, that he'd stopped and looked at the sleeping Euphemia, at the pages of notes he'd made so messily, at the empty wine glasses and the shrunken candle, and felt an emptiness in his gut he hadn't felt since his last nights in Gheel.

But tonight, at this assembly, he'd shut out these thoughts of failure. 'It's a very well-run operation,' Alexander answered Stewart as dispassionately as Euphemia had once answered him. *I'll betray no confidences, either.* Many of the wealthier fathers in the town had scarcely restrained themselves from flinging their unwed daughters in his way since his heroics of that day, for all he was only a *mind-doctor*. His host didn't disappoint him.

'You'll be thinking of running the place yourself one day, I'd imagine? An ambitious young man like you?' The beefy Mr Stewart's eyes bulged through fat and wrinkles: Alexander was reminded of Bulckers, briefly, then shooed the thought away. No: this man had no seductive qualities. God only knew how he'd persuaded his attractive wife to look twice at him. His money had been diverting enough for her, he supposed.

A breathless young woman, in a sparkling and new-fashioned dress, curtsied and turned in line with a gentleman opposite. Perhaps it was the permanence of the end result, but none of the Elizabeths or Florences or Claras that Alexander had led around the floor when he first attended this local dance made the blood pound in his ears. Not until he'd spied the creature called Philomena Stewart, bubbling and rippling the waters around her with her pale brown eyes and short, cropped hair. The sparkling band she wore round her head, with its garish and outsize feather, indicated a frivolous woman with too much interest in fashion, perhaps. But there was a wariness in those pale eyes that spoke of disappointed hopes, and that contrast of foolish indulgence on the one hand, and bitter experience on the other, suited him where it might have warned others. No – the combination would do very well for him, and that night in bed he'd had an unusually innocent epiphany, where he'd pictured the healthy boys she'd give him, the grand house she'd tend, how she'd fill his glass with wine of an evening, and see that fresh clothes were stored in his closet. A domestic scene that made him forget the darker parts of his past, that he was the son of Anne Balfour, the brother of Thomas Balfour. That he was the kind of man whom dangerous individuals approached to make a deal in dark closes.

'Oh, I wouldn't care to look so far ahead yet, Mr Stewart.' Alexander spoke modestly, he hoped, rather than lightly. After all, Philomena was an heiress, an only daughter. Stewart's money would be useful in Alexander's profession, for his plans.

'But you're an ambitious man?'

If he only knew. Alexander smiled at the man's misplaced anxiety and raised his glass instead. What would be the best answer for his purpose? The dance was coming to an end, and Philomena Stewart was eyeing him from the floor. In a moment she'd pin him down for the evening. But it wouldn't do him good to be so easily caught.

'Thoughts of ambition are diverted by attractive sights. And so they should, sometimes, don't you agree?' he said at last, nodding in her direction. Her father was a greedy man, and not just for his belly. Philomena was twenty-three. Mr Stewart no longer had time to be so choosy about prospective sons-in-law.

'That they are!' He needn't be so pleased with himself, Alexander thought, the heat and noise in the room suddenly making him nauseous and more quarrelsome, and he struggled to locate the source of his bad mood.

'Where are you going?' Philomena hurried to his side after he'd made his excuses to the surprised Mr Stewart.

'A sudden headache, that's all. I've been working too hard, my dear.' Alexander smiled wanly. The disappointment and anxiety in her eyes made his belly lurch with a new sense of power. An older sister or a wiser mother might have told her not to make her feelings for him quite so plain. No wonder she was still available.

'But I wanted...' she began, but he silenced her with a wave of his hand.

'Not tonight, another time. Let me be, you'll enjoy your evening more without me.'

Her large brown eyes filled with tears. It was too easy.

'Let me think when I am home how beautiful you are, and promise me you won't let another capture your heart,' he said, and this did the trick. She smiled and nodded, let him raise her hand to his lips. He held her there like that for a moment, then left the hall without looking back at her once, such was his hurry to return to the asylum.

But it was as if Philomena's disappointment had infected him. Fear of being too radical, a disappointment in himself, had him pacing his office floor and drinking more of the whisky he kept in the desk drawer, longer than he intended and by sunrise he was still there, stretched out on the divan, unable to sleep.

When the maid Agnes knocked on his door a few hours later to tell him 'a lady' wished to see him, he had washed and shaved but his temper had barely improved. Not Philomena, surely? This was an unpleasant surprise, and would take her enthusiasm for him too far: nothing smelt so sour, even from the prettiest and most eligible of young women, as desperation.

But it was a tall, thin, small-breasted, androgynous figure with pale skin and dark, fine hair who entered his office. The kind who never attracted much attention, he mistakenly imagined. Lines and shadows under her eyes had him judging her age to be twenty-eight, thirty possibly. Her exhaustion could not be misinterpreted, however. And as she approached his desk he found himself musing unexpectedly on a choirboy face and dark green-brown eyes, on a pale pink mouth he wanted, suddenly, to smudge somehow. What blood and semen and mother's milk had gone into the creation of the boy-woman standing in front of him who was inexplicably making his nerves tingle, was something he'd always wonder long after their first meeting. He'd never satisfy himself with an answer about her, not if he lived to the end of the century.

But on that day, he didn't know what was to come. How could he, when so little sign of it was given? And if even he had, it might have made little difference. Yes, that was the thought he'd comfort himself with in the years ahead: that perhaps he wouldn't have walked away from his fate even if he'd had the choice.

6.

Broughty Ferry, October 1823

I gripped David's sealed letter in my hand like a shipwrecked soul clinging to wreckage, all the way from Christy's to Montrose. A dour-looking couple from Dundee accompanied me on the trip, talking mournfully of their newly-married daughter and her betrayal with this inconsiderate move to another town, for which the only compensation would be a grandchild in nine months' time. But I was safe, even if my patience was tried. Christy was happy to be left alone with my girls; and they are safe with her, for the time being.

Last night was my first at the inn: I shouldn't wonder my sleep was troubled by yet another dream. I shouldn't have come north, my dream mother said: I must go back now, straightaway. She was pale and tearful, and I wanted to comfort her. *Take care of him,* she urged me but I couldn't listen. Even when she thrust her book at me: *And let us consider one another to provoke unto love and good works. Not forsaking the assembling of ourselves, as the manner of some is: but exalting one another and so much the more, as ye see the day approaching.*

The assembling of ourselves. *Put me back together.* But on this damp, dreich morning I have worse thoughts; worse than any dream that troubles me for being consciously made. There will be no sun and freedom for me, as Mary's husband had once suggested. That third path – the worst path – still tempts me, and if I take it I'm lost forever and my mother knows it. *Not forsaking the assembling of ourselves.*

The phial is still in my pocket but it's almost empty: twenty drops taken before I leave the inn makes my slow journey across fields soaked by last night's rain less of a trial, and I don't care about the muddy mess of my hems, or my sodden shoes. The air is heavy and suits my mood, as though it's commiserating with me. I should be more cheerful, but the twists in my belly revel in the uncertainty even my phial can do little to ease: I have no idea what to expect of the director of an asylum, am wary of what horrors I may encounter. Everyone knows the stories.

But too soon, hazy though my perception still is, I arrive at the stone stairs to the asylum building and think only, *you can still run away.* And I am still standing there when a dour, plain, harelipped woman I discover later is called Agnes opens the door before I can make my escape and I'm captured.

Captured, though, by some kind of magical place I could never have pictured. But that is still to come. 'My name is Isabella Booth,' I enunciate as clearly as I can to this miserable creature: she is the kind of servant I would imagine worked here. 'I wish to speak with the Director of this hospital.' Yes, I may call it *hospital*, but it will be like none I've seen before. Agnes only nods as if I've been expected all along, and then it begins. My gasps and wonderment as she leads me through corridors, up stairways. I am astounded; there is no other word for it. What a gentle tyranny in its grandeur and homeliness, in these great windows and their pale patterned drapes, in the gleaming wooden floor and clean, whitened walls! What a welcome of light and reflection! We pass a picture lying on the floor under its broken hook, its hilltop scene on its side. There are no marks on the wall to signal the space it once occupied: this is a place without shadows. A great white vase of blue flowers gives off a sweet, majestic scent that fills my head. Deception or comfort? My cottage in London is all dark, mean corners, so let it be deception, I think. *Go on, then: deceive me.*

Agnes urges me, limping, along a whitewashed corridor. Her left leg is shorter than the right: did God think to grant her no good fortune?

'I'm in no hurry,' I reassure her as we crawl along: this way I can peek through glass windows, make myself ready for the horrors inside, the wretches I'll spy in all their derangement and distress, a thousand Davids at their worst. And that's when I notice the quiet – where are the screams and howls of these mad folk? There's a scuffle and some shouts far off, but the moment passes and they're gone. 'Is it always so silent here?' I ask Agnes, but she only shrugs.

We pass a room where twelve women of various ages and sizes sit in three rows facing a great window. Ugly women. Plain women. Beautiful women. Sitting stiffly in identical plain grey dresses, their hair tied back as if the black, brown, fair, red plumage among them is excessive and needs restraint. Dress codes to aid the calming of the mind and the easing of mental pain? Or to ensure conformity and good behaviour? I want to know what their madness has made them do. 'Why are these women here?' I ask Agnes, but again she doesn't answer me.

One woman sits apart from the rest, fat and kindly looking, swathed in black. She reads from a large book. The chairs are hard and straight-backed but no one fidgets in discomfort the way I used to in church as a girl. There's a fire in the large grate though, and a vase of purple and yellow flowers blooms on the table in the middle of the room. A gentle kind of schoolroom: what are these women here to learn, I wonder, but I'm too curious. One of the younger women looks over her shoulder at me: *we're not exhibits at a fair*. Agnes mutters something and indicates I should move on, but in the next room eight girls, their novice faces scrubbed clean, have their hands raised to make charcoal drawings on paper set on easels and I stop again, press my fingers against the glass.

'I'm sorry,' I whisper to Agnes. 'I don't want to disturb anybody, I promise.' Her strong fingers pull mine from the window as she draws me past a kitchen where four more young women, one of them with terrible, vivid pockmarks on her face, stand sullenly by a large, polished stove. An older woman with a splattered apron directs them to lift their wooden spoons and one by one they stir the great copper pot bubbling on the stove. I glance through the window beyond them to a group of men, also uniformed, hoeing weeds.

What a perfect microcosm of the world, I think: women sew and cook and paint, men till the soil. No doubt there will be a library somewhere for men like David to sit still and study, just as they would at home, and there'll be an Isabella near the kitchen, ready to serve him his supper. So these doctors believe more domestic habits may right the troubled minds of men and women! I can tell them that a little hoeing and some pretty flowers won't prevent a man from believing his wife is a whore, or from striking her in his madness.

And learning to cook won't stop a woman from being haunted by ghosts that promise to drive her mad.

'This is a pretty kind of madness,' I murmur at the silent Agnes. 'Such men and women cannot be seriously ill, surely? A rest, perhaps, away from their families, their loved ones, their friends, is all they need. Their distress cannot be so great.' I cough at more vases of lilies and roses in the hallway and through the quiet comes the sound of an organ being played: a hymn I recognize. I stifle the urge to hum along. The home, the church: great institutions combined in one building. A home to end all homes, full of reverence and comfort, moral reminders of better ways to live, and their rewards. Our men of science are no different from other men, I think. They too want to be close to God, for they believe they're in the service of something greater than themselves, and that this will make them great, too.

As the absurdly young Dr Balfour must also believe, I think after we stop at last and Agnes knocks on a door. The Director, Dr Browne, is away, he explains. He looks annoyed to be disturbed and seems to have slept as badly as I have. Suddenly, the splendour of this place recedes and I'm less sure if it is right indeed for David. If this *doctor* would be right. 'I wish only to view the house and its grounds. For a relative,' I say, as I finger my phial lightly through my skirts. My throat aches for the burn; my limbs are heavy and I see only one opportunity: there is no jug in the room.

'May I have a little water?'

And the thing is done. Dr Balfour apologizes and rather than call Agnes back, rushes from the room, asking me to wait only a moment or two. It's long enough: I tilt back my head but there are only ten drops left, possibly less. My restoration is incomplete. The room shimmers around me as my legs and arms loosen. I wait for my head to clear but the fog doesn't lift.

'For you,' he returns, panting, with a cup. 'I am still settling in...' and he waves his hand at the room behind him. I try not to show my disappointment, or my lack of faith in his powers.

I speak as clearly as I can through the muddle my mind has become. 'I want only a proper sense of it all. Before I divulge anything more.'

'Of course,' he says. 'We are here to serve,' and I swear he bows, ever so slightly. Is he mocking me? 'Naturally you will wish to see what we have here. Let me explain what we do. This is not a place of restraint, as you can see for yourself. We wish only to return the mind to its proper sphere.'

But I've heard these words before. *Conolly*. Management and reason. Sound principles. Does he have nothing more for me than a pleasant house to hold my husband for a few days?

'We are revolutionaries here – of the best kind,' he continues. 'Do you understand me, Mrs Booth?'

I shake my head but it hurts to speak. 'We have a new treatment for patients of all kinds of nervous disorders. We invite them to speak to us of their condition. They will go back to childhood, as far back as they can, and tell us everything, not simply how they feel at this present time. But what occurred, how they felt, what they thought – *before*.'

'And how does this help?' I speak at last.

'Think of us not as doctors. Rather as *priests*, hearing a confession. No – that is not quite right. The older faith, forgive me,' he winces, unnecessarily, I think, but he swiftly carries on: 'We are the *intermediaries* who will return an insane mind to sanity. Not a Holy Trinity, but as a scientific trinity, perhaps. A patient, his doctor, and sanity.' He smiles at that, broad, with even teeth. 'It's not so heretical a thought. The mind, the body and the soul are three, after all. We have a surgeon for the body, a minister for the soul. And now we have a mind-doctor – for the mind.'

He cannot know that these words mean something different to me: *Holy Trinity*. My church teaches that the Son is only divine when linked with the human. The human is an essential component of the Trinity.

I know this: I have felt it. I saw it.

Mary, David and myself.

* * *

We should have begun at twelve that windy, bright Sunday. But even in the absence of a clock, I knew we'd gone past that hour. The windows facing northwest were cooking us, lambs of the Lord stewing in the kitchens He liked to pretend were churches. And for this blasphemous thought I was immediately punished, as my hunger pangs worsened and I had to grip my belly to quieten it. Father frowned at my movement but still, nobody had indicated we could start yet.

While we stray we are allured by the charms of novelty. How I shifted about on my narrow wooden seat. Another Elder followed David, then another after him and another, as though they'd all forgotten about the food. My thin summer skirts on the hard chair meant that discomfort and hunger stopped their words reaching my ears, which was surely not their intention. Another time I might have giggled, and saved the thought to take to Mary, who was waiting for us at home, that year of her last summer with us. But I prayed hard instead it would soon be time to eat, and at last He relented and heard my prayers.

David was pressing a large white handkerchief to his fore-head and frowned when he saw me. 'Isabella! What a lovely dress, but suitable for this occasion?' I left it to my father to explain how I'd turned sixteen the day before. 'I knew I'd suffer if I wore it and I am,' I said, smiling. David mirrored my smile: lines carved his face gently, in ways I hadn't noticed before. 'You have an inclination for martyrdom, Isabella,' he said, almost laughing. 'We'll have to watch out for that.'

Later that evening, when David read from his work at our dining table, Robbie sulked at having to endure not only lectures during the day, but also at night, when all he wanted was to catch up on his supper and fill the belly that cabbage soup had only warmed. None of us mentioned Margaret's absence. Only Mary was lively: she wasn't tired or hungry. She leaned across the table towards David when he finished speaking.

'Is that really what appeals to you most about etymology, Mr Booth, its simplicity? For you have produced a difficult book about a simple thing.'

She had the kind of daring that always made me wonder. But it belonged in the home where she'd been brought up.

'Perhaps I have special powers,' David replied, and my father raised his eyebrows. It wasn't easy to know when David was teasing. 'We are a strange mix here, Mary. We are well-educated in parts, we believe in the progress of man, in the cultivation of his mind and his ability to reason. But some still believe in sentiment and sorcery. You'll have encountered both during your time here. It is the old and the new, warring with each other, but the new will win out. The men of enlightenment chase away old wives' tales.'

I bit my lip and the topic changed. We saw again David unexpectedly some days later, when his old-fashioned carriage appeared outside our window. I turned to Mary, panicked.

'Father's not at home – can you entertain him until I make myself presentable?' Sixteen years old and hurrying to my room, splashing cold water on my face, combing my hair, fixing it back up again, patting my cheeks before I could leave, hoping my steady pace would calm the beating inside me. My shallow breath as I descended the stairs. My nervous steps to the drawing room and its partially open door. How the curtains had been drawn against the sunlight to protect the furnishings. And Mary's face as she stood in front of David. Her knowing smile as he lifted his left hand and brushed it against her cheek.

Desire rose in my throat; hot hands ran over my body, lots of hands, lots of fingers and I gasped as I took two steps back and stopped. Then I set my foot down on the floor, forced myself forward and pushed at the drawing room door. 'Isabella, how well you look. Another lovely dress that compliments you,' he said. Pain and longing made me happy to tell a lie. 'Thank you,' I smiled back. 'But it's not mine. It belongs to Mary.' I was making an offer to them both, even if I didn't quite realize it, and neither did they. Two days later David left for London. When he returned, Mary had already gone home for the last time.

Mary, David, myself.

Another trinity.

But I can tell the young doctor nothing of this, of course. I can only thank him and promise to return the next day.

7.

Montrose, October 1823

The asylum might have been everything Alexander had hoped for, but until Browne returned there had been little for him to do. He had only four patients, besides Euphemia, who interested him beyond the run of melancholia sufferers and might test his theories. John MacLaverty was a young labourer from the town who tried to kill himself one night by falling on an upturned pitchfork, the day after his father died, and who had not spoken a word since. Marion McBride was a middle-aged spinster from Dumfries who held a kitchen knife to her elderly mother's throat and drew blood before a neighbour stopped her. William Alexander was a teacher from Edinburgh who developed a paranoia about his pupils and locked himself in a school-room, whereupon he destroyed most of the furniture until he could be restrained; and Caroline Angus was a wealthy young wife who had tried to smother her baby. They hinted at homicidal mania but had been saved from incarceration by a mixture of good fortune, rare compassion on the part of the authorities, and their own previous good character.

'Gaps waiting to be filled,' he'd thought as he'd read Browne's case notes. The Director hadn't delved much beyond asking for a description of symptoms, though. Changes in behaviour, diet, sleeping patterns, physical ailments, were logged in files. Browne's main concern was the operation of the asylum, the new way of *housing* patients. Architecture and atmosphere were enough to effect a cure.

But exercise, a strict diet, company, attention, pleasant surroundings that freed patients of responsibility and therefore of worry, were only the beginning, not the end. '*For some of them, all the linen sheets and fresh bowls of flowers in the world will never be enough to "make them want to be good",*' Alexander had written up in his first notes.

Within those four patients who had committed, or wanted to commit, an act of violence, would be evidence of trauma, he knew it. He had their endings: now to trace their beginnings. So he hadn't abandoned Crichton after that day of the fire; and Crichton hadn't abandoned *him*. Childhood trauma was still the key. *Observation, sympathy, trust*, the method. He'd be the Esquirol to Browne's Pinel. What was lacking in patients' lives was presently addressed adequately enough: those who couldn't read were taught to read; those who had no practical skills were shown how to weave or mend shoes; those with no experience of fine music were encouraged to listen and learn to appreciate it. All to 'build the mind anew'.

But that required an erasure of what had gone before, not a delving in to it. A radical departure. His professional ambitions might have gone beyond a comfortable general practice, but as his recent epiphany had shown him, Alexander also had the attitude of a good bourgeois: a house, a respectable wife and obedient children, sons, preferably, to carry on his name. With perhaps a little secret affair or two: what was the harm, after all?

It was with radicalism at the forefront of his mind that Alexander initially dismissed the unusual-looking woman who had appeared briefly in his office the day before. He was almost disappointed to find her in front of him again this morning, shaking her gloveless hand. She had nothing to offer him, he was quite sure.

Oddness rather than predictability began their meeting though, as she stumbled over his name as if it was the first time they'd been introduced. Indeed, it was as though she scarcely remembered their brief encounter and a thought struck him. He stared at her face until she blushed.

'I'm simply "doctor", Mrs Booth, not "professor". Not yet.' *Bulckers' techniques.*

'I've insulted you, I'm so sorry...'

The blush on her pale choirboy's cheeks made him forgive her interruption. He directed her to the easy chair in front of his desk; his offer to take her coat was politely refused. 'I'm flattered you imagine I've reached that distinction,' he joked as he settled himself opposite her. She was too restless: the way she scratched at her hands and her neck, the constriction of her pupils, the tapping of her heel against the floor. How had he missed this before? All were indications of the potential patient. The dark circles under her eyes suggested it, too. Then she said, 'You are much younger than I expected,' which made him laugh.

'They cast us off when we reach thirty years of age.' His second joke failed to ease her, either.

'If we are fortunate enough to reach it,' she murmured.

Again Alexander followed Bulckers' example: sympathetic but patrician, playing the father to this melancholy choirboy. 'I am concerned, Mrs Booth,' he said, his elbows light on his polished desk. 'You are tired, you have clearly not been taking good care of yourself. Do you have children?'

She nodded, surprised by the directness of his question. *They always were.* 'How are they to manage,' he continued in the same careful tone, 'if their mother is unwell?'

'How do you know I am unwell? Is it so obvious?'

He thought he saw tears in her eyes but it might have been the light. He reached across the desk and opened his palms: she was clutching a letter.

'My dear lady, you have come to the right place...' but he couldn't finish his sentence because, to his immense annoyance, she actually began to laugh. *At him?* Small teeth made her look childlike.

'Tell me, doctor,' she said, 'is it because you are an expert or because I am such a specimen, that you know these things?' But he knew how to deal with that attitude.

'Mrs Booth,' he said, looking at her sternly now. *Like a disappointed father.* 'I am in the business of restoring a mind to itself, as I told you yesterday. I do not play games.' Yes: Bulckers' chiding, pedagogical tone had her blushing again for her own presumption. 'So please – tell me this time what brings you here,' he said. *The routine story.* Trapped in an unhappy marriage, perhaps. Hence the use of laudanum that he could see in her every movement. Maybe a hint of the hereditary principle: a melancholy mother? To make it a little more interesting. 'Tell me what ails you.'

'Not me,' she said, her chin raised. 'I'm here for my husband. He suffers attacks of epilepsy.'

Not what he was expecting, but not what interested him, either.

'And there are other... difficult things that cause him... shame,' she said, at last. Alexander stifled a sigh and opened his notebook. The action caused her to straighten up, as he expected. He could have been writing anything, but they never considered that.

'Before I ask you about these "difficult things",' he said, 'perhaps you can tell me a little about him. His profession, for instance. His age.'

She nodded, more eager now. 'He is fifty-five years of age. We have been married for nine years and have two children. David is a scholar, presently engaged in work on an etymological dictionary.'

Another overtaxed, over-zealous man of letters, the type Browne liked. And again, not for him. Alexander rested his pen against the inkstand. 'Does he know you're here?'

She nodded again. 'It's his request – that I look over this place for him. He asked me to give you this.' At last she surrendered the sealed letter in her hand and smoothed the soiled and crumpled corners that suggested she had once thought of throwing it away.

'His epilepsy began four years ago,' she continued. 'It occurred perhaps only every nine months or so, until recently. Now I am recording weeks, even days, between attacks.'

This, too, did not interest him. 'But before they even began, I noticed things.' She wasn't capable of registering his lack of interest: her voice had grown low with self-absorption and her eyes had weakened their focus. 'His mistaken beliefs in me. His angry moods. His confusions...' Yes, how like a confessor a doctor was indeed, whatever their faith, he thought.

'This has been difficult for you,' he said when she paused at last. Her husband's letter would contain more of the same, no doubt: details of his fits, his diet and so on. Alexander began mentally to plan for the evening: a surprise visit to Philomena, perhaps. Or would it be better to keep her waiting? People rushed when they were bored, though, and that was how they missed things. He didn't notice Isabella staring at the books in his glass case.

'Pinel,' she indicated. 'I have it, too. I've read everything I can find,' she said, as if by way of explanation. 'Combe and Locke, too, I veer from phrenology to philosophy and back again but none of it helps. Don't you think we give too much importance to feeling, Dr Balfour?' But she answered her own question before he could. 'Rousseau was wrong. Too much feeling makes us mad, not savage. It does not return us to our natural states, it distorts them.'

He picked her up on this, hopeful for something more. 'You believe your husband is mad?' She had no hope of a cure, she said. 'Don't believe those who associate epilepsy with madness,' he continued. 'We may not cure his epilepsy but we can cure his madness. It would be a straightforward case, from what you tell me.'

She raised her eyebrows. 'Straightforward? You think what I have told you is straightforward?'

He wanted to quash that superior tone her reading had doubtless given her. *God forbid more women take up the practice!* 'You understand about the nervous system?' he asked her. 'The nerves receive stimuli from the external environment, which they transmit in the form of sensations to the brain. If a man's nerves are impaired, if his environment is hostile to him, then nervous symptoms can ensue.'

He'd always found that women preferred neurological explanations first. Words they needed explained to them, terms they'd never heard of and had to be interpreted for them: well, that was why men like him were there.

'His environment is *hostile* to him?' She leaned back, disbelieving. Alexander frowned. She would be a difficult wife indeed. He wouldn't lose his patience. 'You mean by that – me? It is my fault?'

'This is no use, without a proper examination of your husband,' he said, calmly. But she shook her head.

'You don't understand anything about him,' she said. 'Everything is governed by his madness. His moods. How he will greet you. How he will speak to you, think of you. Whether it will be a good day or a bad day, not just for him but for all of us, depends on it. We orbit around him: our lives are controlled by this... evil. I can have no thought that is not him and his needs, and even that is not enough; for the more I do the more he complains and the more he demands of me.'

An unhappy wife's complaints, after all. He was disappointed again. Well, he'd ask her a few more questions then show her out, fix an appointment for her husband. He'd be rid of her after a few more perfunctory questions that he could submit to Browne in a satisfactory report on his return. Alexander stifled another sigh. 'How did you come to meet your husband, Mrs Booth?'

'He was married to my sister before she died,' she said, simply. Such common family mixes, he reflected. Deaths in childbirth, unexplained diseases, repeated pregnancies. But more, not fewer, husbands must have married a spinster sister-in-law. He knew commonality did not make a thing easier to bear though, and he wondered how she had struggled with this connection to her husband's past. Perhaps that was what was

138

there in the shaking hand lifting the cup to her lips; in the dark smudges under her eyes. What a too-close familial connection would do... But he only asked her if she took anything for her distress, waiting to see if she would admit it. Her dry mouth, the way she fought to take a breath. Her self-absorption, the way she twisted his enquiries about her husband round to her own state of mind, signified melancholia, which she treated with the drug. Perhaps there was more to learn, after all.

'He wanted me to see this place,' she continued. 'That's a hopeful sign, isn't it? That he knows there's something wrong with him and wants to put it right?'

It was rare for any possibly psychotic individual to turn himself over to the control of any asylum, even to a place as liberated as this, as Alexander knew. He'd heard of Mary Lamb, of course, the celebrated children's writer. She was also a murderess, who had stabbed her mother to death over twenty-five years ago. She was thirty-two years old then, an overworked spinster daughter who took on sole care for her elderly parents, both of whom were invalids by the time of her breakdown. Apparently, because her behaviour on the day of the attack was so strange and worrisome, her brother had fetched the physician Charles Pitcairn to attend her, a man with no expertise in mental matters and who would prove to be quite useless to her. For it was shortly after his visit that she attacked and fatally wounded her mother at dinner: her brother, Charles, restrained her, then admitted her to Fisher house, in Islington, where she was confined until the parish authorities considered she was well enough to be released. On one condition: that her brother assumed absolute care for her.

Her mania had taken on the form of extreme violence, obviously, but also delusions, where she imagined she was alive in an age almost a hundred years previously. Her speech was also considerably altered and disjointed. Very often during a manic phase she would have to be restrained in a strait-jacket, for her own safety as well as that of others. Alexander would often imagine why her diseased mind made her commit matricide; what *childhood experience* had brought on this desire to murder the woman who had given her life?

Hers was a case he had contemplated many times. He liked to think that, if he could have interviewed her over a period of time, he would have established causes, patterns and experiences in childhood that would have explained her mania, her desire to kill. But far more extraordinary to him than the care her brother took of her – and Charles himself had not been so stable, having also spent time in an asylum – was her ability *to acknowledge her state of mind in advance* of subsequent manic episodes. That she could not only tell very clearly when such an episode was approaching, even while she was lucid and calm, as she could be for periods at a time, but would actually remove herself from her brother's care and *voluntarily take herself* to a private madhouse, in her case, at Hoxton.

Was David Booth another Mary Lamb? Offering himself up to the authorities, in anticipation of a manic episode? The connection appealed to him.

So when he reached out for the letter, he thought he knew what to expect. He broke the seal with confidence, not considering for a moment why a man might seal a letter he had entrusted to his wife, and read the following:

Willow Cottage,
Richmond, London,
September 28th 1823

To Doctor William Browne,
The Medical Superintendent,
The Royal Lunatic Asylum, Infirmary and Dispensary,
Montrose

My dear Sir,

I must express my deepest gratitude for your kind reply to my previous letter. It is with great difficulty and much

140

sadness that I write to you again, but please be assured I do so only from the gravest of concern for the health of my dearest wife, Isabella Baxter Booth.

It is several months now since the first evidence of her distressed state of mind became apparent, and in the last weeks has reached a pitch where I fear for her own safety. My wife, as you may remember from my last communication with you, is of a highly nervous disposition. She is very well educated and extremely principled, but her most recent behaviour shows how far she has removed herself from those principles, and from the care of those who love her most.

In short, what I have to tell you will shock you, but I must trust to your experience of such matters and be as meticulous as possible. I cannot shirk from my duty. I have found my dear wife walking alone along our street in a state of complete undress, late at night, on several occasions. When I have questioned her, she has been unable to give an account of herself or of her actions, and indeed often resists my injunctions to her to return home straightaway. She has spent entire nights away from our home, and, I fear, in the most dangerous and dubious company. Alternately, she has come to me at night, with what I can only describe as the wanton intentions of another kind of woman entirely, not the behaviour of a Christian woman.

She is also very tearful, often and for no reason; she is awake at all hours of the day and her appetite has diminished completely. She is extremely neglectful of our two young children, to the extent that I have been forced to ask my father-in-law for aid on many occasions, as I cannot keep them in the house with her. She raves, for minutes at a time, quite incoherently, and then will be found in what I believe is described as a catatonic state. Worse – and I hesitate to mention this, but clarity and truth are important

– she insists that the ghost of her dead sister appears regularly before her.

I hope to persuade her to visit you when she returns to her family home in Broughty Ferry next week, where she will be in the care of her sister. I have not taken her family into my confidence, for fear they might persuade her otherwise. But I believe there is every possibility she will come, of her own volition, to see you, once I have spoken with her. She still retains some respect for me and will listen to what I say.

It is my greatest hope that a stay in your radical establishment, for whatever length of time you may consider appropriate, will provide her with the care she requires, and will return her to full health. I have asked a lay person from our faith to speak with her, in the hope that he could reach her, but to no avail. I have no other recourse but this.

Yours, etc.

David Booth, Esq.

Alexander sat for some moments in silence. This would require the greatest care and attention. Isabella herself had already acknowledged some of the behavioural aspects detailed in David Booth's letter: her inability to sleep, her lack of appetite. She was also a laudanum addict. He had a delicious moment of imagining her husband's description of her, dishabille and wanton, dancing along a dark road on a summer's night into the waiting arms of some young man. Could it be true? Or was *Isabella* the voluntary patient he sought, unable to admit her own troubles, concocting a story about her husband as a kind of subconscious attempt to admit herself?

It seemed extraordinarily deceptive but if David Booth was telling the truth, why was his wife making up such a story about him? His letter insisted that 'she still retains some respect for me and will listen to what I say', which pointed either to wilful self-delusion or a complete innocence on his part as to what his wife was about.

We can only work with what is presented to us. He should have known better: he should have run away. Someone was playing a trick on him, either Isabella or her husband: enough of a reason to dismiss her. But Alexander paid no heed to the warnings in front of him. He made his choice and thought only of the tricks he might have to play instead.

And so this is what he said, after he finished reading the letter a third time.

Part Three:

Montrose

1.

Montrose, October 1823

Noises made by the inn at night keep sleep at bay, remind me why I'm here. So this is his fault, after all, and I've failed and must blame him even though I've tried hard not to. But resentment glows inside like hot stone, whilst forgiveness is dull and cold and no comfort at all. So maybe I don't need to hug the blanket quite as close as I listen and watch for them. Doors are bolted; chairs clatter in a far-off room. Muffled voices rise and pitch with the scuff of well-worn boots on stone. A laugh, short and sharp, breaks through the night, and somebody groans, a guttural sound like a dying animal. Bedsprings come creaking from another direction. The light under the door will be doused soon. I shiver and reflect, *what a useless traveller you'd have made, after all. How would you have made it as far as the Continent, all the way to Italy with Mary and her husband?* Changing my mind all those years ago wasn't the wrong decision I've long thought it was, perhaps, and I almost want to laugh.

But I'm afraid here alone in the dark in this friendless little inn: my mind won't rest. Even the fire in the grate, still bright, can't disturb the dark that rejoices at my fear. Then drapery drags soft and heavy over the floorboards, and I'm suddenly brave and ask out loud, 'who is it?' but she's too cowardly or too mocking to reply, so I know it must be her. Mary's husband used to swear that furniture moved by itself when he stayed alone in his room, and Claire swore the very same. Well, she didn't like to be left out, did she? Mary told me once in that grim voice she kept specially for her step-sister. Mary, Claire and Shelley. That 'trinity'. A second one. David and I taught her something then, even though we didn't mean to, about belonging to a threesome.

Perhaps it's Mary's husband who's been making the noise all along. Haunting those of us who sleep alone.

A slithering, sucking sound this time and so I must light the candle and prove it to myself. Its shimmery light shows everything is just as it was. Dress and stays, underclothes on the chair. Shoes by the bed, coat on the hook on the back of the door. Travelling bag beside the dresser; the jug and basin on top. The curtains closed. Nothing altered.

I blow out the candle and something soft strokes my hand. Of course, only she would dare. But she can't stop me going back to the asylum tomorrow. I'd been unsure earlier when I came back here so tired I made straight for bed. His pomposity, his confidence; they don't match a youthful face or that strange delicacy about it. *I know the diabolical when I see it.* I thought maybe I'd caught a glimpse at one moment, but then it was gone, so I can't be certain. I might have been a little scared of him but not of him doing me harm. His words were confusing: I thought I'd read enough but he led me into a new area and I didn't know how to wind my way back out again onto more familiar paths. Perhaps that's why he'll be good for David. My knowledge is too mean to help him.

Is this what it means to have power, I wonder, as I cringe in my little bed in the night in a way I'm sure *he* cannot be doing. Yes, I doubt very much that 'my' mind-doctor is as confused at this moment as I am. But will he pity my powerlessness or take advantage of it? Whatever I want for myself, I don't want David to suffer. I want him to be well. We've done each other harm: I'm making it right.

A sigh that sounds like joy: Margaret. She thinks she's winning, but he has David's letter now. Perhaps he knows the diabolical when he sees it, too. *How would Dr Balfour greet you as a widow? Or a murderess?* Margaret whispers. Her pleasure spreads through the room before the crash happens and the chair tips over. She sighs again, as if my visit to the asylum has made her happy when I know it hasn't. I dip down under the unfamiliar blanket and close my eyes, tight.

* * *

Dinner was late: my fault. One trigger amongst many. Like the milk, sour on the shift under my dress that he hated, too. My baby was just put to bed, out of my arms and leaving me feeling the loss of her that always had me wondering what to do next. Trying to hold a needle to finish his shirt when I was so clumsy was pointless: I gave it up. I was never this way after Izzy but Kathy made me all fingers and thumbs. I missed numbers, too. They taunted my tired eyes with a language I couldn't understand. I'd hunt for an hour or two when I could place an order for beef, send out washing, but time hid from me and I had no energy for games. Nothing would ever be done, no task completed. Dirt and mess grew in our cottage and David retreated to his room, writing, unmindful of it all. The house was my responsibility. Sums for cotton and linen and muslin and calico; repairs to smocks and shirts and breeches and handkerchiefs; orders for the candles and coal and wood, cheese and butter and eggs and milk and fish and game, soap and starch, wine and cider. But those lists didn't respect me. Like the mess, they grew as much as they pleased, as our income shrank under my husband's old debts and his new ambitions.

I couldn't make him understand the burden. What wife can? I didn't come to keeping house and having babies with ease. He didn't care that we stabled no horse, or that I grew our vegetables, or that we never entertained. But we couldn't slip down any further or we'd never get up again. My worries were real, not 'irrational fancies'. Leasing Barns o' Woodside gave us some money for our cottage and David one opportunity to make his name in London. But a roof and prospects leave little room for anything else.

Kathy's touch of colic had tapped our shrinking purse for remedies and robbed me of a night's sleep when I stood at the range that evening, stirring a pot of hambone soup that didn't smell right. I was less nervous now of colours and smells changing: what food was meant to do. Before Richmond, I'd never poached an egg or a fish, had never chopped a carrot or skinned a chicken. I was surprised to like it. On his good days, I could even be adventurous. Not today: I sniffed our soup and wrinkled my nose. Was the ham off, or was I too weary to tell? Food didn't taste the same after Kathy's birth. I couldn't trust myself. Neither could he.

David's familiar distracted step was on the stair, irregular, as though he'd had a thought that stopped him and needed to be sounded out before he could continue again. So maybe something wasn't right with it. I'd have to dish it up and let us take our chance. Bowls edged out the papers he'd spread on the table and he muttered, as though they were jewels whose value I didn't appreciate. I thought to say something, but changed my mind. He wouldn't hear.

Kathy made me invisible to everyone's but her baby's eyes. Even Izzy seemed not to see me. David supping at his soup without a glance in my direction made no change. No word about any strange smell or taste, either. I was alone in that, too. I lifted my spoon, let it clatter against the bowl.

'Did you not hear what I said?' He glanced only sideways at me, but at least it was a start. 'I have nothing left – the bill for Kathy was high enough, and now we have nothing left for the rest of the week.' I pointed to his soup: he was almost done. 'That was the last of the ham. I don't even know if I should have used it. We'll all be ill with it.'

He frowned, then sniffed the air. My hand went automatically to the damp, loose cloth at my breast. My appetite had returned but I'd been too busy with Kathy and Izzy to eat. All my dresses, let out for Kathy, were still too big. 'I need some help, David. I need to know that you…'

He pushed the empty bowl aside and broke off a piece of bread for himself. He could smell me and my daughter. Our disruption of his life.

'You need to know what?' he said at last, after he'd chewed a number of times and swallowed: keeping me waiting.

'I need to know that you still love me.'

That wasn't what I'd meant to say. I'd meant to ask about money for more help around the house: for his shirts to be sent out with the laundry, just for a few months; for a few hours' work in the kitchen that some girl could provide, cheaply, that would let me catch up on my sleep.

'We are husband and wife, Bella. In Christ's eyes we are bound to one another.' If I imagined the coldness of his tone, it wasn't without reason.

'That's not what I meant. I don't mean you have a duty to love me.'

'But I do.' He tore off more bread and chewed slowly. 'As, in fact, you do me. Therefore I cannot imagine in what capacity I could have failed you.'

'You haven't failed me.'

'Then why would you even ask me such a question?'

He'd had enough. He began to gather up his papers. I put out my hand to stop him and he flinched as my skin touched his.

'You see?' I couldn't contain it any longer. Days and weeks bitten back, until now. 'What is wrong with me? Why won't you even look at me? How could I have suddenly become so repulsive to you?'

He shook his arm free. 'You are tired, Isabella. I have work to do.'

The decanter of wine was almost empty but he poured the rest of it into a glass and drank it straight down. I covered my leaking breast with my hand once again.

'What's the matter, David? Is it because of Margaret?'

His hand supported his brow, the heaviness of his burden clearly growing with every word I uttered and confirming my suspicion: he regretted marrying me.

'You say you have seen her,' he sighed, as though we'd gone over this too many times. 'That she appeared to you. I believe you, as you know. So let us leave the matter there.'

When he turned I read the regret more clearly than if it had been painted in letters across his face. *If my father could see this, would he tell me that we need only to talk about our troubles, like any married couple?* A child wanting her father. He wouldn't leave me here if he knew.

'Why did you marry me?' I caught his sleeve as he opened the door. It was a pitiful, pleading gesture and he only shook his head. Impatience, yes, and contempt; that was there, too. I repeated my question, my voice steady this time, pitched too low for him to dismiss.

'Why did you marry me?'

At last he looked at me properly. 'I thought we were compatible, a good match.'

'We *were*? You don't think so now?'

Spring rain fell to feed my kitchen garden, my carefully tended plants breathing at the moment my own breath stopped. The candles flickered, unfriendly: one of them was almost down to the wick. It sputtered at me as though I was a child to be scolded.

'These questions do not help, Isabella. Place your trust in Christ to help us,' he murmured.

But I was the one who suffered his strange, silent moods; I who, time after time, managed his rudeness to the tradesmen that called, who excused his odd expressions to our neighbours when they tried to be friendly. I the one disappointed in my expectations: did he think I rejoiced to be cooking and cleaning with my own bare hands? I, who had to compete with a rival. Yet I was faithful in my dreams. *What has he to complain of me?*

'Do you think our marriage was a mistake?'

I hadn't thought it until I said the words: my mind flitted to my baby, asleep upstairs beside her sister, knowing nothing about what, or who, had brought them into being.

'Do you?'

He couldn't answer: clearly, he thought so, too.

'Am I a mistake?' I shrieked with sheer frustration: he covered my mouth with his hand and forced me against the wall. I thought he might strike me, then he let go.

'I fear that you do not bring out what is best in me,' he said, as I touched my bruised mouth. 'If I keep away from you, then perhaps that is the reason. I fear contamination from your – propensities to emotion. You are not restrained, Isabella. You are not – proper. You infect me with it.'

'What in heaven do you mean by that? I am diseased in some way?' My voice was getting louder again: I couldn't control myself. He was right: I feared for what I was, what I might do.

'I mean, morally,' he said, with perfect calm. 'If I seem strange sometimes to you, then perhaps you should look to yourself. Ask what influence you might have over me. How you exercise it.'

'David, you're not a child. How could I influence you? You know so much more than I do. I think you want to trick or tease me.'

'I assure you I am not teasing. There's a demon at work in you, Bella. It leads you into wicked ways. I have to help you, yes, I will help you.'

'Is that why you married me? You were trying to save me? From what?'

For a moment I thought he might grab at me again. But instead, he smiled and shook his head. There was no more wine, but a little brandy in the kitchen. When I returned with the bottle, he was still standing by the table. He held his hands out to me, but now I wouldn't touch him.

'Of course I love you, Isabella,' he said. 'You are my wife. We must simply work harder to understand each other better.'

I kept my hands by my side, then Kathy began to cry and he took up the rest of his papers. As he left the room, I called out, 'we will speak about this again', but he didn't reply. The hambone soup turned in my stomach and Kathy continued to cry, but I made no move to go up to her. The next day, David left us for Scotland on an urgent visit he'd forgotten to inform me about, he said, and the following week, this conversation between us still circling my mind, Mary paid her final visit to me.

2.

Montrose asylum, October 1823

Alexander sat still in the silent gloom of his office and waited for his heart to assume its normal rhythm. Would anything ever be the same again? His 'eureka' moment, after all! Showing him for a fool, doubting it into near extinction by his opposition to all things romantic. He shook his head and laughed a little at himself. *And all thanks to a woman.* He smiled again as if he couldn't believe something so preposterous. 'But who cares about the source?' he said aloud, and got out of the chair to pace his office once more. The confluence of sex and medical theory didn't alarm him that night, but on many nights after this one he'd think often to himself that it should have. In the latter years of his life especially, after he read a new paper, or came across a new appointment, he'd ponder that moment when he'd stood on the edge of a precipice and thought only of how he would fly above the darkness below, and he would shiver.

But for now, all Alexander did was pause by the window, pull the drapes apart and peer through the black of an autumn night. Even in his moment of triumph, he felt sadness rather than anger for his mentor and the theories he now realized finally were mistaken ones indeed. *Crichton.* 'Look at child-hood? Looking at childhood yields nothing!' he frowned at his reflection in the window. 'No wonder Euphemia was a dead end. It was for this.' And after all, he assured himself further, when a twinge of doubt at this easy rejection of his faith in Crichton made his shoulder twitch, what was a new generation for, if not to revise and renew what had gone before? It was meant to be: it was natural. He could still be grateful to the great man's wisdom even if he no longer represented the right path.

The red wine shimmered in its glass as he poured out more from the decanter on his desk. He was a little drunk, he knew, and should have gone back to his room at the inn hours ago. But he was too preoccupied to be shut up alone there, or to have to make conversation with any of the inn's irritating residents, who might decide to join him by the fire for some gossip about the 'mad folks up at the hospital'. Only his office would do. He ran his forefinger over the indented titles of the books on his desk, the celebrated names of their authors. Cheyne, Whytt, Cullen, Duncan, Morison, Crichton, Ferriar, Abercrombie. A roll-call of genius. *The Treatise of Nervous Diseases. An Essay, Medical, Philosophical and Clerical on Drunkenness and its effects on the Human Body. An Essay Towards a Theory of Apparitions. Hygeia. Inquiries concerning the Intellectual Powers and the Investigation of Truth.* And now he'd join them.

At Edinburgh, his lecturers had enjoyed reminding their students every day of Cullen's legacy: the classification of neuroses, the Comata, Adynamiae, Spasmi, Vesaniae. One man: what one man could do had begun to obsess Alexander from that moment. He might have thrown himself into every excursion to the nearest inn, made himself the first to arrive and the last to leave as though he didn't have to care, but his constitution demanded a soaking of his own 'neuroses' and it masked his studying. His eagerness to know more wouldn't have won many favours with Hepburn and the others, who were only there because their fathers wanted them to carry on a practice, he knew that. He couldn't have them suspect he wasn't one of them, so he carried his passion for these great men who were discovering something new every day in secret, bound inside his coat, as Duncan and Morison billowed past on their way to the Surgeon's Hall. Neither man had the look of a hero: the students liked to joke that Duncan's nose turned corners before he did, and that Morison resembled a spinster who was better with her needle. Yet they carried an air of achievement about them. *Let other men travel to the four corners of the globe and bring back their strange creatures, their exotic plants*, Alexander used to think quietly to himself. *We have no need to travel: the mind is our globe, what it's capable of, how well it functions, how badly it can let a man down*. He could still remember the day he held a new copy of Cooke's *Treatise* in his bare hands, turning it over in the light, before he stepped back into the close and tucked it away. That he never lost it once on his many nights out was nothing short of a miracle.

He took another deep gulp of his wine. Since Isabella had left, he'd been forming a seamless little narrative of titles, appointments and honours in his head. Cullen stood out among the many, why not Alexander Balfour? Whatever mix of work and good fortune that lit on one man while others stayed in the shade, would light on him, too – opportunity was what made the difference! He knew genius didn't exist in a vacuum, even if history insisted on it. But she would be the cause of his greatness. He knew it, he could feel it.

'No battle is ever clear-cut: it's a medieval campaign where you can't tell friend from foe in the scrum,' he'd said pomp- ously and drunkenly to Hepburn early one morning after a full night's carousing. Hepburn had been teasing him about his future in Gheel, and this was the closest Alexander had ever been to belief in a given moment that changed a man's fate. Perhaps he'd always been a romantic, after all. 'Am I scav- enging in the dirt, looking for a buckle or a pin to show me the moment the battle changes and winning turns into defeat?' He'd accosted Hepburn in Cockburn Street like a marauder, and they'd both fallen down with laughing. 'Then I'll get down into the dirt and soil my hands until they blister and my eyes are so tired with searching that I wouldn't know a treasure if I saw it,' he'd said, and mimed the action, Hepburn copying him drunkenly as market girls hurried past.

He breathed in hard, puffed out his chest and stretched his arms. He'd acted quickly today, sensing glory, and he could be proud of that. It was after he'd read her husband's letter that he'd told Isabella he could help David Booth, and free of charge, too. That she herself was disturbed in her reason was quite evident at that point because in her distraction she'd fainted, just as he was explaining something of the history of epilepsy to her. Or was it at the mention of her husband's illness?

Whatever the cause, he'd been far too intrigued to let her go just yet. Already now he was craving her company a little, and it was only a few hours since she'd left. He hadn't any clear designs on her, only the damage that had been done to her clever mind interested him. And that choirboy face, perhaps, with its pink mouth that begged for the artist's thumb to smudge it fat and wide.

Because Isabella, not her husband, would be his patient. And without her even knowing it. 'Such a stroke of genius,' he made to congratulate himself again, and once more his heart skipped a beat and he put a palm to his chest. The wine wasn't doing the trick, after all. He should go to the inn and sleep it off if he could at this late hour. He took up his tweed coat and doused the candles. The corridor was quiet; once again he'd creep silently through the night as everyone else lay sleeping. What kind of night creature was he, he wondered as he made his way down the central staircase, his heels hitting hard on the wood as though he was determined he shouldn't be alone after all and wanted to wake everyone up instead. He paused to take up one of the lit candles by the door, as well as a glass lantern and held it in his hand as he eased himself out of the front door.

* * *

It was what she'd said. She might have been staring into some kind of mental abyss but she nevertheless had been very aware of her surroundings when she recovered from her fainting fit, aware to the point of combativeness, and she'd surprised him.

'You have more women than men here, I believe,' she'd said. 'I only saw a few working in the garden. There are no others? Men are less likely to be mad, then?'

The ratio of male to female patients in the asylum at that time was actually sixty to forty, but as Browne had indicated in his notes, it was the female mind that had the greater propensity for madness. What Isabella saw was a quantity not yet there. But it would be, and soon.

'Not all male patients prefer the outdoors,' Alexander had informed her, patiently. 'Some who do will have been working further away than the immediate gardens.'

'So men *are* more likely to be mad than women?' she'd persisted. Her persistence would always be a character trait he disliked but one he'd never manage to subdue.

'I'm afraid not. The weaker sex, the stress placed on women during their childbearing years...' he'd reeled off the list easily.

'Why are there so many men here then as you say, if that is not the case? If women are more prone to madness?' He didn't believe she was confused; at that moment he'd thought she was just being difficult, and he disliked that aspect of her, too.

'The pressure on men to compete and succeed is greater,' he'd replied. It was another easy answer. Her sex obsession wouldn't take her so far, he'd wanted to tell her but didn't. He wouldn't treat her like an equal, however clever she thought she was. 'The pressure of the modern world. The damage done to great minds by extensive study.'

Isabella had stared at him, green eyes narrowed. He'd cursed himself for choosing the wrong tone to take with her, and thought again of Bulckers and his techniques. 'You really believe that men's minds are more capable of greatness than women's?' she'd asked. But he'd already given her his answer:

whose was the greater mind here, the frail housewife's or the doctor's? She shrugged without waiting for his reply. 'I suppose it is so. Running a household with only a few pennies to spare is no great strain, compared with the pressure to compete and succeed, as you say. And studying pamphlets on the workings of the mind so that you can better understand your disturbed husband: no, that's not damaging to a woman's mind at all. It's the fault of our *children*: breaking our minds while they fill our wombs. How clever you are, Dr Balfour.'

Her bitterness and sarcasm would make an ugly woman of her in a few decades' time, Alexander thought, as he sipped his tea and tried to stare her down. She was fidgeting now, and scratching once again at her neck. But he didn't make excuses about his workload to get away from her.

Why not? Because what she had just said changed everything. With one single sentence she altered the course of his career. *To better understand your disturbed husband – no, that is not damaging to a woman's mind at all!* Her words carved a place in his brain, had him counting possible papers, books even, based on his brilliant, innovative case study *where the madness of a male spouse infects and causes madness in the female.* A romantic theory, of course: why he'd almost missed it at first. Everyone was 'infected' all the time by mental sickness, be it lovesickness or homesickness. It was a metaphor for a real condition.

But Alexander understood no metaphor by it at all. Now at last he realized what a gift his fondness for the literal was to be for him. *A literal infection.* Robert Whytt had had no notion of an actual nervous system, although he was the first to argue for the nerves when he wrote *Observations on the Nature, Causes and Cure of those disorders which have been commonly called Nervous Hypochondriac or Hysteric, To Which are prefixed some remarks on the Sympathy of the Nerves.* He'd shown that pain in the stomach made for pain in the head – not new, Galen had argued it, too. But in Galen, pain in the head was caused by vapours arising from the stomach. He'd had no notion of nerves that run throughout the body, connecting it in every way. Whytt had developed that 'sympathy' of the nerves, acting upon each other, linked to each other, creating a system of consent between various parts of the body, a system that Cullen had then expanded.

But the part of that theory that Cullen had smothered, he, Alexander Balfour would expand and claim for his own! *A sympathy of the nerves*, taken further to a notion of infection. The infection of madness! He would be the successor to Whytt and Cullen, after all. What fame was to be found in the study of the mind! Not just for mind-doctors like him, but the fame of those who suffered mental agonies. Samuel Johnson and the 'black bile'. Robert Burns and William Cowper. Oliver Goldsmith and Thomas Gray. Johnson's amanuensis, James Boswell, who self-medicated with alcohol to keep his own melancholy at bay. Boswell thought melancholy a disease of the artistic mind. How delighted he was to find that Aristotle considered 'melancholy to be the concomitant of distinguished genius'. Ergo, all melancholics must be geniuses. 'If it gave the revolting little show-off some comfort...' Alexander chuckled to himself. But Browne believed it, too. Men of genius overtaxed and exhausted themselves in their desire to be immortal.

Browne attributed madness in thirteen of the cases Alexander looked at, to the reading of novels alone. What about that particular choice of reading material might aid the rush to immortality, he'd wondered at first, before realizing, of course: the notion of a specific path. That lives weren't pointless, without a beginning, a middle and an end. That they made sense. A life that made no sense was the very definition of madness, after all.

Alexander was to make sense of Isabella's story. To give it meaning, and in doing so, give his own life meaning, too. Give it fame and fortune and glory! His path to glory, as he saw it that night, depended utterly on his rejection of David Booth's letter, of course. He made his choice, and it lit up the fields before him better than any candle might.

3.

Montrose, October 1823

I was alone and back once more in Scotland when Kathy was just a newborn and Izzy my closest companion. David had stayed in London during the final stages of my confinement; he couldn't bear to be close to such a grotesque thing as I was, my belly and breasts bulging like some obscene fertility goddess. It was best I left his sight until it was over. He didn't complain when I removed myself to Christy's for the birth, and he didn't visit.

I think my father must have said something then, whilst he was in London. Something to Shelley, or to Mary herself, I never knew which. But she took her opportunity and made her suggestion in a final letter she sent to me from London, which should have shocked me. Perhaps, at any other time, it might have done. Did my father have any idea what his gossiping nearly brought about? *'Come with us to the Continent... belong to our large and disreputable party,'* Mary wrote. To go to the Continent with her and Shelley! With Claire and her baby Allegra, that grand, infamous poet's bastard daughter. Does he think of her now, cold and dead at only five years old? While he arms for battle in Cephalonia? And the two nurses for little William and baby Clara. I'd hardly be noticed in that melee with my babies. Mary's words were those of one new mother to another so that I should best understand

her: '*you can still have the courage to live as you wish! It's not too late.*'
It was three years since I'd seen her yet she could forgive me for
disassociating myself from her, and still want to come to me in
my distress. I packed my bags, gathered up my babies and headed
back down south.

David wasn't happier to see me after the birth, as I'd hoped.
Sudden, fierce accusations from him after Kathy was born that
ran from, 'where have you been?' to 'is she mine?' rained down
on me so fast they made me dizzy. The days he spent locked
in his study until the stench forced me to break the lock and
confront the detritus he'd made of his latest work, the stained
clothes he'd flung from him, the dark patches on the floorboards where he'd chosen to relieve himself. All of them indications my husband had gone well beyond occasional flashes
of bad temper or worrying switches of mood. He needed more
rest from us. Or we from him.

Mary was too dangerous, said the man who hid himself for
six days in a single room that burned with a hundred candles
while he bayed at the moon. He'd written to me from London
about his visits to her and her husband. '*They have a little child,
"Miss Auburn", of which your father could not procure the history.
Is she not Jane's? She and Mary live with Shelley alternately when
he is in London and in these cases, Mr Godwin tells me that they
have never been able to persuade Claire to sleep a night under her
mother's roof. She has, says Mr Godwin (with great simplicity) an
unconquerable fear of ghosts and will not sleep in a room alone. She
therefore goes to Shelley's lodgings every night.*'

I never knew Claire, now in a land of ice and wild bears.
We might have kept each other company. She'd understand the
ivy grip of entwined families.

Perhaps, I wrote back to Mary when I was in London, it
wasn't so serious or so irrevocable a step if I did leave with her
for the Continent. Perhaps David could even join us once we
were there? The community her husband proposed where like-
minded families would live together without possessions or
fear of disgrace was not objectionable, in principle.

My father and her husband had struck up a sort of friendship these past few months, in spite of David's misgivings about his morals. Surely I'd still have my father's support, I thought. Both men were without funds but they were lovers of words, of freedom and beauty.

Quarrels over money are the quarrels of much of the world, I think. My father's timing was disastrous, quarrelling with Shelley just then and reminding him what his status meant. Mary's timing, on the other hand, had been perfect. And so I made my decision in her favour. I packed up my belongings once again, and got my babies ready for our flight to the Continent. Only, my strange, difficult, baying husband changed himself for the better that day, and in doing so, he changed my mind. I stayed where I was.

Change, alas, for too short a time.

My husband didn't appear to me in my dreams afterwards, though. Mary's husband did. Even though I'd never met him, I knew who he was. A man with soft curls that wound about a strong, feminine face would appear to me after that time and reproach me again and again for my cowardice.

One day, after David's first fit, I went looking and found George Combe in David's copy of *The Scots Magazine*. Combe's essay on the science of phrenology confirmed an initial interest I had. When his fits began, I read everything Conolly recommended. Franz Joseph Gall. Johann Spurzheim. Theories that shapes of the head pointed to characteristics like guile, pride, circumspection, affection. Even a fondness for language and colours. Numbers. A carnivorous desire that could lead to murder. Covetousness that led to stealing.

I see myself that day, insisting almost coquettishly that David consider the essay. My provocative pose: one hand on my hip, one hand holding up the magazine: why did I approach him this way? I thought he could be cajoled, that teasing would work. His concentration on my body during my little speech made me believe my strategy had won him over. Before he grabbed the magazine from my hand. 'What do you think you can teach me? Who do you think you are, in relation to me? It's your duty to learn from me. Don't presume to think you have anything to teach me!' His first harsh words, my stumbling as he heaved at my waist. The ripped pages fluttered down on me as I lay on the floor, clasping my side. Another book clattered at my head before he slammed the bedroom door. When I eventually sat up, it was to gaze on the cover of a tract written by Mary's father. He hated this new science as much as David did.

Emotion doesn't come from the heart; it comes from the brain. The brain is where it begins and where it ends. The brain predicted how my baby would grow, who she would become. So every day, since she was born, I've watched Kathy for jealousy of her big sister, or for some kind of mistaken belief in the world. That's what it indicates, that little egg shape near the crown of her head that her father has, too. Once Kathy is old enough to know, then she can police herself. Her father will end his days having others do it for him, but I won't have that for my baby girl.

* * *

Oh, but I'm too groggy this morning for another visit to the asylum and I groan as I rise stiffly out of bed, groan as I wash and dress. How Margaret worked on me through the night, my own sister and her devilish ways! But my little phial, my own form of the sacrament, deep in my pocket is empty, and so I have another reason for my return. He is a doctor, after all. He can replenish me.

This time I am better prepared and my good, rarely worn shoes click loudly on the polished floors as I accompany the limping Agnes once again. For all this light and calmness, I don't understand why someone as clever and ambitious as Dr Balfour wants to be an asylum director. This is no challenge. Madness is no route to fame and fortune, I heard Conolly once say.

Temptation exists in this Garden of Eden, though: to slip away, take a chair for myself and join these women in their strange classrooms. *You are not strong enough alone!* Temptation always calls to weakness and makes my hand reach for the nearest door, push it open... but that is when the screaming begins.

Agnes flattens me against the wall as a woman flies past, her long grey hair flowing free, her face streaked with dirt and tears. Dark figures at the end of the corridor restrain her arms and still her head for a brace. 'But they're hurting her! They are hurting her!' I struggle against the weight of Agnes's hard, masculine body; the women in the room stand up, one raises her palm to her chest, but they do not panic, they do not run to the door. I watch helplessly as two middle-aged, ordinary-looking men pass my way with the woman, who is quiet now in her neck brace and strapped arms. Her face shows no sign of bruising or cuts, of harm done, and I lack comforting words to offer her.

This is no place for David, or for me, after all. 'I've made a mistake, I have to leave,' I say as Agnes releases me. 'Tell Dr Balfour I cannot see him today,' and I hurry along the corridor back the way we came. At the front door, though, Dr Balfour himself appears.

'Mrs Booth! My apologies, I was called away for a moment but I have returned in time. You're not leaving?' He's blocking my path but to push past him seems melodramatic, unnecessary, so I mutter something about feeling unwell. 'Then let me escort you to my office where I can have a look at you. You are a little pale – Agnes, bring tea to my room, please.'

It startles me, his grasp on my arm, his push at my body. His hand is surprisingly small on my sleeve, delicate, like a woman's. When did a man last show care for me? When was a man's force meant to do me good?

'I'm so sorry, I can't stay,' I babble like a child as we march along the corridors. 'My husband has made a great mistake; we cannot waste any more of your time, please forgive me.'

But his office door closes behind me. I can't step out and join those fleeing women or I will be restrained, too.

'I don't understand,' he says and I trace humour in his voice. 'There's no need for you to leave so soon. You've only just arrived. And you mustn't be shocked by anything you saw: it's never so bad as it appears. Besides, I suspect you have seen worse?'

I don't answer at first, hide my shaking hands behind my back. 'The calmness of this place is an illusion,' I say at last, in a rush. 'The brightness, the flowers in the vases, the simple dresses. You want to pretend it's another home, but home has enough terrors of its own. So what have you done to convince them? What have you done to them?'

Righteous anger is always best. Outrage and shame and pity: I have them all in plentiful supply, too much for any medical man. So I think until he pulls my hands out from behind me and holds them tight. 'Yes,' he is saying, 'some of the men and women are given medicine to help calm them. But we prefer to rely on other kinds of help as much as possible. Routine, tasks that give a sense of purpose and achievement.'

His touch warms: I can't be warmed. *You will not be saved.* 'And the woman I saw screaming just now? Who was trying to escape?'

'Her name is Alice Robertson and she arrived only yesterday.' He lets go of me, returns to his desk. 'It can take time to adjust, to get used to this place. That's only natural. She'll be fine, and will be cared for, I promise you.'

'You can't promise anything. Nobody can,' I say and defeat is in my voice, the slope of my shoulders, my need for his hand once again in mine. 'My husband has been – unclear. I'm sorry. I can't imagine why he thought such a place would do for him.'

But he pulls at short red curls and my gaze falls on two bottles on his desk with labels I can't make out. 'An alcoholic remedy for a distressed patient this morning,' he nods. 'As I said, the occasional use of medicine...' He takes a deep breath, rubs his hair again. I'm at the door, there's nothing he can say. The office is warm and my head hurts. The glare of the sunlight on the polished desk dazzles me. 'Have you eaten today?' A kind tone, then tutting just like Aggie would have done. 'Then we'll get you something before we begin.'

'Begin? What?'

'What you have to tell me: how to make your husband well,' he says, and as I shield my eyes from the sun to see him better, to trace this man telling me how he can save us, his outline resembles a devil, and a child's devil at that. Hunched over his papers on the desk, with wayward red curls and red beard, a long pen held between his fingers just like a toasting fork. I forget my fears and the harsh, blinding sun and where I am and how to get away, and instead I laugh. He's talking of 'contralateral lesions in the brain' and 'forms of apoplexy like epilepsy' and 'precise correlations with clinical symptoms': a mixture for a devil doctor and that makes me pitch and roll, laughing, at the strange words that come at me like waves.

'Mrs Booth! Mrs Booth! Can you hear me?'

The room is still; his face is close to mine and I blink in the light. He gives me water and I apologize, my mouth dry and sticky.

'I've expected far too much from you. I had no idea how ill you were.'

'I'm well, really.' His devilish ways have disappeared.

'I alarmed you again with medical terms, it was my fault,' he says. 'I'll proceed more slowly, I promise.' And he fusses more as my head clears and my belly gripes. 'I told you that you were hungry,' a flash of white, even teeth fixes me and makes me hungry, too, for something more. 'Let me take you to our dining room, feed your body first and your mind after,' he jokes and my body, lighter now, takes in his words.

And on that day, the conversation between us begins.

4.

Montrose asylum, October 1823

Alexander could hardly wait to begin. He'd risen early and almost ran to the hospital, his head surprisingly clear after so much red wine the night before. Excitement had made him clumsy earlier, had him cursing himself for almost letting Isabella slip away when she took fright at a patient's antics. He knew now he had to be careful with her, be more alert. He looked around his office and wondered how to make it more comfortable for her. She was fed and rested and lying on the divan for now; but who knew how unsettled her mind had become due to that morning's fright?

'And you're sure you feel strong enough?' he began, and took the liberty of holding her hand in his own, on the pretext of taking her temperature. He knew she'd find the touch reassuring and it worked: her eyes were bright and her breathing a little rapid, but otherwise, the frail look of yesterday was gone. 'I'll not push you too far,' he promised and she nodded. He smiled as he turned his back on her, ran a hand over his head. Yes; this would require careful handling. *Make her as impatient to begin as you are.*

The brightness of the morning had given over to rain, and the room darkened as he took his time making notes. His fingers shook as he headed the notepaper and made his list, but

Isabella couldn't see that from the divan. He sensed her puzzlement at the delay but counted slowly to ten in his head to still his own racing heartbeat. He would burst with it soon, if he wasn't careful. 'Whytt's diagnoses,' he muttered, then paused for a moment before speaking apparently only to himself again.

He was still working out his dilemma: he couldn't frighten her, she was here voluntarily, but he needed to be frank. Impatience alone wouldn't make her reveal everything. He thought of Bulckers; how to tease the answers from her? But when he got up at last after some minutes at his desk and she turned to face him, he doubted he could fool her with a seductive manner. She required truth, or something close to it, at least.

'There's no other way, Mrs Booth, although I've tried. I can't afford to spare your blushes or avoid delicate questions. Do you understand what I'm saying?' Yes: plain speaking was best; her cheeks may have reddened but she didn't look away.

'You may ask me anything,' she sighed, and raised her eyebrows in an expression almost of defeat. 'If it helps my husband. I won't shy from it.'

'Very well, I'll begin,' he said. 'If it's easier for you, focus upon another spot in the room. You needn't look at me.' His voice grew softer; some of Bulckers' effects after all, then. She took his advice and lay on her side, facing the window. Light rain dotted the panes.

'I'm ready,' she said, but he thought the resoluteness in her voice sounded false. He took a deep breath.

'We are agreed I will establish first the effects of your husband's mental disorder on you yourself, yes? Before I establish the exact nature of your husband's condition?'

'Yes,' she replied, quietly. *Not so resolute now.* He pulled his chair closer, crossed his legs and laid the bundle of notepaper on his lap. Pencil would do for now; he'd write up his notes in ink once she'd gone.

'Then we'll begin. First, have you ever experienced uncommon feelings of cold or pains in different parts of the body?'

'Yes.'

'Where?'

'My legs, sometimes. My hands at night, when they should be warm. Along my shoulders.'

He began to scribble.

'What about cravings for food?'

'Occasionally.'

'Any particular kind?'

'Anything hot, sharp. Lemon.'

'And the last time you vomited – was it dark or pale?'

A pause. She cleared her throat. 'Dark.'

'What about the shade of your urine? Is it dark or pale?'

Another cough. 'Pale,' she whispered. He fought the temptation to make her repeat it, more loudly this time.

'Do you have a history of asthma?' he asked.

'No.'

'Do you suffer regularly any nervous coughing or palpitations?'

'On occasions, yes. Not regularly, exactly. The palpitations come and go.'

'Is there ever a quickening of your pulse?'

'Yes.'

'Without any obvious reason?'

She hesitated.

'Yes. It's been happening more often lately, too.'

'Any regular headaches or giddiness?'

'Yes, both.'

'Does your sight ever dim or darken?'

'Sometimes.'

'Do you suffer frequently from a lack of energy or nightmares?'

'Yes, both,' she said again.

So she satisfied most of Whytt's points on hysteria. Alexander frowned at the scribbles he could barely make out through the gloom. Did that make her a hysteric, affected by her husband's behaviour merely, or was it more than that? Whytt's

171

theories were based on experiments conducted on frogs, by cutting off their heads and making them respond to pain after death. He'd made his assessments from the *physical* effects only, to establish how voluntary and involuntary motion depended upon the nerves. Alexander made a clicking noise with his tongue. The room was almost in complete darkness now but he was still too distracted in thought to light a candle. *If one part of the body could affect another through the nervous system, why could one* mind *not affect another?* he pondered, and stopped writing. The nervous system had no part to play, of course: nerves didn't fly through the air. They weren't contagious. But Whytt had said, 'All sympathy and consent supposes feeling.' No: Alexander was certain now that neurological studies wouldn't provide him with the proof he needed. His own brand of 'sympathy' theory didn't rely on tests on decapitated frogs. His was a theory concerned with the mind, not the brain.

'Is that all?' she asked suddenly and sat up. He'd almost forgotten she was there. He got up to light the candles on his desk. The room's dimensions swooped and he stretched his neck, felt the top of his spine click.

'Yes, yes, that's fine for today,' he said, helping her to her feet. Her arm was slight over his, and he judged she weighed hardly more than a child. He caught her breath, sweet and musty, as he bent down. 'So little?' she asked. 'We'll continue tomorrow, and for longer. Please be prepared this time: I insist on the heartiest breakfast you can manage. Food is good for you.'

She smiled at his advice and inclined her head. 'I promise, doctor. I will be well tomorrow.'

Was she being coquettish with him? Almost. He'd go along with it then, he thought, and joked with her as he helped her on with her coat. But he was reluctant to let her go: why he'd barely scratched the surface really, and dissatisfaction swelled in his belly almost before she'd left the room.

Instead, he made himself sit at his desk and be composed. The air was filled with the violet scent she'd carried in with her. 'The mind as a sympathetic host,' Alexander went over it again. 'Sympathy can not only host madness, but in doing so, can reproduce it as well... the mind as a receptacle, waiting for the transference of madness...'

He was missing the necessary experience. He'd never observed a married couple before, only patients in isolation away from their families and loved ones in Gheel. How was he to gain what he needed?

He hadn't been over-protective when he told Isabella to eat heartily; his worry about her paleness and her thin bones came from self-interest: his new case couldn't be ill in body as well as in mind. Passing out as she had done twice now wasn't helpful, he had to keep her healthy. Not so healthy that her symptoms disappeared, of course: she would have to return to her husband where he could observe them both, together. It wouldn't be possible to have them both installed at Montrose at the same time, even if the husband agreed to it, to help his wife.

The Infection of Madness. Insanity and the Sympathetic Fallacy. The great contributions he was going to make, the attention they'd attract on publication... and suddenly, Alexander coughed and sat up straight in his chair. What was he thinking? Chiding himself for foolish daydreams dreamed far too soon, he picked up Isabella's notes. Those healthy families at Gheel hadn't become insane when housing patients, had they? So why not them, but this woman, if she had been healthy before? And he had overlooked something much closer to him. It was a heavy burden, indeed, that of the mad brother. There was one who broke down and one who did not. Why had not he been so infected?

The mad brother. *Thomas.* The great fly in his ointment. For if a sane man had lived by a mad brother all his life, why wasn't he infected by his brother's affliction, the way Isabella had been by her husband? Why was the father not infected by his mad wife? What could have made Isabella more susceptible than a sane brother, a sane father? A more sympathetic host body?

Yes: it was in the body that the answer had to lie. Isabella was more susceptible because she was female. *That* was her weakness. The Gheel families were, of course, married couples: no woman on her own ever housed an insane patient. The strength of the male mind was essential to the partnership. Woman was the civilizing force, it was said, 'infecting' the savage male with her sensibility, her domesticity, and so taming him as a result. A poor theory that he'd always sniffed at. His theory would turn that notion on its head.

He couldn't settle, not now. He wouldn't stay for his evening meal, but fastened his coat, ran downstairs into the rain and took the road away from the asylum into town. Heavier spattering from above hit his lips and he licked them, thirstily. He was hot and dry with anticipation: too much, as he should have known. If only he'd left her alone that night, if he hadn't gone to the inn... but he believed now that greatness could be forged in a single night. The romance of discovery: fortune could turn on a kiss, after all.

But Isabella wasn't altogether pleased when Alexander chanced upon her that evening so soon after they'd parted. *Not so predictable a woman, then.* When he shoved open the inn door and shook the drops from his tweed coat, a blast of wind showered rain over the woman sitting alone at the fire. But he showed her a smile wide enough to swallow down the world and turned out the palms of his hands. 'I was headed elsewhere but this sudden deluge gave me no choice...' he began. She was standing up now, less affronted and, he mistakenly thought, more fearful. He carried on. 'And gave me this opportunity – I admit it, Mrs Booth, I wanted to speak to you again.'

He gave his order to the girl for a whisky and suggested Isabella join him. The remains of a meat pie on her plate, and a glass with traces of red wine were still evident: he'd persuade her to more.

He lowered his voice in the quiet of the inn, slid close. Her eyebrows were thin but not arched and exaggerated the olive green of her eyes. They still showed exhaustion: she would be easy. 'I can't deny I'm concerned...' he began, the way he liked to. How eager women were for care and attention, grabbing it as soon as it was offered. Which was why they so rarely got what they needed. 'You've come all this way, alone, and naturally you're anxious,' he soothed, honey on bitter fruit. 'There are few wives who would make such an effort, I think.'

Again, though, she wrong-footed him. 'I think you cannot be right,' she frowned. 'It's very little and exactly what *most* wives would do. I've made no sacrifice. I want to know everything.'

He tried again. 'I only meant... I've seen this before.' Sympathy and sensibility. Whytt didn't recommend the combination as a strategy for wooing women, though he might have done. 'You're not the first to suffer this way. I see human suffering even when it's hidden from me. You are a good wife.'

More argument where there should have been agreement.

'No, I'm not. I've failed him,' she cried out, suddenly. 'I only make things worse for him.'

Alexander made her sip some wine then took a risk, resting her hand in his open palm. She didn't pull away and the touch let his enthusiasm out too soon, as he promised her, 'We'll work together. You need to trust me. We can cure him.' She shook her head again and withdrew her hand. Her hair was untidy and thin around her face. He'd tire of this feminine game soon but he wasn't done yet.

'I don't mean to insult you, Dr Balfour,' she said, with a spirit that irritated him, 'but specialists, doctor friends, they all promised the same thing and his behaviour only gets worse. I don't believe in a "cure" any more. My only hope is less of this... nightmare. Some containment of it, at best, some *management* of it.'

Did she mean the enforced incarceration of her husband? 'It's not a question of blind faith,' he said. 'We have evidence to offer believers and unbelievers both...' But she interrupted him with some remarkable words. 'Sometimes,' she muttered, 'I think he is making me mad himself.'

How had she divined the diagnosis he'd made? Of course she hadn't, it was a throwaway remark. He experienced an odd moment of self-doubt and downed his whisky. 'I don't mean,' she said, 'that I am literally mad. A fine thing to say to the superintendent of a madhouse...' But he wouldn't interrupt the coming confession. 'Sometimes...' she hesitated again. 'Sometimes I see things that are not there. Perhaps I am a little mad, after all,' she ended, a sad smile on her face. He nodded, sympathetically. If her madness was deceiving a husband and tricking a mind-doctor, that was an option he had to consider, but he still preferred to believe her husband's letter was the real trick.

'Can you be sure?' was all Alexander said, finally. The fire in his face was cooling. 'You say you see things – can you be more specific?'

'Oh yes,' she sighed, heavily. 'I have always seen them. Ever since I was young.'

A morbid disposition like his own then, only he didn't see ghosts. He waited.

'My dead sister,' she said, at last. 'Myself.'

John Ferriar's *An Essay Towards A Theory of Apparitions*. Less a theory than a series of cases.

'I see myself standing in the distance,' she continued. 'I don't turn round and show my face, but it's me. I know it is.'

A *'partial affection of the brain may exist,'* Ferriar wrote, *'which renders the patient liable to such imaginary impressions, either of sight or sound, without disordering his judgment or memory...'* The mind and the brain. What had so disordered Isabella's mind was not, he was sure, some 'partial affection of the brain'. Her brain, had it been cut open at that moment, would have revealed nothing. But Ferriar did write of a Scotswoman who kept catching glimpses of her own self, always turned away from her. Special circumstances of time and place; a morbid disposition; religious melancholy; the fancy of 'second sight' so particular to this northern part of the world, where 'seers' believe they are witnesses to future events they can predict, usually the death of someone close. They all contributed to spectral illusions, as Ferriar persuasively argued. It was, he said, like looking at the sun: the sun would leave an imprint on the eye, so that when one looked away, the glare of the orb still lingered. Likewise, an object, presented to the mind, especially a tired mind, could be retained as an image. That image could become anything in the mind thereafter, disrupting thought, preventing true sight. Dreams, recollected impressions.

'I've read,' he said, to comfort her as she was shivering in spite of the fire and the wine, as much as to impress her, 'of an individual who fancied he saw spiders crawling over his bed. He would see them on his clothes, on his body. At the worst, they would cover the entire floor and walls of his home. These impressions took place even while he was convinced of their fallacy. His visions were not accompanied by any signs of delirium. He wasn't "out of his mind". He wasn't mad.'

Isabella sat up straight, rewarded him with a small smile. 'I've had a sensation like that before, too... So I'm not mad? I was convinced that my mind had broken at last...'

He returned her smile: an appealing thing, if a little lop-sided, but transforming nevertheless. 'Some believe it is a sign that the brain is agitated in some way,' he explained. 'But what causes that agitation, it is difficult to say.'

'You say – "some"? Is that not what you believe?'

'I know that people can be convinced they have seen demons, and that these demons have spoken to them. And yet the brain itself, when a post-mortem has been conducted, has been shown to be perfect in every respect. Where is the agitation?'

'Are you saying I simply have an overactive imagination?'

'No – but you may have certain – susceptibilities. Some people have an especially morbid disposition, others a religious melancholy, that may make them more likely to see apparitions of a sort. I detect a certain morbidity in you... but perhaps that is not enough to explain your experiences.'

'So you don't believe in ghosts, Dr Balfour?'

'Only in a mind that believes it is seeing ghosts, Mrs Booth.'

She sat back and studied Alexander whilst he tried not to gulp back his second whisky. 'This "morbid disposition" or "religious melancholy" that you spoke of... Can it be challenged? Altered?' she asked.

He spoke with the conviction of his profession.

'Of course.'

'Tell me then, Dr Balfour...'

'Alexander, please.'

'What about witchcraft? Do you believe in the bewitching of a soul?'

Belief demanded respect from many people, but not from him. He'd have to be careful here.

'I think people believe they can be bewitched,' he said at last. 'That's what I challenge: the belief, not the bewitching.'

Isabella nodded: there was a grace in the gesture he hadn't noticed about her before and he felt the urge to take her hand again.

'Then I'll tell you what I see and you can undo it,' she said. 'Take my beliefs away. I don't want them. They haven't done what they should. Another day, perhaps, Dr Balfour.'

She held up her hand to dismiss him, as she had dismissed his request to call him by his Christian name. He wasn't ready to go. 'Tomorrow morning,' he insisted. 'I will go gently with you, I promise you.'

Doctors' promises, empty as lovers' ones. He had to leave – she was already making for the stairs. 'I'm afraid my sudden appearance this evening has only added to the strain of the day. Let me leave you in peace,' he called after her. The red wine had taken its toll. He fastened his damp coat against the rain, which was still battering the darkness outside. It had begun.

5.

Montrose, October 1823

The drizzle keeps up as though it fears to stop, and it has even dampened the wind into silence, unusually for this coastline. And if nature is out of sorts, why should not I be? I'm not inclined to face the charming Dr Balfour today. *Alexander.* So I'll wash and dress and sit in this bare little room whose lack of homeliness makes me feel like a stranger in my own land, a stranger to my own self's troubles. I'll listen to unfamiliar noises downstairs of more travellers seeking the right path, and watch the clock reach the appointed hour. And still I'll sit. *I sigh when he sighs. I laugh when he laughs.* Yes: I'm in danger of becoming more of a stranger to myself than I ever was. Because I know that one day I'll look on that ghostly image and I won't recognize her; that's my real fear. And I cannot tell Dr Balfour – *Alexander* – this. Or what I tried once to do to my husband. I can't tell anyone.

So I dip the nib into ink instead, ignore the banging that has begun behind my eyes, and do as he advised me yesterday. Try to make a record of my situation: begin with my name, my home, my station in life. And progress, slowly, to what he means: what, or who, I see. When, and 'in what circumstances'. What 'circumstances' might they be? I see what isn't there when I'm with my children, my husband, in my own home, surrounded by loved ones who cannot protect me.

I'm just about to give up and retire again to bed, away from a task I'll never complete, even though it's not even noon, when the innkeeper's wife raps righteously on my door. Yes, indeed, this place is full of strangers who will not leave a body alone. Dr Balfour. Mrs McPherson. I don't seek them out. I may have to engage with the world but I don't want to shake its hand.

She knocks again, that self-important rap, and calls out for the whole inn to hear. 'Mrs Booth! Ah've a message fer ye!' I open the door to her foolish face, cocked to one side; she waves a white note at me. 'Jes' delivered this minute.' I thank her but she wedges herself in the doorway. 'I hope ye're well, Mrs Booth? It's no richt for a fine young lass like yersel' to be in a strange toon on her ain. I only said yon to Mr McPherson.'

'I am well, thank you.' My quiet tone to shame her loud one. 'My business here will not take me much longer.'

'Business!' she laughs and I swear the walls shake with it. 'The way lassies talk these days. The only "business" ah've ever kent wis yon place. But yer business'd be michty grand?' She eyes my fading wool dress, the patched coat draped on the bed. My respectable accent tells her I've fallen down in the world, so she'll speak to me how she pleases. I imagine lifting the china jug on the washstand and cracking it over her head. *How the walls will shake, then!*

'I am on business for my husband.' She presses on the door but my foot is firm behind it. 'On family business. Nothing grand.'

'That wis yon new doctor popped in here last nicht, wasn't it? You'll have met him up at yon place?' She raises her eyebrows and leers, all crooked yellow teeth and gaps. She's been spying on me. Listening, no doubt, to our conversation. You have to watch out for evil, spiteful women. Witches like this one, with rotten teeth and evil looks.

'My husband has an elderly aunt who requires rest,' I fight the witch with lies. She won't catch me. 'How much you remind me of her,' I add, and as she gasps and steps back, I slam shut the door. No witch will trick me! I hear her scrabbling in the hallway, her footsteps as she stumbles away, frustrated no doubt that I didn't give her what she came for.

The letter from Alexander twists in my fingers. I break the seal and smooth it out on the bed. His hand is nondescript, professional.

> Dear Mrs Booth,
>
> I trust that your missing our appointment this morning is not the result of some illness you have contracted through the night? If so, please do let me know at once, as I will not be easy until I know that you are quite well. I hesitate to ascribe your absence to an unwillingness to meet me today, but if it is so, I can only apologize for anything I may have said that has upset or angered you. Your husband's case is especially important to me. I only wish to help. We have a great deal to discuss, and so I would urge you to make another appointment with me. I will be here this evening at six. I will wait for a communication from you indicating your illness; otherwise I will expect you then.
>
> Yours,
>
> Alexander Balfour.

They have conspired, my landlady and my doctor. I've been too congenial, let him think I'll bend to his will, and she, his messenger, colludes in it. Well, I'll not wait until six o'clock. I'll make for the asylum right now and tell him to his face that I don't want his help. Except for the refilling of my little phial: he owes me that, at least. *Put him in his place.* I breathe deeply and the dream of escape promised by a foreign land where Izzy and Kathy may live unpolluted by madness rises through me. Eden is where their father is absent, and I promised it to them once before. I can't let them down again.

I check the clock: a quarter after one already. He won't expect me. Red and yellow leaves are drowning in the drizzle and collecting in slushy piles beneath my window. An end to all things, then. My gloves are missing, and so is my hat but I'll walk without them and ignore the stares of the Mrs McPhersons of this town as I take to its streets. The air's misty with damp: the sea is too close. But I make my way, as purposeful now as I was reluctant before, and ignore the heaviness of my soaking hem, the leaking of my boots. I pretend to enjoy being hatless when suddenly I remember that I left it at the asylum yesterday. So that will be my excuse: I forgot my hat. Even a mind-doctor can understand a foolish woman's need for her hat.

And that's how I plan it, only when I enter his office after the same slow meander through the hospital with Agnes that shouldn't have me breathing this hard, I can't remember why I've come. He apologizes, is nervous, he didn't expect me, he says, and now I'm sorry for what I've done. Papers tumble from his hands: his office is a terrible mess with even more papers on the floor; on his desk, books are scattered everywhere.

But this is a scene, I reassure him with a smile I hadn't planned to give him so soon, *that I am well used to*. There's a boyishness to his confusion that makes me want to comfort him and tell him not to care so much. To hold him close, hunched over his desk as he is, ease those short curls back from his forehead. *Yes: this is madness*. He is there to save me, not the other way round.

'I'm alarming you for some reason, I'm making you fearful,' I manage to say. But our intimacy of last night has gone. Today we are awkward with each other, strangers, for all that urge I have to pull him to me. He is too young, he lacks experience. I've made a mistake: I've misunderstood. 'I should leave you. Forget that I came – forgive me for disturbing you,' I murmur as I grip the door handle. My legs are trembling; my hair sticks to the back of my neck. Sweat and drizzle from outside are still on my cheeks: I hear his steps across the room and then his hand is brushing my cheek dry. He is not a boy. I hold my breath.

'I've been a bachelor so long,' he says at last, looking around him, 'that I've grown uncouth. I get lost in my work and this, as you see, is the result.' He waves his hand around the room; I don't follow it. 'I was sure I wouldn't see you again after you missed our appointment. Please, can I apologize for the note I sent you? It was written in haste...'

I smile when he smiles: I sigh when he sighs. The weakness in his eyes weakens me, too, makes me say, 'I had to see you. After last night, I couldn't think...' But as he pulls me away from the door he slips on some papers, lands heavily on his arm. 'You're hurt – your hand,' and I rush to sink down beside him. His breath is musty from milky tea, but his odour carries that mix of whisky and rain from last night at the inn, too. Our sudden closeness isn't right but my hand stretches out towards him nevertheless, strokes his curls before shock at what I'm doing chases my fingers away. He catches them though, and presses them against his lips.

A knock at the door stops it all. Her master tangled with me on the floor in the midst of papers and books and mess finally brings a new expression to Agnes's face. 'I tripped,' he says, simply, and eases himself up slowly. 'Mrs Booth is not quite strong enough to hold me up, I fear: I hope I haven't hurt you, too?' Agnes silently places the tray on a chair, clears a space on his desk. It was a dream only. A hallucination of some kind. My delusions: because he is formal once again. 'Forgive me, Mrs Booth,' he says. 'I've grown uncouth, as I said. It is the lack of female company, that is all. It makes me forgetful of – the ordinary kindness and gentleness of women...' But he's not sincere: the sly look in his eyes shows he's making a fool of me.

'You have plenty of women working here. You have women patients. You are surrounded by women every day.' And I catch my jealous tone.

'That's not what I mean. I mean the company of women like you,' he says, but it's not enough: I'm alert to him now.

'You are pioneering new methods that are based on kindness and concern,' I reply. 'I cannot believe that you know nothing of kind ways.'

'The assistants here are very good women, that's true,' he says, pouring out the lukewarm tea. How long is it since Agnes brought it? 'Please, have this. I mean more – society. Manners in the real world. I step so rarely out of the world of work that I forget how to behave sometimes.'

'I came to tell you that I was leaving.'

'We were clear between us last night; something made you change your mind before you came here? Something I said to you, perhaps?'

'It was nothing you said. I had a dream, last night, after you left. About someone I never met, but he gave me advice once, and in my dream he was advising me again.'

'He?'

His turn to be jealous. 'My friend's husband. He's dead now.'

'And what did he advise you to do?' But I won't give that away so soon. 'You are agitated,' he says, gently. My hands twist in my lap. 'I have something that may help,' he says, and unlocks the glass cabinet behind his desk. He removes a bottle from the shelf. 'Only a very few drops, on the tongue like that, yes. There you are.' The familiar taste: I am open again, at ease with myself, relieved and grateful. 'We are human beings: we are meant to feel,' he says, suddenly. 'And the more gifted of us feels more intensely.'

'Do you believe that? Or do you excuse self-indulgence?' I say, remembering David's silences, his moods and violent out-bursts: *because he is a gifted man.* 'Isn't there a danger of feeling and nothing else? If man is a progressive creature then where will the human race end? With a world of feeling creatures, too sensitive to move?'

He laughs then, and so do I. His office is warmed by unexpected sunshine breaking through cloud and I confide again: intimacy is restored. 'Feeling for others,' I shrug a little as he resumes his seat beside me, 'is what our church taught. Christian feeling. My friend's husband had a different idea. But his notion of moral responsibility applied only to his work.

184

Not to my friend...' I stop at the primness and anger in my voice. 'I mean, it is easy for man to have feeling for his fellow creatures. But can he show it to those closest to him?'

'We don't think so differently, you know,' he says. 'God's world is there to be apprehended by those with eyes to see it. But what is the self? The self cannot be seen: it must be felt to be known. The way that beauty is, love is.'

Pinpricks in my shoulders. 'God allows us to know beauty, to feel love. God gives us our selves.'

I've lost him again. He gets up to pace about the room. 'The self is located in the mind: immaterial, yet felt and known.'

'Like God,' I say. 'Immaterial, yet felt...'

'Not like God: we are made to feel by nerves, not by God. Nerves make us anxious or happy, well or unwell.'

'Is pain a feeling or a sensation?'

He stops at that. 'That is a scientific question and a good one,' he says. 'And the answer may tell us where the self is located: in the mind, as I believe.'

'Ah,' I say, and pout a little at what I'm about to say. 'As you *believe*...'

His eyes narrow. 'Your friend's husband...?'

'Was a poet,' I reply. 'A minor one, who will be forgotten.'

'You disliked him?'

'I never met him but yes – I disliked him. He was a force that blew into people's lives and unsettled them. He didn't care what effect he had: my friend's sister fell in love with him and killed herself. His first wife was in love with him and killed herself.'

'Not a fortunate man,' he smiles at me.

'Not fortunate women,' I smile back, his mirror image. 'He may have written of grace and light and beauty and love, but he cheated and lied and manipulated and corrupted. He won over my father and would have stolen from him...'

'The worst kind of blackguard, then... so why are you dreaming of him?'

'*Leaves dead / Are driven, like ghosts from an enchanter flee-ing...* have you ever heard anything so beautiful?'

'His words have the power to make you feel.'

'And that is why feeling is dangerous. It blinds us to the truth of a person.' My cheeks ache and throb with the self-pity I gulp back. 'He tried to persuade me to leave my husband for the Continent. Kathy was a baby. David... would not come near me. I disgusted him. Me, the baby. He left us, to work.' My throat is too tight to continue. *Is pain a feeling or a sensation?*

Like Izzy, like the stranger I hallucinated back in Richmond, he has speaking eyes, too, is all openness.

'But you didn't go to the Continent with them?'

He must know better, shut away here with these quiet, dutiful, mad women: he must know what they really are. That sewing and painting and cooking are only disguises for what lingers beneath, hiding the sluts and witches inside. Treacherous, vile-smelling hags that all women are to their husbands, who suffer the revelation of their filth for the rest of their lives...

'...Isabella? Isabella, don't close your eyes. Tell me. You said you didn't leave him. Why not?'

I open to his voice, kind and knowing. 'No, I didn't say that. I told him I was leaving him. He persuaded me to stay.'

'I want you to stay here,' his breath strokes my ear. 'You're not well enough to stay at the inn. You shall stay here. Not as a patient. As my guest. I will tend to you.'

Go. Stay. Go.

'I cannot...'

'Isabella.' His grip tightens around my shoulders: another to hold and insist. 'Stay here. Let me help you.' And now an image of the inn at night with all my belongings and the wicked Mrs McPherson still inside, silent and full of flame, before human cries sound in the darkness as fire washes over them, appears in my mind's eye. *I'm a seer* and this is what I see, what gives me no choice but to reach for his hand.

6.

Montrose asylum, October 1823

Was it just as Alexander had suspected? Was she playing a game with him, after all? Was that why she hadn't come at the hour they'd agreed? Her little bid for power. No matter, she'd lose in that, he comforted himself. He'd always been able to play this game better than most. She was no match for him.

All the same, after he'd penned his note to her asking why she hadn't come to him as arranged, he was frustrated enough to swipe the books and papers from his desk in a fit of doubt and bad temper. How much she'd intrigued him the previous night at the inn – he had barely slept for thinking about her. He'd thought he disliked her; he'd thought he was immune, after Marie, controlling himself with Euphemia. But he didn't dislike her at all. He wanted her for more than she could tell him. More than a patient, more than an inspiration: confusion had him composing three notes before settling on a final fourth.

Perhaps he should take something for his own state, calm his nerves, the jangling of his heart as though it had come loose inside him... he took out his key, unlocked one of the doors on the bookshelf and reached for a dark bottle. An overwhelming need to gain control, or lose it, he couldn't decide. Waiting was an art he'd always struggled to master, and he'd have to learn it better if he was to succeed in this profession. To know when to reveal and when to hold back; the self and its secrets. Isabella's secrets. 'What is a self without them, after all?' he muttered, as he scuffed at a few more pages on the floor. 'What is she?'

How could a man learn so well the secrets of the self? *What can be learned at our mother's knee...* Something rose in his throat and he gagged, spat the mixture on to the floor. To his surprise, his hands were shaking. It was no good: he had to get out, the office was stifling him. His own self, *his own secrets*. Come back to haunt him.

The cool autumn air didn't blow away unpleasant thoughts as he'd hoped. The asylum's gardens were already growing small in the distance as Alexander made his way towards the sea, but what had spiked him so suddenly in his office had followed him all the way. *What can be learned at our mother's knee.* Well, it wasn't as if he hadn't known he was the less favoured brother, poor compensation for his mother when Thomas was sent away to school. Was that when it began? How he'd tried everything he could think of; he'd wander alone the meadows several streets from his house, a child of only eight years, to pick her favourite wild flowers. He'd spend hours memorizing her favourite poems to recite, words he was barely old enough to understand. Everything his elder brother used to do for her, he'd made his own burden.

Nothing ever touched her: it was as if he didn't exist. She'd barely glance in his direction when he entered her room. If he attempted to take her hand, she'd brush him away. Once, he cried for her: he'd fallen outside in the street, scraping his knee badly enough to cause tears. He wanted only for her to hold him, kiss away his pain. But she shut the parlour door and left him to snivel his way along the hall to his own room.

One day, though, his mother began to notice him, after all. At last he got what he'd been longing for: to be the object of her administrations, her soft touches. She taught him how to be a gentleman: how to flirt, to praise, to withhold affection, to give it back again. To play with someone's emotions, toy with them until they had what they needed.

He was her handsome prince, her angel sent to save her. And so she'd send for him at all times. At *all* times: in bed, getting dressed, bathing even. He was embarrassed on those occasions and would look away. 'Are you ashamed of your mother, darling boy?' she'd tease him, and demand that he hold the garments she was shedding or taking up. Occasionally, when she was in her bath, he'd have to hold her towel out for her as she stepped out.

She'd make him wait for her as she dressed behind a screen, but he'd hear her moan and know what she was doing. Once, she placed a mirror in the corner so he could watch her if he wanted to. He pretended not to see the flash of her breast, the mound of hair between her legs; he pretended not to hear her pleasure but he couldn't stop himself growing hard at the sounds. When she appeared in front of him at last, she touched his hardness, slipped her hand inside his trousers. She wore a transparent nightdress: she pressed his hand to her breast, worked his fingers against her nipples. It became routine between them after that: once, she even took him in her mouth. He told her no, but his hardness said otherwise.

A dirty little tale of a mother's perverted love. What was forbidden. He stood at the edge of the fields, the beach ahead of him, the incoming tide bright and forceful. Even now, he still craved the scent of jasmine his mother soaked herself in those nights; he still craved the touch of a woman who knew how to work him with her fingers. He craved the disgust he felt and he craved his loathing of her. He would crave it all until he died, he knew that.

He could wash it away. Step down on to the sand and walk towards the angry water that would take it away. He stumbled as his boots sank deep and soft, wiped tears that the wind whipped from his eyes. The sea was vast enough to wipe it out; he'd heard it said that drowning was a speedy end, only a moment or two of pain. What would that mean for him, against years of it? He thought suddenly of Isabella – she might have changed her mind and come, after all. She might be waiting there for him right now, with her choirboy eyes, her small breasts and her narrow hips. Fucking her would be like fucking a delicate young boy, he thought: what could be purer? And he wanted nothing so much as purity.

Raindrops joined the tears on his cheeks. He wasn't a monster of perversion, out to destroy a married woman. He was a great man, and if what made him great was darker than some imagined, then it was darker for everyone. He was a man, not a demon or a devil. He pissed and shat and drank and fucked and lost like every man until obliteration. That was all. He was a man. But few attempted to go beyond their limits, make themselves great. He was one of the greats – he had to remember that.

He took the miniature portrait he'd carried with him for so long from his pocket and looked at it one last time. Without another thought he hurled it at the waves, which swallowed it in an instant, then turned and headed back to his office and Isabella.

7.

Montrose asylum, October 1823

Two winters before Mary came to stay, everything froze. The first week of frost, with a bitter wind in the days that followed, scored our windows and iced the firs; the second week trapped our breath and nipped through our mufflers, made us pad our boots and pull our hats tighter. By the third, it seemed that nothing green would live again, and we'd never be warm. Robbie, Christy and I went down to the Tay because we heard there was skating on it: with or without skates, so many people in different coloured coats and hats were falling, laughing, pushing about the ice. The sea was beaten for once, and I was glad. That a little ice could be so freeing! My curious eye spotted courting couples holding each other in ways they could never have done without attracting disapproval; I counted children running free from the supervision of their parents or schoolteachers. It wasn't a festival's anarchy but something of that spirit made Robbie yell out, and Christy and I chase him on to the ice. I was afraid at first that it wouldn't hold so many of us. But I forgot, soon enough. Stalls made a brisk trade by the shore, selling hot tea and pies. We raided our little boxes at home for a few pennies.

By the fourth week, we could hardly wait for our fun on the ice, but when we reached the shoreline, the vendors and skating couples had vanished. A line of fishermen and their wives stood further out, stamping their feet in the cold. A great trawler was shaking and shuddering as the ice cut into it, and the sea tried to suck it down below. Eventually, Robbie asked, 'Where are the men? Did they get off the boat?' One old woman in black shook her head. People began to shout and slide about on the ice: the trawler was sinking at last. We weren't close enough to see the men on board; whoever they were, they were going down, too. In a rush, as though the sea was gobbling it up in one mouthful, the boat lurched downwards, tipped up to its stern, and plunged. Screams and shouts did no good: Christy held on to Robbie because he would have gone to them, those men who would soon be frozen forever under the icy water, and whose faces we would never see.

The cold weather held for many more days but we didn't play on the ice again. We gathered collections instead for the families of the men lost on the trawler, and Christy, Margaret and I knitted shawls for their children. I'd been right to hate it, after all. But the knowledge I was right gave me no comfort: like Christy and Robert, I, too, dreamt for many weeks of our house tipping up, plunging down into dark icy depths, and taking us all with it.

* * *

It's my third full day here already; an anniversary of sorts. No little phial, just more recounting of my family's history. Without an answer to the many 'whys' he has. It's not new, he assures me. Mandeville in *A Treatise of the Hypochondriack and the Hysterick* advised nervous patients to talk, and there are plenty of examples of talking, he says. James Boswell is one he has mentioned. It's as though he doesn't have faith in his own ability to make me trust him. So he invokes this litany of old men, this proof of precedence. When, in fact, I'm happy to talk.

But his ways are strange. Our very first 'session' together, as he calls them, I am still trying to understand. After I hardly slept my first night here, with so many thoughts to keep me awake and footsteps pattering through the corridor outside my room, I took comfort in the fitfulness of this place. It seemed to keep me company. After breakfast I waited on a chair outside his door, like a good patient attending her doctor. His voice was low inside. The older woman who emerged wasn't at peace but her agitation softened the hardness of her features. Her hands were strong, I could see; the hands of a murderess. So there was worse than me.

'It's your birthday today.' He had the notes on his desk and I was surprised. His dark and stainless coat and trousers were new, I could tell, and his red beard trimmed, with his curls brushed back and wetted down. I felt small, afraid of what he'd think.

'I don't expect anything,' I said, sounding sullen, which I didn't mean at all, and he strode over to the window, pulled the drapes together to darken the room.

'Why don't you expect anything? Do you think you are not worthy of love?' he asked, again to my surprise. It sounded more like a plea, or even a reproach. My mother had asked it once towards the end, in her delusion, I told him. She wasn't speaking to anybody in particular: I'd thought she meant God, whom she was about to face and was frightened. Alexander stroked my hair. 'Poor Isabella,' he said. 'How do you think of her now?'

But the touch didn't draw me the way he intended. I was too baffled by the anger that rose up in me. 'Tell me why you agreed to stay here; tell me why you volunteered yourself into my care,' he asked, settling down in this chair as I lay on the divan. But I didn't volunteer myself. He'd sent a carriage to the inn for Agnes to collect my things. Didn't he remember? 'You must know yourself better than this,' he said. 'For I can act only on your desires. I can't make you want what you don't desire.'

But that wasn't true, either. He made me want things I didn't dare to want, like his touch deep inside me. I want to know what he knows: I'm weaker when I'm with him, as though he sucks the strength out of me. But then I'm stronger, too, for what I learn with him. The way to reach a soul. My home, he told me, was my mother, my father, my sisters, my brother. He didn't ask about Mary. Or David. Or Mary, David and me.

'And my husband and my children?' I asked.

'We all belong to the world,' he said. 'We are all Caesar's wife; we are all above suspicion. When we are a family.'

He disturbed me with this suggestion of innocence. I wasn't innocent, sitting on his lap that very day as I was, letting his thumb caress and part my lips until I closed my eyes, took his fingers in my mouth. *I am not above suspicion.* 'Think of me as a most trusted, most intimate brother, who wants to know his sister in the closest of ways,' he murmured in my ear, his hand squeezing my breast. 'We are all a family.'

When I returned to my room much later, trembling all over and amazed at myself, my boldness, *my sinfulness,* I could only sit in the gloom. My mother, Margaret: they're as familiar to him now after all I've told him.

Walking the corridors alone to his office and back to my room is my practice at first. 'You'll become like a creature in a zoo, unable to appreciate space when you are finally released,' he said and ordered me to the 'schoolroom' to read poetry to the youngest girls here. I didn't want to at first but I'm beginning to like it now. I don't ask about their fears and worries, what brought them here. I leave that to him, and anyway, they're shy of me, believing me to be a teacher or even a doctor of some kind. I try to tell them I'm like them: that we're all lost, waiting to be made innocent again so that we can trust. I ask Alexander what has been done to these girls that they should lose their reason, but he talks only in generalities and advises, 'Your pity for them won't do you any good.'

'We're not allowed to read,' says one red-haired girl called Euphemia to whom I've taken a great liking, when we start with Spenser. 'It will excite and strain us.' And she turns away when I pass out the books, gazes out of the window when another girl begins, haltingly, to read aloud. My girls. *We are all a family*. And one day we'll return to them, take up our places again and hope that whatever was done to make us lose our reason will not resume.

But how are we to prevent it? Everything here robs us of responsibility for our own actions, I tell him. I eat when the bell tells me to; I sleep when Agnes takes me to my room and blows out the candle. I read to the girls: his order. *How will this stop me losing my reason when I go back to him?* Alexander is not always right. 'Have faith in me,' he says, but I lost my faith many years ago and won't go looking for it again. We are combative: the day before yesterday he challenged me: 'Picture the soul and tell me what you see.'

But it was a trick and made me miserable. 'Picture the falseness of a wife and tell me what you see,' I replied. He glanced away, but didn't blush. His room smelt of camphor and the drapes were closed but still I could see the whiteness of his skin, the paleness of his eyes fringed by dark red. 'Then tell me the worst a wife can think,' he said, and so I told him.

These days seem like dreams. Nothing here has its place in the real world. I come into his room and the norms of society disappear: we have our own laws and the freedom makes me happy. Except yesterday, when I brought an intruder into our midst and something happened.

This place keeps cats: two black and one ginger. Two are mouse-catchers, but the ginger tom is too old for the chase and has made a friend of me instead. When I knocked on Alexander's door yesterday for our 'session', it followed me in. It curled by my skirts and slipped through the door. I cradled it in my arms, let its purring vibrate against my skin.

'Leave it outside,' he said, without looking up from his desk. The room smelt stale: the windows were shut and the remains of last night's meal had dried on plates on the floor. I goaded him but he carried on writing without acknowledging me. 'I said to leave it outside,' he said at last, still not looking up.

'Are you going to look at me, Alexander?' I said. 'Address me properly?'

'In a minute. Don't disturb me,' he said, and carried on scribbling.

The tom's back was bony. 'You care more about that beast than you do about me,' he said, looking up at last. 'I should leave the two of you together.'

'How ridiculous you are to be jealous of a cat.'

'Then if you won't get rid of it, I will.'

The tom lay curled on my lap, sensing nothing from his approach. He didn't lift it or push it as I feared he would: he simply watched it for a moment, then bent down and flicked it hard on the nose with his forefinger. It woke up, offended and complaining. 'At last,' he said, as I let it out. He went back to his desk and continued writing for some fifteen minutes. Just as I was about to leave and go back to my room, he called me, 'Come here, my girl, my Isabella,' and before the sentence was complete, I'd risen and, just like my little tom, scampered over to his lap and his caresses. There's little left to tell him about myself, and he wants David's story from him. I thought I heard scratching at the door: the tom, concerned about me, perhaps. But I ignored it.

Last night, I expected to hear it at my bedroom door, and when I went downstairs for breakfast, I expected to see it begging for scraps as usual. But the master – the doctor – had ordered it to be taken away and destroyed, I was told. It was old, the maid said. Too old to do its job. Nobody wanted it any more.

He was jealous of a cat. Does that give me power, or take it away? Surely there is nothing for him to take.

* * *

Eight days in all: three since my elderly, fond tom was taken from me. Two days since I woke in a fever, with a rash all over my hands and body that Alexander couldn't convince me, though he stayed with me throughout the night, didn't exist. My hallucinations will stop when the rash is gone from my sight, he said, but only last night I saw my mother for the second time. She told me it was time for me to go back to London and David, to nurse him properly. *Do your duty.* Love makes me see sores on my body and hear my mother's voice, I decide: for the man I love is not in London and is not my husband. It's not only the delirium and delusion of a broken self.

I think the philosophers must be wrong: the soul is not immaterial at all, but real, material, a child on the ice watching a ship go down, or finding a ring hidden in the sand. The opposite of death: living while others evaporate. My mother, Margaret, Aggie. They've all gone, left nothing of the self behind for me to point to and say: there it is, after all. Except when they appear in my dreams, or I see them ghostly before me, in my garden, or on the stairs. And when I see myself, material but ghostly, too, that can only mean I am evaporating... but Alexander will not permit me to think that. I need to form right principles once again, just like David. But love makes me too sick to grasp the most basic principles.

And in the morning, my rash is gone, just as he said it would be. The hospital is full of new noises, new patients, and I want to be about, helping in the schoolroom again, working with Alexander, confiding in him. Now I am well, I can tell him of my plans: what came to me in my fever. I did it once before. I can do it again.

8.

Montrose asylum, October 1823

They were steps he'd been forced to take, he had no need to reproach himself for any of it. Medicine was the beneficiary, not his own senses. He didn't do these things merely for gratification. Or so Alexander told himself that morning when he woke with a sickly weight in his gut. Over the last few days he'd felt something go rotten inside him, like fruit after too many days in the sun. His relationship with Isabella had ripened and flowered even more than he could have hoped, but now? He was too caught up in her. He couldn't keep away. He couldn't stop thinking, eating, sleeping, breathing her, and it had to stop.

That twisting in his stomach must be where his conscience lay. It wouldn't listen to any of his protestations, but gurned and growled enough to have him wave Agnes's offer of a bowl of porridge away. The thought of bacon and eggs made him feel worse.

'It's time,' he thought. He couldn't delay it a moment longer.

He'd deprived Isabella of her laudanum to see the full effects of her derangement. It resulted in her suffering a short but severe illness, just as he expected, which gave him a few hours to spare away from her. Having a husband of her own wasn't enough protection: already she was building fantasies about their life together, and he was entangled enough to believe in them.

'*The urge to domesticity and routine. Conditions of the female mind*,' he'd written in his notes, trying to rationalize his own feelings, to jolt himself out of her dreams. So once he struggled out of bed, ignoring his head and his stomach, he sent a message with Agnes, then ordered his horse to be saddled and ready for him while he washed and sorted out his finest shirt, his newest coat. His boots needed to be cleaned, which delayed him, and he couldn't find the necktie his father had given him when he first attended university.

The days had turned wintry now and he wished he'd worn a thicker coat. The challenge of Isabella had worn him out, physically and mentally, that's what it was. A boy-woman whose dark green eyes followed him everywhere. He'd lose control completely if he wasn't careful, he thought, as the wind dived down inside his collar and chilled his rolling belly. The note he'd given Agnes to deliver had said it all, ardent lover as he was.

'*Will you grant me an audience this afternoon, for I have something particular to discuss with you?*'

Alexander might have been the one who rode seven miles over fields and badly prepared roads that day, but it was *her* features that showed the glow and heat of exertion when he reached the grey faux-manor that her father had had built especially for his small family. He was surprised but he couldn't help be pleased to see that they were alone, too. She was a woman of enough independent spirit indeed, he thought, if she'd commanded her own parents' absence. Or perhaps they were simply happy to collude in it. Philomena Stewart might have been pretty and bubbly but she was also twenty-three years old, he reminded himself again. They wouldn't dare intrude upon her last chance.

The drawing room was shaded by a great oak growing too close to the bay window, and whose dying yellow leaves stuck to the glass.

'Autumn came too soon this year,' Philomena pouted. He spread his new coat-tails at the other end of a gilt-edged chaise longue that had seen better days (was her father's money running out? He hoped not), and settled back, crossed one leg over the other. It was a slight liberty but he was in the mood to dare. After all, he was about to give up his freedom. A few last moments of fun were all he had. 'They're not happy to leave us.' So she was clever, at least, at the rules of this game, and Alexander couldn't help wondering how much practice she'd had. Whatever experience was there, though, didn't put him off or wipe the tender, fond smile from his face.

'It's trying indeed when we cannot control the timing of great events,' he said at last. 'We may wish for longer but are so rarely granted it.' He could afford to tease her: her blushes didn't indicate innocence.

'You must feel quite suffocated at times,' she said, as she sat at the opposite end of the chaise longue. She had to turn to face him, her prettiest angle, and the line of her chin caught the light. He smiled again. 'Working and living at the asylum every day like that. A man of ambition must require proper space?'

So she didn't waste time, either: Alexander liked that, too. She was as direct about his prospects and his ability to support her as she could be: he was enough of an answer to her prayers. But she wasn't going to sell herself in the marriage market quite so cheaply: she had at least to be sure that basic standards would be met.

'What a coincidence you should mention it,' he said, and allowed a little breathlessness into his voice as he got up and paced about the room. He wouldn't look directly at her, as though the sight was too much, her beauty too great. But he could still tell the high spots of pink on her pale but still full cheeks; the glitter in her eyes; the bud of a nose and low, even forehead. She'd be a suitably decorative thing, he thought, and a very pleasing sight after a day spent in the company of Crazy Janes, suicidal girls and distracted old maids. He was done, finally, with horse-faced young women; Isabella had brought about that change, at least. No: he wanted a pretty ornament to give him pretty sons to play on the pretty green beside their pretty house. 'For I've been making enquiries about suitable properties: suitable for my status and any future needs,' he added, and she blushed again. They'd have a lifetime of skirting around subjects too delicate to discuss openly, he thought, and that satisfied him, too.

'A pleasing view is a most important thing,' she said, nodding at the bay window.

It was time for him to be bold.

'I agree, but we needn't look out of the window for that, not when there are far more pleasing views closer to hand,' he said, as he stopped by her at last. Her shoulders twitched; her bosom was covered but he detected a quiver beneath the lace. 'I'm in haste, I know,' he said, slipping to one knee on the floor. 'I'm only afraid some other will carry you away while I obey society's rules and smother my feelings. Dear Philomena – ever since I came here, I have been dazzled by your beauty and unable to think of anything else...'

But she didn't allow him to finish. She was twenty-three, after all. She put a finger to his lips, bade him stand up, and lightly kissed his cheek.

'We can postpone our announcement for the sake of propriety – such a quick engagement would only cause gossip,' she insisted.

'If you are sure, my dearest girl...'

But she was quite firm and Alexander needed only to urge a few more pretend wishes on her. 'Let me give you something – my mother's ring,' he said, after he kissed her chastely on the cheek. He wouldn't be permitted to enjoy her before his wedding night, of course, but that was no matter. 'Keep it close by you, to please me, until then,' he added. The ring held a small sapphire; she gasped and promised, 'But of course, dear Alexander,' and then it was done. He stayed a little longer but not too much; her parents would be nearby and would want to know what was happening. He promised her to meet with them again soon, to ask for her father's permission properly. 'For now, it is our secret,' he whispered in her ear, and felt her tremble beside him. 'But I will see your father soon.'

When he headed back to the asylum that evening, it was with the light step of a man who had struck the best bargain and more easily than he could have imagined. Why – he could indulge himself with Isabella now as much as he pleased. Not, of course, that any of it mattered: she'd caught him nevertheless, but in a different way. She was his muse, not his nemesis. She wouldn't bring him down; he wouldn't lose face through an affair with a married woman. He could breathe again. Isabella had only steered him on to the right path for his career. She was a tool for him to use. He couldn't get carried away.

Any hint of future failure was far away that afternoon. Any possibility that he'd been diverted on to the wrong path, that his name wouldn't be remembered, that he'd fallen in love with the wrong woman: it was all safely put in hand. And appropriately, all was safely quiet when he arrived back at the hospital; he rode over darkening fields with no intimation of calamity whatsoever, then let himself in and hurried to his office. He would check on Isabella's state as soon as he'd completed some notes. But when he reached his door, Agnes appeared out of the gloom as though she'd been waiting for him all this time.

'Euphemia Ross again,' she spoke with her characteristic difficulty. 'The infirmary.' Her few words gave him no time to stop. The infirmary, where the medicines were naturally kept, was one of the few locked parts of the building. Lunatics were wily folks, after all. He'd forgotten his keys in his hurry, though, and when he got there he had to bang on the outer door for Mrs Munro. His stupidity made him angry and he was short with her when she arrived.

'We found her in the schoolroom,' she said, as she let him in.

'Arson again?'

'No – another fit. The girl needs to be watched every hour of the day.'

'No reproofs from you,' he snapped at her for her cheek. 'I'm ahead of this, and have someone in mind for the task. Now remember your place here.' The woman was ready to argue but he shushed her as he approached Euphemia's bed.

She was fast asleep. She'd been much calmer since their sessions ended, and whilst she hadn't given him what he had been looking for, she touched something in him nonetheless. Alexander grazed her high forehead with his palm, and took her pulse. She woke at his touch and whispered, 'When will it stop? When will I be well?'

He told her not to talk. 'I'll ask Mrs Booth to move into your room,' he continued, gently. 'You like her, and she can watch over you. You'll never be alone, I promise. We will observe and take note.'

Her incurable epilepsy had alienated the very parents who were meant to love her. She shouldn't have had to stay here, he was sure she was never insane. But as long as she was afflicted this way, and he couldn't persuade her devout parents that there was no shame in epilepsy, that it wasn't the mark of the Devil, she'd spend the rest of her life here. He was no monster: he wouldn't wish that fate on any child. He could make some of her days here a little more palatable for her, at least.

She was saying something again now, something he couldn't catch, and he leaned in closer. 'Speak up, Euphemia, what is the matter?'

'I saw you,' she spoke clearly enough for him to hear this time. 'I saw you with Mrs Booth. I saw you kiss her.'

He leaned forward. Euphemia's small eyes widened.

'I have to tell what I saw...'

'No, you saw nothing, Euphemia.' He bent down closer and whispered in her ear, gripped her hand. 'You saw nothing and you will say nothing. You're a deranged young woman. Who do you think will listen to you?'

He let her go and signalled to Mrs Munro.

'She's delusional,' he muttered. 'Keep her in isolation and don't listen to a word she says. I'll draw up a special menu for her and visit her daily.'

'Of course, Dr Balfour,' Mrs Munro spoke quietly, laid her hand on Euphemia's arm, which was twitching. The girl's eyes were shut fast.

'Remember – complete isolation,' he said before he hurried from the room. There was no time to lose – he had to return Isabella to London, after all, the sooner the better. It wouldn't be long before he followed her there.

9.

Montrose asylum, October 1823

My last days here in Montrose. The sickest and happiest time of my life spent in an asylum: the irony is not lost on me. So love is a madness that infects us. His eager talk slips into my ears. The urgent flicks at dark red curls fix in my consciousness and make me sick with love for more of his ways: his springing step, his casual cruelty, his moments of doubt. How he delights in a detail and never sits still long enough. I'm like a girl on her sixteenth birthday, when she begins to know what she is. When I began to know what I was: a wife. But that was the wrong kind of knowledge, the kind that brings madness.

His are feminine qualities and make me wonder as I wait for the switch that always surprises me, for all my expectations. And there it is: the command in his voice and the threat in his eyes that remind me, sometimes, of David. I shouldn't be drawn to it as much as I am. Yet the change is deep enough for me to know it's all part of him. He's not split in two, like light from dark or hot from cold. He's his own demon, and his own saviour. They may separate the mind from the brain, these duallists, but a dream, a ghost, a sensation, a rash, all belong to the same person, to whoever sees them or dreams them or feels them. I think madness is dormant in all of us, men as much as women, until something or someone sparks it into life. Unwatched, it catches us off guard and begins to grow. And we can feed it, if we choose.

Do I really mean that? Our free will is part of our madness? I haven't given up the religious philosophers yet, then. I'm not convinced, much as I love him, of his theory: David didn't infect me. *He merely gave life to what was already there inside me.* It's not his fault: but is it mine? Could I have stopped it?

I don't know, which is why I must trust Alexander, even though he tells lies, and not only about my cat. For instance, he never told me Agnes isn't an assistant here at all but a patient. Euphemia told me, and her illness isn't of the lying kind. Why not allow me the knowledge, if I'm required to trust him? His residence in Gheel was without adventure, he said. But he's called me 'Marie' by mistake, and on two intimate occasions. Her name wasn't said the Scottish way. I've never asked who she is because I know what she must have been to him and I don't want to hear more lies. I want him fully formed and honest, to have come into being the moment I saw him. I'm jealous of a past in which I played no part.

'Tell me when you first began to fall in love with your brother-in-law,' he says. The drapes are shut as always and the hospital is worn out by the industry and drama of the day. Even the mad need a rest from themselves. I'm lying still on the divan this time, and he's far from me, turned away, not even looking. I've done my hair specially, the way he likes it, but today he's scarcely noticed and I'm peevish now. So I won't rise to the provocation in his use of 'brother-in-law'. Instead, I'm shy suddenly of confiding these details more than any others, and especially if he has no more regard for me. Is he tired of me already? Panic rises in my throat. He'll judge my actions girlish no matter how much he says he doesn't want to set himself against me. I'm not his patient, I'm always reminding him, but he insists anyway. 'Do you not know a mind-doctor has never asked questions before? Are you aware of the part you're playing in this overthrow of centuries of bad practice?' he says. 'We are making history, Isabella. You and I.' And the dancing in my belly spins faster and gets wilder at the thought of eternal bonds.

'Was it before or after your sister died?' How he enjoys my resistance. One poet says love is a torment, whilst another laughs at it. How to describe its danger though, the choices it lures us into making: that is the real task. These times with him alone make me forget my girls, you see, and that is dangerous. He'd have me go back to David so he could analyse him and make a case of him; a short-term solution until I can leave him and we can be together. I wouldn't say yes but I agreed just the same. Dangerous, indeed.

'I don't know,' I deliberately whisper in the still of his room to make him come closer. Our sessions are always in the evenings, after I've read poetry to the girls and he's interviewed his patients. Perhaps I'd have been a teacher if I hadn't married David. A plain schoolmistress or a despised governess: isn't that the choice? But I'm neither, here. In the madhouse, I'm the mother of Izzy and Kathy, a sister to Christy and Robbie, a carer to my husband, a damaged and sick soul to myself.

I like the variety, though; my many roles don't confuse me. Part of my sympathetic tendencies, he says. We women are more 'sympathetic', I tell him, because the world insists on it. He tuts at me. 'No more Wollstonecraft for you!' But I think he wouldn't want to spend his life with a foolish woman, for all he laughs at my reading too much. No mere bauble for him.

'It was always there?' He is prodding a little more. I might make a little story of it for him, spin it as Scheherazade once did into a thousand and one nights to save herself. So where to begin? What would he want to hear, make him want to save my soul? He presses me to expose myself and I, sympathetic body as I am, reply and say, 'Yes, while Margaret was alive.' Like a guilty child caught taking something that doesn't belong to her. When I turn to look into the single candle beside me, he is there above it, and his smile hovers and he continues, 'And when she became ill? Were you glad?'

But the story that interests him isn't the one that interests me. I want the story of my escape. What would have happened to me if I'd left for Italy that year when Mary invited me. What would I have done? I would have held Mary's hand as she looked down onto the beach where her husband's body was being burned. Perhaps I would have persuaded him never to sail the boat in the first place. My hatred of the sea would have convinced him to wait. He'd have listened to me. But then I remember: he wasn't with Mary when he set sail that day. He was sailing to her. So there's only so much I can do to change the story of a life before it's no longer about Mary's husband but just some man who bears his name.

'I wasn't glad she was ill. But I was happy when he came to see us, alone,' I say. Intimate questions have answers wrapped inside them. The purpose of my testimony isn't to inform him, it's to make me voice what stays buried, to dig it up like a dog with an old bone he can present to his master.

'And your mother? Whose death was worse for you?' he asks, thinking it a competition. The room is warm and sweet-smelling; I gaze at the bare ceiling, devoid of the simplest rose sculpture. My skills are not motor skills: I'm not good with my hands. Sewing, cooking, making things. My talents are the sensory ones: memory, learning. I can tell him a story: I can lie, too. Where is morality located in the brain? I want to ask him. Is there a tiny piece of the cerebrum that is marked for good and for evil? And if that piece is too large, am I a storyteller or a liar? *You see, Alexander, I have learned your words.*

The candle flame flickers in his eyes. 'I never recovered from the loss of my mother. She was everything to me,' I say and he's satisfied with the lie. *I could tell you anything at all, and you would believe me.* He writes it all down very quickly, and I wonder if I should tell him more.

'Did you resent Margaret taking your mother's place?' he asks next.

I doubt his intelligence if he can be so obvious. Perhaps he's laying a trap for me with this too-clear path, luring me into a forest he knows I don't want to enter. I have the truth elsewhere, all in my journal, locked inside my box. For me alone. Not even Alexander will ever read it. So I shake my head and say, 'Enough,' swing my legs over the side of the divan and he stops writing, pours me a glass of wine instead.

Our sessions always begin and end with too much wine. On our third-last session, I'm dulled by red wine and lie back on the divan. I'm a siren, he says, a calypso, and I close my eyes and giggle because I can't hold a note. His fingers flutter at my neck. 'What do you want most in the world, Isabella?' He whispers butterfly kisses, his light fingers worry at my shoulder for a lock of hair. A lightness of touch that implies what we are doing doesn't matter. 'A little memento,' he says, but I miss the warning, am too busy picturing the lock of hair cut and hidden inside a tiny gold case, and so the pain comes as a shock. 'You've bitten me!' I cry out.

His laugh, too full of wine, angers me as I search my appearance in the glass, and even with only one candle to see by, I can make out the brown-red bruise too well. 'It's just my mark on you, Isabella,' he shrugs.

'Like a branding. I'm not some beast on a farm.'

'Now I really know you are mine.'

'And so will everyone else. It wasn't your right, I gave you no permission.'

'O my America, my newfound land,' he whispers, as his fingers tiptoe along my neck and down to my breast. But I am nothing new, and now I'm marked, soiled goods. My mood doesn't ease with his touch, and I leave him without saying anything more.

The next evening I refuse to see him at our usual hour, but when he knocks at my door I let him in. 'I have a special favour to ask of you,' he says, that same sly look still there in his eyes. An apology's what I expect but my anger is pointless so I throw it away, a thing not wanted by either of us. He tells me his favour and I can't say yes. But a weak part of me wants it: the part he knows.

My room lies in the guest quarters. The mother of the hospital director, Mr Browne, often stays here when she visits her son and I'm mindful of these touches a woman needs: pretty cushions, pleasing images on the walls, a soft rug by the bed. It's fashionable, too, with its very own water closet that contains a large white porcelain bath. Only the smartest, richest houses in London have such things. When I smoothed my fingers over the delicate, cold surface, and thought of the washstand in my room at my home, how I'd sponge myself down every morning, I was ashamed that material things could matter so much to me. 'No need for a chamber pot,' he had said, taking liberties as usual.

'A new kind of privacy: what kind of world needs this much privacy?' I wondered. 'Where might it lead, when we already hide so much?' But he wasn't interested in pondering the morality of this new bathroom. It'll be mine again when we return here from London. I know he's looking for a house for us both, for us to share with my girls. David is far away: it's easy to imagine he doesn't matter any more.

It is essential he doesn't matter this evening. I call for Agnes to fill the bath, just as he's instructed. The door of the mahogany armoire clicks shut just as she enters and I imagine his eyes glinting in its dark interior until she leaves, and he can open it. I begin to undress just as he has bid me.

How easily another's need can override our own. *You're a Baxter. We don't hide.* I forget myself too easily when I'm with him. I undo the ribbon from my hair just as he's asked, and bend down to unbutton my boots. I roll down my stockings, then lift my dress over my head. I work in profile, in the lit doorway of the bathroom. The armoire creaks as I play his game. I even giggle, once, when a knot sticks and I have to squeeze my arm through the opening of my shift. The bath water is as lukewarm as I am bold, and I stand still in it, ready to remove my shift entirely. I hear nothing more.

Actaeon watched Diana while she bathed, and she turned him into a stag and hunted him down with his own dogs for his gall. Praxiteles carved a statue of Venus after he watched her drying herself. The statue was set up in a circular room so that everyone could gaze on her from all sides. I lie down at last in the warm water and wonder if it's our nakedness that makes men want to watch women bathing. Or if they like to see us attending to ourselves, as if they aren't there. The secrets of a woman's toilette – are they so marvellous? And do they expect to be punished for discovering them?

The water grows cold quickly though, so my bath is soon done. I stand in the doorway, dry myself carefully. I wind my hair up in the towel, naked as I am, and turn round. The armoire door clicks: he's got whatever it was that he wanted, and is gone. I fashion a scarf of muslin for my neck – the cold weather, I told Agnes earlier in the day, who didn't care and hadn't asked, had given me a sore throat – as the bath water has made the mark on my neck as livid as ever. Now I've been exposed in every way. *I am shameless.*

On our last day together before I leave for Broughty Ferry and my girls and then London, we drink and eat together and he lies beside me on the divan and holds me in his arms until sun-up.

✵ ✵ ✵

The night Izzy was born, David left *me*. He tried to ignore my growing belly, just as he would later with Kathy. But I was delighted to achieve what my sister hadn't. I adored my new clumsiness. The straining at my clothes, even the cravings for potatoes mashed in butter and rosemary, or for bowls of peas soaked in mint. As I grew, Barns o'Woodside shrank: I'd dream of growing until I burst through its walls. A monstrous mother, leaking milk in showers. Perhaps David dreamt it, too. Women in that state can unnerve and frighten men of genius. Repel them but fascinate them, too. My voice grew louder as my belly swelled; I gave orders about food and cleanliness, times and dates, which he didn't contradict. I turned our household upside down, bent it to my will.

Until, of course, the time came to send for the midwife. I knew what was happening when I heard the door slam, and I started up, but she wouldn't let me go after him. I waited all that day and the next. Izzy had shocked me, ripping my body apart, puncturing my new power and making me whimper as I clutched her hard. My father's presents of fruit and flowers, and the neighbours dropping by with homemade pies and soups, made me wonder if it would be this way forever. My empty but inflated belly pinned me to the bed. My husband was gone; my pitiful state invited unwanted gifts although nobody knew he'd left us. And each night, as I lay Izzy down beside me and stayed awake, terrified I'd crush her in my sleep, I listened for the latch on the door.

First three, then four, weeks passed in this way. He was never coming back. I had no more excuses when my father and Christy came to visit, and began to panic about the future. Would my father take us in? Was this a punishment for marrying him? Was Margaret looking down at me, enjoying my abandonment?

It was the middle of December, at least. Nobody wanted to be out in dark afternoons, making a special effort to visit. I kept to myself during my lying-in. Several times I thought of grabbing up my baby in my arms to go looking for him, like some cast-off kitchen maid. But I was a Baxter, I kept telling myself. *We don't hide.* The days smothered out the light, my stock of candles ran down and my good baby, sucking at my breast, began to sicken. She was drinking in my fear and worry: it was time I told my father the truth.

It was on the thirty-seventh day, at nine in the evening, when the garden gate creaked opened, and the latch clicked. I rose up out of the parlour chair, Izzy colicky in my arms, and stood in the hallway. His hair was matted, grey whiskers covered his face. His clothes were stained and crushed. He sank to his knees in front of me, his head in his hands, and begged my forgiveness. He would be the husband and father I expected him to be; the husband and father he expected of himself.

I covered for his weakness, and my own. No one would know what a mistake I had made, marrying this man of genius, this weakest of men. Not until Kathy was born, and I would stay far from him in my sister's house in Scotland, while he remained in our Richmond cottage. The only person I ever told about what he did on the day of Izzy's birth was Mary... Mary, who had too many problems of her own to be shocked at mine. But it shamed me to tell her. It shamed me every time I thought of her.

Part Four:

London

1.

Holborn, November 1823

The letter from France had made it all the way to Montrose, only to turn back again for Holborn. Its sensitive, shaky script still lay exposed on the side table after two whole days. Alexander had read it once and meant to throw it away. Sleepy by a meagre fire in the drawing room, he rubbed his eyes again. His dreams showed things he didn't want to see.

Her first words wouldn't leave him alone, either. '*I am sorry to have to tell you that your father died yesterday morning, suddenly, of a brain haemorrhage. He spoke of you, his only son, many times and I...*' The 'only son' jarred him. Well, he hadn't meant to mend their quarrel. There was no such thing as 'too late'. Not for him.

He'd carried a glass of red wine and a plate of sourdough bread and Brie through the silent house to the first floor. He bit down now but the bread was stale and the cheese like rubber; the kitchen maid his father had employed and whose name he couldn't remember had a very fetching smile but not much talent for food if this was any evidence, he thought. Alexander swallowed what he could, then twisted in his chair by the window to stare down through the dark at passing figures on the streets below.

The house had been empty for two months, he'd found out when he arrived. His father had lately been in the habit of making short trips over the Channel, they told him, and everything was arranged to manage smoothly without him. He hadn't wanted to inform his father of his arrival as he'd travelled south: he was in London to see his soon-to-be patient, David Booth. He was here for his career. Not family. Not his father. In fact, relief at his father's absence, he decided, was probably the greatest emotion he'd experienced over the last couple of days.

He'd inherit everything now. Thomas wasn't in a fit state and anyway, that 'only son' effectively disowned him. *Thomas.* Alexander shivered. Where to start? When? How long had it been? Three, four years? As long as that? He brushed his lips with his knuckles, just the way he did when he was small. It didn't ease his fear.

And what about Isabella, David Booth? He'd only just been able to silence Euphemia Ross before he left Montrose, but his feelings for Isabella had taken something of a new turn lately. Struggling to make the headway with his new theories that their beginning had promised, he found himself wanting to blame her. And the artificiality of some of her answers in their last sessions together: she wasn't giving him the truth. *Families get in the way of work*, he decided as he sat, picking at the whiskers on his chin. His belly rumbled. 'Families cause the work, then get in the way of it,' he said to himself. 'Families *are* the work. Yes: families are the work…'

It was a thought that hadn't occurred to him before. He gulped back the last of the wine and wished he'd brought up more from the kitchen – he didn't feel like trekking back downstairs again, and he didn't want the kitchen maid to catch the guilty look on his face. He stretched; his limbs felt heavy and stiff. He reached for the watch in his pocket and his fingertips caught the edge of Isabella's invitation to dinner.

Too many letters. Too many women. Too many claims on him! Time to head out for a tavern, other bodies, some night air.

When Alexander stepped outside in his familiar heavy tweed, the cold air nipped at his face and he coughed loudly enough for two passing figures to turn in curiosity. He stamped his feet at them. Where to this time? In spite of the new gas-lamps his path was smothered enough to deprive him of the choice. And so he kept walking without clear direction, though it was cold enough for snow and not weather for wandering, tucked his chin low inside his collar. Cover gently those misdeeds; cover the tracks of those who might not scruple to use their own brothers for themselves... maybe the night would swallow him up and that would be a good thing. *But then the greatest of the mind-doctors would be lost forever.* Flattery was always warming.

'Remember first principles,' he muttered and cast his mind back to Montrose. Isabella's intensity of feeling; her future plans for them both; how she could make him feel, when he wanted to be in control. She kept a daily journal, she'd told him, locked inside a wooden box she took everywhere with her. He needed to see what she wrote in that journal. Withholding it from him was evidence of her hysteria, was it not? 'Hysteria' came from the Greek word for 'womb' for a reason, he thought. Isabella hadn't inherited her 'disease'. She'd been infected with it, had it planted inside her by her spouse. So she couldn't have been pretending. Could she?

The possibility of performance, of fakery, was a constant threat, Bulckers had warned him about that. Watch for hysteria that begins with an epileptic type of attack, he'd said. Be careful when touching a certain part of the body – under the breast perhaps, or the leg. That might trigger off a hysterical attack that would only be the simulation of epilepsy, not epilepsy itself.

No, Isabella told the truth, he was sure, except in those last days... 'Women feign insanity all the time,' Bulckers had said, a sly smile on his lips, 'and for lots of reasons.' To attract the attention of a spouse or a parent, to commit themselves to a doctor's care. Sometimes to ward off an unwanted suitor, or to get their hands on a spouse's money. It wasn't without precedence, a wife trying to do away with her husband, however much Defoe might have condemned the wickedness of husbands sending unwanted wives off to lunatic asylums. It was Bulckers again who'd told him once about a poor tradesman whose wife had wanted to shut him up in an asylum. He'd visited their home unexpectedly whilst the lady was absent. Bulckers had met her husband on the stairs, and with some difficulty had persuaded him into his parlour, that he might talk to him. The man had evidently become suspicious of the intentions of strangers, but after a little quiet conversation he'd become more confident, and told of a domestic situation that Bulckers said would make any man insane. She'd arrived home, though, and had begun to abuse her husband enough to make him frantic and run from the room. 'Now,' said his wife, 'you can see what a state he's in: he does this twenty times a day; there's no living with him.' Bulckers asked to talk to the poor man without his wife being present but she insisted on staying. The wife had learnt her part well, Bulckers said – she'd had her husband committed three or four times already. The paper was lying on the table waiting for him to sign it. He refused. When he called some days later to ask about the man, he was gone. Probably his wife had found another doctor to sign the crucial pledge and put her husband away for a fifth time.

Ah, the inherent weakness and wickedness of women! *The wife seeking to put away the husband.* Alexander wondered what had made that particular story, out of the many Bulckers had told him, stick in his mind the most. Was he frightened he'd missed something? He was panting now, far from familiar city streets, and shoved a freezing fist inside his coat. He needed a drink badly. He'd definitely come north out of the heart of the city, he knew that much; south would have taken him to the new Bethlem hospital at Lambeth; far, far southwest towards Isabella. He leant against a low-slung building and looked up at a bedraggled tavern sign. This place would do, wherever it was.

He opened the door, only to be hit so hard in the belly that he immediately fell backwards. A fat hand reached out and grabbed his elbow.

'Wait now, I said!' a man's beery breath was in his face. 'Take your time!'

A hatless boy in black, standing in front of him, smiled. 'My son, Edward,' the beery voice said. Fat hands that belonged to thick arms and heavy shoulders. A cheerful face wreathed in dark whiskers. The boy in black laughed for no reason Alexander could see and mumbled something behind his fist at his father, who shook his head, teased his son's ear fondly. 'And tell your mother I'll be an hour yet.'

'An apology wouldn't go amiss,' Alexander grumbled as the boy vanished out the door. 'Teach your son some manners.'

The stranger chuckled. He was younger than he looked, the shy shame gave it away. Alexander stood straight, satisfied to find himself easily a foot taller than this rude individual who agreed, cheerily enough, 'Indeed, he needs them. His mother has that care but she's a soft-hearted woman. So let me offer you a drink for your trouble.'

The inn was dim but warm and he didn't want to be back out in the cold. He nodded at this foolish, short, fat man who couldn't control his children. 'John Conolly.' A beefy but clean hand extended to him.

'Alexander Balfour,' he answered. The handshake was firm, the skin soft; a gentleman's hand.

'A Scots name but an English voice.' Conolly rubbed his chin, rasped his fat fingers through his beard as he offered Alexander a seat. There were only two other men in the place, both bent low over the hearth.

'An Irish name but an English voice,' he countered. *His* voice was too loud here, Alexander thought.

'So it's true, and I won't deny my heritage. Tell me, then, what makes you the man you are?' The man named Conolly heaved good-humouredly at his beer, fat fingers glued to the beaker. His possessiveness bothered him. 'You're a gentleman, I can see that.'

'A doctor,' Alexander muttered. The beer was musty and not what he wanted. He thought of the bitterness of jenever and wished he'd insisted on something like it. Already Conolly had had his own way and that annoyed him, too. He drank the sooner to finish it and leave. 'A mind-doctor. At the Montrose Royal Lunatic Asylum,' he said at last, resistance in his voice. *Wipe the smile off your face.* But Conolly raised bushy eyebrows the colour of mahogany and surprised him.

'You're a man after my own heart then! Or profession... almost.' The man was laughing at him; Alexander forced down the last of his beer. 'For I am a mind-doctor, too!'

He beamed – disingenuously, Alexander felt. The beer made him belch; he should have eaten that bread and cheese earlier. Too hungry to leave now, he called out for food.

'Not at this hour; let me take you to my home. We'll feed you there,' Conolly insisted.

'Not at all, I want something simple only, here will do.'

'For another of my profession? The meat is terrible here – get your coat!'

The weak son of a weak man. Conolly would brook no opposition, and pulled Alexander through the quiet and dark, their footsteps muffled by frozen grass and mud, talking every step of the way to a rambling shack of a house that once might have been called comfortable, on the edge of a village. He was a mind-doctor, indeed, Conolly confided; why, he'd been north, too, to asylums in many of the great cities. He'd observed it all, and could draw only one conclusion.

Even though it was near midnight and freezing, the front door of Conolly's house was wide open enough to let chickens that ran in and out of the house during the day carry on being chased by children who should have been asleep. Alexander removed his hat to the genteel-looking woman who welcomed him in and he wondered how often strangers were brought to her home at all hours. She seemed to bear it with humour: a gentleman wouldn't show her what he really thought.

'This way, Balfour.' Conolly guided him past the chaos in the hallway and into a barely presentable room where faded wallpaper hung down in strips and weak candlelight couldn't hide the chicken droppings clustered in the corners of the uncarpeted floor. He wouldn't eat a thing in this pigsty, but Conolly's wife appeared with plates of mutton and potatoes, and hunger overcame his repugnance nevertheless. Conolly poured a dark brew into two cloudy glasses and thrust one at him.

'I'm a different kind of mind-doctor, though,' he began. *You don't say*, Alexander thought, his mouth full of meat. 'I believe only in the power of home cure.'

He swallowed. 'Not, I think, in *every* case,' he muttered.

'Oh yes.' Conolly wasn't easily undermined. 'In every case.'

'No establishment will do?'

'None whatsoever.'

'No matter how radical?'

'No matter how radical.'

Alexander would finish eating his fill then he'd leave. If he wasn't poisoned by the lack of hygiene in the place first. He frowned as Conolly topped up his glass. 'A home brew but a fine one,' he said. It tasted of cat piss, Alexander thought.

'You know at least of the Tuke experiment in York?'

'Of course,' Conolly shrugged. Nothing seemed to throw the man off. 'No chains, no corporal punishment, I know of it,' he continued. 'But still they use the straitjacket! It's an experiment, after the death of that young girl at the York asylum. Just an experiment.'

'What are we scientists without our experiments?'

'Facts, Balfour, when we are presented with the obvious. Tuke recreates the family model in its grounds. There is a "father" and a "mother" to look over the patients, there is a hearth for them to gather round. And why does it do this? *Because the family environment is the one that works best.*'

He spat bits of bread and mutton on the table in his enthusiasm, making Alexander flinch and hate himself for feminine squeamishness. 'So I say, stay with your family,' he continued. 'Don't opt for this false one set in the confines of a stranger's establishment. Too few asylums offer kindness and care. Too many rely on fear.'

Warmth rose in Alexander's belly, his throat. He was feeling better than he had these last few days. A miracle brew indeed. 'So what of Gheel?' he said, unable to keep the triumph out of his voice. The air in the parlour was stagnant; the candles flickered unhealthily. *Just like this place and like his ideas*, he thought. Conolly looked as puzzled as Alexander had expected. 'A community where the insane are housed with the sane. You'd approve of it: patients in family homes. Only the most disturbed, the most dangerous, are excluded, and those who are very greatly troubled, reside in the asylum building until they are ready to be transferred to a family home.'

'Well, then, I'm delighted to hear of it!' Conolly's exclamation didn't match his expression, though. 'But why not leave them with their own families in the first place?'

'In the home, where the madness originated? How can this help them or those who care for them?' *Thomas.* 'The success rate at Gheel is high,' Alexander rushed on. 'It's my aim to introduce Gheel's methods to Montrose.'

Thomas. Home. A man like Conolly would have rescued him long ago. And placed him in greater danger? Guilt didn't come easily to Alexander; he choked on it. Conolly patted his back until the lump of mutton went down. 'I've seen the workings of the asylum in Glasgow and Stratford and Warwick, Dr Balfour. I'll never be impressed by what they do. Even more kindly institutions like your own, however much they are watered down by new methods. Restraint chairs, leg-locks, leather straps, screw-gags,' Conolly reeled off the list as though Alexander had invented them himself. 'Applied to those too powerless to assert themselves.'

'Which is why the profession needs men – like us.' Why was he flattering this man, Alexander wondered. For a moment, he could even picture them joining forces. *Shouldn't we radicals stick together?* But he was forgetting: he was no radical.

'Even Cullen believed in fear,' Conolly continued as if he hadn't spoken, made the gesture.

So he's a zealot who revels in isolation, Alexander decided, forgetting also that *men of genius walk alone.*

'Fear and punishment to keep lunatics in order. Morison believes it. People who are not naturally cruel become habituated to severity until all feelings of humanity are forgotten: it works on the gaolers of these poor souls and on the inmates themselves. I've never seen a kind word, or a sympathetic gesture, made by physicians on their rounds towards their patients. They observe, but they don't interfere, they don't empathize.'

Conolly was no more interested in the words of the mad than any of the men he criticized. But why Alexander should feel such disappointment at his opinions, he couldn't fathom. *A miracle brew.* Yes: he was being slowly poisoned, that was it. Or perhaps it was the warmth of the room, the softness of the candles, the comforting noises of the house. *Family and rescue and safety from harm.* The fantasy wasn't his and was a false one at that, but Conolly's was the voice of the believer. Could he be right?

'And where good is found,' Conolly continued, 'it's too often for the doctors' own glory. Yet they imagine they do it for others' benefit. That only makes them worse.'

He stopped at last, satisfied, sure.

'My brother.' The confession came surprisingly easily, after all. 'Thomas.' Conolly leaned towards him as shadows flickered on the walls and animals sounded nearby. Alexander reached out for something in the gloom and Conolly caught his hand. 'It's up to me now. What to do about him. He's in my charge.' *A soul to save.*

2.

Richmond, November 1823

Alexander is to meet David, at last: which is why I'm too busy this dark, cold evening to be made gloomy by my obligations here. How poor Euphemia cried the day I left, we had become so close. But I've written and told her I'll be back, very soon. Once Alexander has what he wants from David, we'll return there together.

My father's coming tonight, too, and I'll test his loyalty a second time. Promises I want to keep: but only to one person. He thought fear made me shiver that last night and he liked the sense of his own power. But taking charge of my own destiny was what made me tremble. I've known the pain of responsibility before: haven't I borne the disgrace of marrying my dead sister's husband? But the power of it this time: what my little phial once gave me. David's future, as well as my own, is in my hands. For the first time.

My note pricks my leg through my skirts: I'll find a way to pass it to him during the evening. So I'll seat him on my left, and David opposite. My father opposite me.

Christy wasn't happy to let us go, either. Will she be as pleased as Euphemia to see me when I return to be with him? I'm pleasing myself a second time and shocking everyone, she'll say, and she's right. Good women shouldn't please themselves at all, but I'm a sane woman, not a good one, and I've learned what the difference is. All the same, I'll pretend tonight, just as he will, that we're not lovers. Only three weeks of David's testimony to Alexander to endure: surely I can manage that? He won't refuse Alexander's requests to meet after tonight.

And Conolly will help his good friend when my abandonment unseats David completely. Perhaps that's why I'm trying to be kind to him, no matter that he looked so disappointed when he opened the door the day I arrived back here; no matter that he's been rude and cruel every day since. But I can't give time to his comments and remarks, his special requests that only have me running in the wrong direction. 'Why beef and not pork?' 'What have you done with my best shirt?' 'Why did you not invite Conolly, too? Is it too late to send him an invitation?' And the rain hasn't stopped, so there will be mud throughout the house.

'It's not fit,' he says, coming on me in our little dining room, startling my daydreams. He's made no noise on the stairs and I am thinking only of what to wear. Alexander's first sight of me must remind him. The note pricks still and I want to hush him.

'Don't creep up on me like that.' But I'm snapping instead: so much for my kind intentions. I pretend to rearrange the table a little. 'What's not fit? It looks perfectly fine.'

How slow these last few days have been! The houses we passed through the streets all the long way to the green spaces of Richmond when I only wanted to be heading north again; the mix of strangers' voices when all I want to hear is his. David had prepared nothing for my return with the girls, swept no floors, washed not a single cup, never opened a window. It took two whole days of cleaning and cooking and washing just to make it a 'fit' place again and more than once I thought of packing up my girls and leaving anyway, without waiting for Alexander. Despair in the letters I sent have got me sympathy only, though, and a warning to be patient.

So I take a deep breath and try to be calm. The brass candlesticks and good lace tablecloth are laid; the best wine glasses are ready, along with our last few pieces of unbroken china. 'The cushions are dirty,' David insists, his eye drawn down to my hand, resting in Alexander's place. The thickness in his voice and pastiness of his skin are familiar: *not a seizure tonight*, I pray, but I've forgotten: God is closed to me as he is to all unfaithful wives. I mutter that he should rest upstairs but he picks up a candlestick instead, weighs the base in his palm.

'Your sister should be attending tonight,' he says, his eyes on me. 'Or you should absent yourself altogether.' I don't look at the candlestick, and I assume the brisk tone he hates.

'Don't be foolish, David, Christy's in Scotland. How could she be here? And there's nothing unseemly about my attending dinner with my husband, my father and a guest. Who is a respectable medical man.' I don't blame him for disliking this priggish tone, I dislike it myself. And it doesn't help because he shoves the candlestick at my breast, hard, forces me up against the wall.

'You will not eat with us!' His face is pressed against mine, his mouth at my temple. 'You will eat in the kitchen and keep yourself out of our way. I will not have a stranger look at you!' I push at his chest with both fists. He's bony and frail – he ate little when we were away and has scarcely eaten since my return – but madness gives him a supernatural strength. My touch makes him raise his fist up behind his head, but I'm ready for the blow.

'I won't eat in the kitchen like a servant!' I shout back at him. 'You cannot tell me what to do! I'm not what you think: I'm not afraid of you. So strike me if that's what you want. Hit me as hard as you like! Let my father see what kind of man you are.'

He lifts his hand higher, trembling, blinking, lost to who he is, and pity fills me instead. 'I'm the only one here who has met Dr Balfour, David. He's not a stranger. It's my duty to attend dinner and look after our guests,' I say, as reasonably as I can. But the Devil is in his eyes, they cleave to the candlelight and burn with the flame. This may be my last moment on earth.

My father and Alexander will arrive to find me bludgeoned on the hearth, a lunatic man still gripping a bloody candlestick in his hand. But my imagination plays false: the light leaves his eyes and he lowers his hand.

'Forgive me, Bella,' he sighs, his shaking hand passing over his brow. He drops the candlestick on the table and I move quickly to snatch it up. 'Don't be afraid of me. Of course you will be with us. What makes me say these things...' Why did this come to our door, I think for the thousandth time. *We might have been happy. We did not deserve this.* And a strange thing happens: tears clot my eyes, salt my cheeks and lips. He raises his hand again but this time to brush my face as gently as a mother with a baby. 'What I've done to you, my dear Bella...' he whispers. I put my arms around him then lead him upstairs, where I dab his brow with a little cold water. How will I bear to leave him to the care of others, I wonder. Yet I have to, and the thought finishes my tears at last.

A duplicitous life isn't a healthy life, Alexander had said, the second time he called me 'Marie'. The wine, I assumed. Thinking one thing and feeling another; feeling one thing and saying another, and I wondered why this woman, whoever she was, had caused him to behave in a duplicitous way. But then he said religion causes duplicity in us, too, and so I forgot her. How many, do you think, sit in a church pew and think of other things, he said. The shoes they have bought or the picnic they are planning or the smile that someone special has given them. 'We were raised to be forever cleaved in two,' he told me. 'It is science that will restore people to themselves, science that will mend the tear. Science that will restore the self that religion and madness have broken apart.'

I hum to smother the pity and when I escape David for my own room, I gaze at my sleeping girls and try on the dress I've had laundered and mended for this evening. I'll think of myself as a whole being then as Alexander says, mended so and not split in two the way an axe splits wood. The pearl necklace that once belonged to my mother gleams at my throat as I hum and dance and restore to myself its wholeness. Before God, my husband and madness cut me in two.

A presumptuous knock at the door has me rushing downstairs to meet it. It's only my father. 'Bella, my girl, don't keep us on the doorstep, it's an awful night,' his voice calls from the darkness outside. *Us*. I peer past him to the other figure in the gloom: yes, he's no different for the weeks that have kept us apart. 'Don't tell me the girls are in their beds already?' he frowns, banging his hands on his arms to keep out the cold. 'I haven't missed them? Och, that's no good.' Will my father want to leave London, too, once I have gone? Will my girls lure him back north, away from David, no matter how badly he feels for him? 'I've got a wee present for them, I wanted to see their faces when I gave it them.'

I laugh but David is already on the stairs. 'They see you all the time, and you are always giving them presents,' I smile and heave my father's coat off his shoulders, breathe in the smell of tobacco and coffee, his favourite things.

'I know, I know,' he shakes his head. 'But they're the best of wee girls and who else do I have to spoil now?' Alexander is passing me to shake hands with my husband, positioned at the bottom of the stairs, clean and smart in his best shirt. There's no trace of the disturbance earlier on his face. My husband: the man of learning. *Men of enlightenment will chase away old wives' tales*. I usher into the dining room these three learned men, each as painfully close to me as it's possible to be. Father. Husband. Lover.

'You're late,' I scold, 'so we must begin our meal straightaway, or the beef will dry out and the potatoes will be cold.'

But it's only when our plates are filled and we're sitting round the table that I realize I've left my note in my other dress. 'My friend Conolly should have been here,' David is saying. I catch an odd look on Alexander's face. 'Then we would enjoy a good argument, Dr Balfour. Confinement in a madhouse is always unjustifiable, according to him. That would not do for your profession, would it, if his views were to be taken up?'

I take a sip of wine as Alexander, too merry, laughs and says, 'But I don't believe *you'd* agree with him, would you, Mr Booth?'

David's face whitens, and I panic at the thought of a fit, but he answers steadily enough. 'Conolly and I like to disagree. I believe that, in certain cases, confinement is necessary. And Isabella was most impressed with your establishment, weren't you?' He turns to me and I nod.

Alexander merely smiles strangely, as though he has secret thoughts. David knows nothing of my long stay there; he thinks I was at Christy's and visited Montrose only briefly. My deception is written on my face and so I keep it lowered. 'Oh, we don't use words like "confine", for our establishment,' Alexander says, breezily, 'however much we are in control of a patient's freedom. It's not a prison.'

'We use the same word when a woman enters the last stage of pregnancy,' I volunteer, the wine making me bold. 'We call it "confinement". Why do we do that? Is it an imprisoning state?'

My father leans back, not shocked, but not full, either: the beef wasn't too dry, but there was too little fat, which is his favourite part. He'll eat more cheese later to compensate, if we have enough. Alexander raises his eyebrows at me. *Our fathers are like boys, don't you know that?* I want to say to him. One day he'll know that for himself: when he is a father. When I give him children. I shiver, press my belly against the table edge.

'From the Latin, *confinia* meaning "end", or "limit",' David is saying. He's last to finish his plate, patting potato carefully on to his fork. 'Because she is at the end of her time. Nothing to do with imprisonment.'

My father winks across the table at me. 'Is there something you should be telling us, Bella? A wee brother or sister for the girls, maybe?'

David looks at me now, too, as if I'm a stranger, and Alexander coughs unnecessarily: I gather up the plates and make much noise doing so. 'I'd very much like to meet Mr Conolly while I'm in London.' Alexander directs himself at

David again, while I wrestle my husband's plate from him. 'I've heard good things of him, for all his dislike of institutions. I'd like to persuade him to another point of view, have him visit us in Montrose, perhaps.'

I must leave them but I hear my husband say, 'I'm sure that could be arranged: he's a busy man with a large family, but he is intellectually curious as the best men are. You will find him hard to persuade, though. He's not weak in his views.'

When I return, David is still speaking. 'My wife tells me you expect one day to have mostly female patients in your hospital. Is that correct? Is there something about the female mind that makes it more susceptible to madness?'

I'd suggested to David this dinner for Alexander by way of a trick. His angry jibes at the hospital he'd never seen, and which he'd wanted me to visit on his behalf, puzzled me how best to reassure him. Surely he'd be easier in his mind, I reasoned with him, if he made the acquaintance of its assistant director. Reason to excuse my faithlessness: how we use any means at our disposal, we unfaithful wives.

Alexander replies, 'It's my belief that women are the more susceptible sex. But men are too much in the world, sometimes.'

My father chuckles at that. 'I couldn't laugh at it at the time, for he sorely tried me, Mary's husband,' he says. 'But if ever there was a man "too much in the world", it was him.'

'He wasn't mad,' I correct him, hastily, before David speaks, and Alexander asks to hear more about him.

'*She Walks in Beauty like the night.* Is that not his?'

I glance at David, who says, too happy at the thought he might be confused with another, 'No, that is his friend. An even worse rake and languishing in Greece, I believe.' There's a flush in David's cheek: wine and conversation. He's enjoying himself but God won't forgive me for my lies. I may smile across the table at my father, who can't imagine how deceitful his beloved daughter is, but I know he'll not forgive me for what I'm planning to do.

3.

Holborn, November 1823

He'd almost been late for Isabella's dinner; afterwards, in silent fury in the lone carriage ride back to Holborn, Alexander wished he hadn't gone at all and carried on their pretence. And how could it be anything but a pretence when he'd observed no signs of madness in David Booth at all? Why, the man had argued cogently and in an articulate manner all night! On the contrary, Isabella's behaviour suggested an imbalance of the mental faculties. She might have been a little drunk, he understood that, and nervous at his presence. But her fidgeting, her strange expressions, her inappropriate interruptions of the conversation, her distracted air: they suggested something else, too. The possibility of being found out a fraud!

He'd have to abandon his 'sympathy' theory after all, if David Booth was as sane as he appeared. So Isabella had merely impersonated the condition of a woman having a nervous breakdown: could it be true? He blushed in the darkness of the carriage to remember how she had convinced him. He hadn't thought her promiscuous, but her husband had accused her of it in his letter and would know her better. Booth's was an original mind; Alexander didn't want to think what such a mind would make of another, so easily duped by a deranged woman, and he bit his lip till it burst and bled.

When Isabella had accompanied Alexander alone to the door at the end of the night, her sneaking caresses had made him want to push her away. He'd thought of Marie and the mistake he'd made before. Only Booth had saved him; and Conolly, of course.

Anger wasn't conducive to research, he reminded himself. *Prejudices the mind!* Passion might aid art, but that didn't help science, either. How had he lost his way? How had he allowed himself to be snared by Isabella? Passion? *A family weakness.*

In spite of his misery, sleep came fast when he finally arrived home, exhausted and troubled. It seemed he had only just shut his eyes, though, when Annie knocked on his bedroom door with a message from Conolly. He'd be later than expected. Alexander groaned and rolled over on his side, the better to warm his chilled face and hands, then remembered. *Thomas!* How could he have forgotten? What Isabella and her lies could do...

But there was too much for him to do to be thinking about her today. And he needed Conolly by his side. Alone, he couldn't face it. *Family obligations.* But Thomas was more than that. Wasn't he? He forced himself out of his warm bed and over to the window, pulled aside the drapes to a fog that hadn't lifted; if anything, it was even thicker. He splashed cold water on his face, pulled on old breeches, the better for the work he'd be doing this morning, as well as a still-soiled shirt and woollen jacket. Somewhere across the city, in a very different kind of room, a man who closely resembled him would be doing the same thing.

If he looked in a mirror, would he still see his brother looking back at him, as he so often did? Alexander couldn't know what the last four years had done to Thomas, but he'd find out soon enough. His fingers trembled, had him fumbling his boot fastenings.

'I'm not setting foot inside the place,' he'd told Conolly. 'They'll have to bring him to me.' How weak he'd looked, weeping on the man's shoulder that night. Sobbing about the fate of his brother until Conolly made him see he must bring him home. The only way to save him – *bring him home.*

Conolly had read his mind and understood; given permission, almost, to bring forth that seed that had begun growing the moment he'd thought about families causing the work. Oh yes, he'd run away from it that night he'd met the mind-doctor, right away from the thought that he'd use his only brother for research. But he hadn't meant to have him at home; he'd meant to visit him in Bethlem, examine him daily, consult with him. Have him transferred to Montrose, possibly.

But Conolly's suggestion had given him power without guilt: take Thomas out of the hospital and into his own home. And examine him and consult with him there as much as he liked. Perhaps later, he'd move him to Montrose, if he went back, after all. He still couldn't decide; he had some time yet before Browne returned, thanks to his father's unexpected death. They all thought of him with sympathy, Mrs Munro's letter had said.

But perhaps Isabella's lies had been leading him here, Alexander wondered, unable to keep her from his mind, after all. Sympathy was a false road, had excited him, had flattered his intelligence. Booth wasn't mad; Isabella was deranged, and Crichton had been right. Perhaps this situation was not so irredeemable, then. And Conolly – he only reinforced that possibility, didn't he? *Analysis and instruction and childhood.* Alexander repeated the words softly under his breath, glad to have them with him still.

'I'll eat up here,' he called down as Annie and the kitchen maid whose name he thought was Kitty but he still couldn't be sure and couldn't be bothered asking, bustled between the delivery men at the door and the kitchen. 'I'll need a large breakfast – Thomas is due at noon.'

Annie was too young for the role he'd given her, but he'd chosen this stocky, country girl for the task for a reason. 'You'll be running your own hospital one day,' she'd said, flattered when he explained why he wanted a smaller household staff, and that he'd chosen her to lead it. 'Food and hygiene – that's all I care about,' he'd said. 'I leave it up to the two of you to arrange it.' An inexperienced but practical girl like Annie would relish the responsibility, and so she did.

'Talk to him,' was what Alexander had wanted Conolly to advise, too, of course, but he wouldn't. His stomach grumbled. *Where is the man?* They could breakfast together before Thomas arrived. He'd make the place as professional as possible; this drawing room would be his own, and in his mother's old room he'd set up his practice, interview patients. It was a good-sized room, away from the noise of the streets at the back of the house. He'd start with Thomas, with the childhood they'd shared. He'd write about madness begun in childhood, specialize and attract patients the world over.

Alexander laughed at himself a little – grandiose schemes weren't halted by lack of sleep, then. But he had a task to perform first, and only a little time. The paper and ink were waiting on the side table, beside his father's mistress's letter that he hadn't yet found the right moment to throw away. What he knew of the final day of Thomas's freedom, what his father had told him: he must write it all down. Caused by a woman, of course, before their mother was dead. For the life of him, though, he couldn't recall the name of the family that had appointed Thomas to tutor their children. Williams? Watson? Wilson? He'd have to ask his brother.

His stomach rumbled again, marking time. He took up the pen: spring, 1820? An unusually warm day in Edinburgh, it would have been then, he remembered; in London it would have been hotter. But his father didn't mention the weather when he told him what had happened. How he'd come from town, strolled back through the heat and noise of the street.

And just like that occasion many years before, the front door was ajar. His father hadn't registered the warning and progressed slowly up the stairs and into the parlour. All was quiet; then he heard it, the animal cry from the rooms above. He'd stood absolutely still: nothing would make his father investigate. *The weak son of a weak man.* The cry came again.

He seemed to be the only person in the house, he'd written to Alexander. An intruder, whom he'd have to tackle alone. So he'd taken up his walking stick, the closest thing he had to a weapon, and ran upstairs shouting, 'Who's there?' Furniture crashed in one of the rooms. 'Open up, whoever you are!' He'd hammered against the door, until he forced the lock and it gave way. In the middle of the room, naked and smeared with dirt and faeces, lay Thomas, shivering on the floor, a white substance dribbling from his lips.

Only later did they find out he'd become involved with his employer's wife. On discovering the affair, her husband had immediately removed his entire family to his father's plantation in Jamaica. Thomas had demanded his lover stay with him, and when she refused he'd had to be bodily removed from the property in his derangement. Somehow, he'd made his way back to his father's house in Holborn, where he had tried to kill himself.

He was taken off to Bethlem. It was the only thing to do, his father said.

It was too late for Alexander to save his mother, but not Thomas. The brother with whom he'd wandered dark lanes beside their home on days their mother was too distracted to care, his father absent at his club or elsewhere. The brother who'd taught him to read before he was taken off to school. The brother who'd cried when they came across butchered rabbits on their way to market. He tried to recall other memories but Thomas slipped too often from his sight, a hazy presence as he grew older. And then he was gone.

How should he be with him now? Brotherly, yes; professional, of course. An uneasy combination. Alexander glanced at the clock. Eleven already. And still no breakfast. He marched to the door, just as Annie appeared below with the tray. 'There's no time,' he called down as he hurried towards her.

'But this isn't for you,' she stopped just at the parlour door. 'It's for sir inside. He's here. He said not to disturb you. *Thomas Balfour*,' she added.

'Alexander?'

He heard the wary voice behind the door and the world stopped. 'Alexander?' He went down the stairs and stood beside Annie, reached for the doorknob, his hands tingling and his heart skipping again, slamming and skipping, slamming and skipping. He couldn't answer. He could only open the door slowly, as someone came into view.

But the man in the room wasn't the one he remembered. When Alexander had last seen Thomas, his brother had a head of dark red curls, just like him. He was taller and broader, his face full, with a hint of the puppy fat that he'd carried ever since he was nine or ten years old. This man was stooped and thin, his sunken cheeks whiskered over with a light brown fuzz. The curls had been shaved from his skull long ago. His eyes were still Thomas's eyes: brown and soft like a dog's. But they were fearful and made Alexander rush, even when he knew that wasn't the best thing to do.

'Thomas!' His arms reached round his once-burly brother easily and he clasped him to him, but Thomas wouldn't clasp back. He stood still, arms by his side; Alexander felt a tremor run through his brother's body as he realized he was shaking, and released him.

'More food, Annie, quickly!' He wished his brother didn't look quite so dazed, or so wondering. 'You do recognize the old place, Thomas? And me?' He'd meant it as a joke but Thomas didn't laugh.

'Of course,' he spoke politely, and stood in the middle of the room.

'Then sit down – you're at home now. You can be comfortable here.'

Thomas took the nearest seat and made no approach to the food Annie placed on the small table beside him. 'Eat, please,' Alexander said. 'I have had nothing myself yet today. What a pair of starving wretches we are. But you begin. I want you to begin.'

He watched as his brother lifted a plate of kidneys and bacon and sat it on his lap. 'Where are the eggs? Annie knows to bring eggs, too,' Alexander tutted, as his brother gingerly pushed a fork at the bacon. 'You had enough to eat – there?' But it was the wrong thing to say. Thomas returned his fork to the plate without letting the bacon touch his lips. 'I apologize, Thomas. I interrupted you. Please, carry on.' His brother lifted the fork, put the bacon in his mouth and chewed slowly as Alexander watched him in silence. 'It is good?' he asked, eventually. Thomas nodded.

'I'd forgotten the taste,' he said, slowly, as though the words were morsels to taste, too.

More food came, and more tea: and all the time, Alexander watched the clock on the mantelpiece for Conolly to come and help with this silent stranger who would give him nothing.

4.

Richmond, November 1823

How happy our house is now. Since dinner for Alexander, I can reassure myself. What tricks absence plays upon our minds! I feared he'd forgotten me, or was growing cold. But I couldn't have been more wrong; his caresses told me so. He still wants me. And so I let my girls run up and down the stairs and call out to each other, as they open doors for leaves to blow in behind them. I don't scold them, and every so often, when they fly past me, I try to catch them, my blood-and-flesh fairies with tugs in their hair and jam smeared on their cheeks. This morning, I crept into their bed and held them tight, even though they wriggled, too big to share with their mama now.

I slept in the chair last night before going in to my girls, but no one visited me. So I'm over the crisis point, as Alexander would say. No more hallucinations, no more need for my little phial, even though my hands shake as I stir the porridge for breakfast. My fact of being female, and therefore weaker and more *susceptible*, is what made me see ghosts in the past. The fault of all women: the fault of our wombs. The mind and the body working in harmony to disrupt the soul. But I'm still female today so why have my ghosts stopped visiting? Where are you now, Margaret? You've tried your worst and failed, I think; or you have what you've always wanted. Have him back;

I have my own now. And my soul is restored to me, too: you won't have that.

I brew more tea on this dark, misty morning and remember the conversation I had with Euphemia before I left Montrose. We'd brew tea just like this, then pick out herbs together and wash them. Her task, not mine, but I couldn't watch without helping. Sudden noises alarmed her and a kitchen is full of clattering, which made me worry they'd bring on another fit, so I'd take her off to the small library once we were done, though she was forbidden to tax her mind with reading. She isn't so little: married at the same age I was when I married David, though she looks not much over twelve years old. She talked of her husband, of his goodness and kindness to her when she was so wicked.

'How well he endured my "fancies",' she said, and her use of that word made me shudder and suspect his goodness for something else. 'I like to read poetry and to write it, too. At home I often forgot to sweep and sew: I wasn't a good wife.' She traced the small scar above her eyebrow with her forefinger: the shape a burn might make. I tried to imagine how it came about without asking her. She was full enough of shame.

'I am "unnatural",' she said: a consequence of her epilepsy. 'My husband, who is so patient, so gentle, said so from the beginning. My parents think it, too: that's why they wanted me married off so quickly. They didn't tell him, so he always said they tricked him. Yet he'd been engaged to my sister first, before she died, so he must have heard talk of my condition.'

I hugged her then. 'We have something in common,' I confided. 'I married my sister's husband, too. Montrose must be full of bad wives and worse sisters,' I joked, surprising myself in my eagerness to make her smile. Her 'speaking eyes', like Izzy's, like *his*. 'But we are all women,' I whispered in her ear. 'There is nothing unnatural about any of us.'

She nodded without believing me, picked at the sore on her chin that she would never leave alone long enough to heal. I tried to find a poem in the library that might convince her, but I couldn't. Too many words about our beauty, our faithfulness, our innocence. And just as many about our ugliness, our deceit and our guilt. So I searched to find what might fill the gap between, and thought of what a woman might write. But I couldn't find any evidence that we compose at all: at least, not in public. In our journals, perhaps, in secret, as I do: or like Euphemia, lost in a trance of words, scribbling them down when she should have been broiling haddock for her husband's breakfast. To be caught doing so is a grievous thing: it means the difference between imprisonment and liberty. How simple it is.

Euphemia wasn't supposed to write while she was at Montrose, but I smuggled paper and ink to her from Alexander's study. I'd slip it into my pockets at the end of our evening session, and next morning would insist on taking Euphemia with me for a turn about the garden. Who will get paper and ink to her now? I don't like to think of her without it. I hope she was careful with her stock. It took so little to make her happy and calm. Perhaps I'll confide in Alexander later and ask him to make sure she has some. Perhaps if I can make it a *womb-like* need, he'll think it a worthy exercise. Or I'll take it to her myself when I return.

Wombs and madness. It exhausts me to think of it. My womb, where the seed of madness lay, incubating like a worm, ready to grow and infect my mind. The mind and the body making my soul sick. But it was my husband's madness that tried to destroy my soul. So I'll remember that. And I have my girls who will be susceptible, too, according to Alexander's theories. Perhaps, together, we can keep them strong and safe from harm.

'Hurry up now,' I say, as I rub their faces with the cloth. 'Hats, too: we're going to market and it's cold outside.' 'What are we getting?' asks Izzy. 'Wait and see,' I reply. Industry and fresh air will make them strong. The day is brightening and we will face it. I will divert their questions about their father with this bright day: keep his madness from them with words I haven't used for a long time. *And deliver us from evil.*

Before I lose my resolve to face the world, we're out in the lane and on our way. Midday is all smoky, November sunlight that makes the lane a mysterious place but we know it blind-folded, my girls and I, so I won't worry about what lurks there. 'Wait for coaches to pass,' I say, once we have left it behind and are on the main market road. Richmond is small and many squeeze through it on their way to town, they will not stop for two girls in this busy world. Too many men shout and too many women push by, but then a friendly hawker raises his hat to the 'young ladies' and makes them smile. 'Will we get something for Papa?' Izzy asks. 'To make him happy to see us?'

'Yes, we can get him something,' I reply, although I doubt much will make him happy to see his poor girls. 'We must prepare though,' I bend down and level her face with mine. 'One day we might not always have him. He might not always have us.'

'What do you mean?' she says, alarmed. I forget that they love him, that I've shielded them from the worst.

'Don't be upset, but you know how he gets ill sometimes.' She nods. 'It may be that one day Papa has to go away – for a rest, perhaps.'

'Can we still visit him?'

'Of course. And you will be brave and help me whenever he is not here with us?' Izzy thinks for a moment then nods confidently, my girl who is too young to doubt herself yet.

'I may have to tell Kathy what to do more often,' she says, a smile at her lips. 'If Papa is not here to do it.' But Kathy hears and protests, 'I will be good! Izzy doesn't have to tell me what to do!' How I'll manage it, the day when we leave him, I'll forget for now. For now, there is only this day, and my girls.

The mess of horses and mud and rotting vegetables that lines our way changes as we approach the green, chattering all the while, but the scents of basil, rosemary and thyme silence us and I tell them to take a deep breath. 'Doesn't that smell nice, girls? Now, I want onions and celery, and you can have pineapple if the boats have been and there is some left.'

'Can we run?' Izzy asks.

'If you don't go too far,' I say. I'm still fearful of the crowd but she grips her sister by the hand and skips through the body of folk, a cluster of neighbours and strangers, never afraid. I'll make a pie with the rest of yesterday's minced beef, I think, as I test the onions and potatoes, look for worms. We have all day, we can take as long as we like. My girls have seen too much already, even if they've buried it. So I'll bake an apple pie for them, too, as a treat, and I call out to them to look out for apple stalls.

Spoiled cabbages, piled up in a dirty corner and selling for next-to-nothing. Traders shouting above the gossip as a dirty little hand reaches out from behind a coat to snatch a blackening cabbage. Flies buzzing round turnips that still carry traces of horse dung. Too much elderberry wine making an unhappy farmer argue for a better price. He lurches and knocks against his load, sending carrots and cauliflower to the ground where a scurry of rags and bare feet make quick work of them, carrying them off beyond his reach.

'He'd have been better to wait till the day was done before getting tipsy,' I whisper to Izzy, now back by my side with her sister, and laughing at the angry man struggling to his feet. A little further and I give them a coin for a toffee apple each from the smoking pot of apple stew, too sweet-smelling for any child to resist. My girls are hardy, more worldly than me: Kathy pats the little terrier that belongs to the ugly old woman with the witch's nose, as apples dip and bob in her urn. This chaos belongs to them, the dirt and the fruit, the stealing and the trading, the good and the bad, because they are not afraid of witches. They are not susceptible: I will prove it to Alexander. This day proves it.

And it's as I contemplate what I will say to him, and gaze around and breathe in my girls' fearless world with all its guddle and cries and laughter, that I catch sight of her: Mary! At first I'm not sure, then I glimpse again that haze of fair hair, her fine features: indeed, it is Mary.

'Mary!' I shout across the bodies between us: can she not hear me? But the sellers chorus too loud beside me, drowning out my voice. 'But she doesn't live anywhere near here,' I'm saying to Izzy. 'Has she come to see us, do you think? She won't find us at home!' I'll have to catch her before she heads out to our empty cottage on a wasted journey. 'Come on,' I say to Kathy. 'Let's catch up with Mama's friend, Mary. That's her, see, in the red coat, the lady with the fair hair. Can you see? Let's hurry after her. Quick now!'

Izzy takes Kathy by the hand once again, and I guide them past gentlewomen and cooks and maids and mothers like me: a sea of women that envelops Mary in crinoline and cotton and wool, then releases her again.

'There she is, girls. Mary!' I shout, but she's too fast for us: her blonde halo dips down into the crowd once more and I think I must have lost her when Izzy grabs my skirt excitedly. 'There she is, Mama, look!' and I see her at last.

Only this time, she's not alone. She is talking to someone. Another woman. A woman I recognize very well. In truth, I could hardly not recognize her. For Mary, so many yards ahead of us, is talking to me. Or, more accurately, to my ghost.

5.

Holborn, November 1823

Another letter. This time, from Philomena. When could they announce their engagement, she wanted to know. He shouldn't have forgotten that day in her drawing room, but it wasn't memorable enough. The liberties he'd taken with her just after Isabella left for London were unremarkable to his experience, but clearly not to hers. Their engagement, she made clear as she struck *her* bargain, would be a short one. A summer wedding was her ideal.

He'd just had breakfast and was deep in thought as he wandered along to his mother's old room, where Thomas would be waiting. A formal engagement would alert Isabella too soon, no matter what he thought of her now. Perhaps a small part of him was still hoping he was wrong about her? If so, he'd have to find ways of delaying Philomena's announcement. Another woman to trouble him: why couldn't the world get along without them, he thought, as exasperated at the confusion he thought he'd laid to rest, as he was at his 'fiancée's' demands.

Fiancée. How would she like to share her home with a deranged brother-in-law he wondered grimly, as he entered his 'consulting room' to find Thomas sitting silently by the window. A blank sheet of paper hung on the easel in front of him. Painting had been his particular talent, but he showed no interest in it now. He'd barely eaten since the morning he arrived, picking only at the meat pie and potatoes Annie made for him the previous evening. Alexander heard him pacing his room that night over the floorboards, like a caged creature who didn't know how to use the space he'd now been granted. He had the devil's own job, too, trying to get him to wash every day – Annie refused to help but had at least cleaned his sheets every morning. 'It'll take time,' he told her when she complained. 'The mind heals slowly.' But even he was impatient. He'd only approached Thomas with a handful of questions so far but even those had been too much for him.

Alexander closed the door and thought he saw a twitch in Thomas's gaunt shoulders, the only sign his brother acknowledged the intrusion. *One gaoler for another: that's what he thinks I am.* It could take years, and his heart closed up. What did Conolly understand of a mad brother? He still hadn't visited. Did he do this all the time? Recommend treatment and then withdraw his help? Alexander remembered David Booth's mention of him: perhaps he could enlighten him about Conolly's methods. He rang for Annie, and when she appeared, gave her a note. Then he positioned himself opposite his brother; Thomas barely registered him. 'Let us talk to one another,' he offered, quietly. But his offer hung in the air between them until lunch, when, finally, with a soft squeeze of those painfully thin shoulders, Alexander gave his brother what he wanted and left him alone.

He still recognized nothing in this stranger who had once roamed messy cobbled streets with him years ago, and it was unlikely, he realized suddenly, that Thomas had been able to record anything of his experiences in a diary or letters. At least Isabella kept a journal where she revealed her true self. But he wasn't supposed to be interested in Isabella any more.

At least the answer to his note, when it arrived shortly after two, gave him some clarity: David Booth would be free to see him at five. The perfect excuse to cut short these disturbing, unproductive consultations with his brother. His heart skipped again. It was torn, like him, and he pictured it in his mind that way: half a heart beating in time to theories about childhood, the other half with Isabella, and neither of them in unison. He placed his palm against the beats; he would settle the matter for good. He had no reason to be anxious.

But still it skipped on. Alexander took up his coat, and stepped outside, intending to hail a hackney carriage, yet knowing only one thing would calm his worries. And so he dallied in a tavern for an hour or so before heading for the cottage in Richmond, where he arrived just as it was getting dark. He tested his breath against his hand when he reached the front door. He wouldn't have a man like Booth guess his weaknesses.

'I apologize for misleading you, but my wife isn't here,' was the first thing Booth said to him as he led him into the tiny parlour. 'At her father's, I imagine.' He frowned. 'Although she might have sent me word. I haven't seen her since last night.' He might be an exacting man to live with, Alexander thought, as he sat down, but he wasn't a mad one.

Booth didn't seem to notice the threadbare state of his chairs, but that wasn't a sign of madness, either. 'It wasn't Isabella I wanted to see,' he said. 'But she's often absent without your knowledge?'

'My wife has habits... but you will know of them. Everything I wrote in my letter was true, Dr Balfour. So why do you want to see me instead? To ascertain if I am a man of my word? Dinner the other night was surely enough to prove my wife's erratic behaviour to you. Although you must have seen enough of it in Montrose.'

For a moment, Alexander thought he saw something like a smile on Booth's face. He couldn't have guessed what had really taken place between them. He shifted in his seat, eager to dispel the tension.

'I wanted to ask what you knew about John Conolly, but of course, we might discuss her,' he said, lightly. 'You're surprised that she's stayed away all night without a word, you must have felt that Montrose had done its work?'

Booth frowned. 'She told me very little of her time there. I observed some improvement when she returned, but...' and here he sighed deeply, rubbed his brow. Alexander waited for him to continue. 'I may not allow her to stay with us. She is bad for our daughters. I think perhaps she should return to Montrose with you.'

Alexander squirmed. 'Montrose may not be the best place...' he murmured. Good lord, were both the husband and the wife conspiring against him? How delighted Isabella would be to hear her husband give her just what she wants, he thought.

'Then where would be? Somewhere in London perhaps?' Booth leaned forward. 'Where would be suitable? And how soon could we arrange the matter?'

'Excuse me, but I wondered – could I have some refreshment?' Alexander needed time. He was surprised to find Booth so unused to the workings of his own home that he barely knew where anything was kept. So Alexander fetched tea from the kitchen; Alexander moved the candle closer, the better to see in the room's darkness.

'I keep everything for my own needs in my room upstairs,' Booth explained, apologetically. Alexander doubted Conolly would have stooped to playing such a subservient role. But he couldn't put it off forever.

'Are you serious about having Isabella committed?'

'Quite serious. The sooner the better.'

Alexander paused. 'Let me talk with her some more,' he said.

'You can do that very well up north, or in any institution here,' Booth countered. 'I want her away from my daughters, before she does them more harm. She has them with her now, you know.'

'But you believe them to be safe, at her father's, do you not? She has not been walking the streets with them.'

Booth shrugged. Alexander looked round the tiny parlour, hoping to distract the man. His gaze alighted on a book, face down and open.

'Ah, *Caleb Williams*,' he said. 'I've read it, but only superficially. I wasn't impressed by its – didacticism. But I can scarcely recall its plot – can you…?'

'It is a tale of motivation.' Booth succumbed to the temptation, as Alexander suspected he might. 'Williams, a servant, discovers that Falkland, his employer, is a murderer. But he uses that knowledge to acquire power over his master without realizing, of course, that he will always be a servant and therefore always powerless. His employer duly entraps him by planting stolen property on him, which leads to his arrest and incarceration.'

'Yes, now I remember,' Alexander said. 'But it was the message Mr Godwin was eager to impose on his public that I resented, I think.'

'It is about the perception of truth.' Booth closed his eyes for a moment. 'And how that perception is often considered more important than truth itself. But only through full and proper knowledge of ourselves can the truth can be uncovered and be said to matter.'

'In that sense, I would agree with you.'

Booth opened his eyes. 'Then the question remains, how do we know when we have reached that point of self-knowledge? How do we know when we have fully understood ourselves, Dr Balfour?'

'You are indeed a man after my own heart, Mr Booth,' Alexander replied. 'The question of the self. The hierarchy of emotion, reason, sensibility and sympathy.'

'My wife's friend's husband: the poet. His "self" was a lyre to be played upon to produce a beautiful tune.' Booth snorted at this.

'You didn't care for him?'

'You didn't mention morals in your list, Dr Balfour. That man had none.'

'I know I'm no poet,' replied Alexander. 'One advocates truth over beauty, does he not? I want stories from people. I hope they will tell me the truth about themselves, but I have to make a narrative out of them, to understand them better.'

'And what do you see in the struggle for power between Williams and Falkland?'

'A battle between all those wedded together for their souls.'

'And do you see...'

But Booth wasn't allowed to continue as at that moment Isabella's father rushed into the room in a state of excitement. 'Is Isabella here?' he cried out. 'What's happened, David? Where are they?'

'Is she not with you?' Booth looked up as Alexander got to his feet. 'I assumed she was visiting you – did she not stay last night?'

Baxter shook his head. 'She was bringing the girls for supper. But they've never arrived.'

Booth began pacing the room. Alexander surveyed the two men dispassionately: this was simply more proof and he'd have to accept the truth of it. The woman was mentally unbalanced; there was no need for him here, no need to converse with Booth. His bouts of epilepsy could not be cured by anything Alexander had to offer. And Isabella could not go with him to Montrose.

'I will leave you,' he said, getting up.

'But we must look for her and the girls!' exclaimed Baxter. 'God knows what has happened to them.'

But he was done here. He had another case which mattered more and which was proving difficult. 'When you find her let me know,' he directed himself at Booth. 'I'll sign whatever needs to be signed.'

'Sign what?' he heard Baxter's raised voice as he stepped out the front door of the cottage. 'What is he supposed to be signing?'

But already Alexander was hurrying down the path, back to his brother.

6.

Richmond, November 1823

I'm not afraid: no, I want to laugh out loud instead. *Yes, I still see them! Where is my cure now, Dr Balfour?* What will he make of this? At least my ghost isn't dressed as I am today. It's dressed as I have been on other occasions, though. I recognize the pale rosebuds on the skirt and bodice, even from this distance, and the false hem that still has the skirt skimming the ankles too high. My ghost wears no hat like me, but its coat is my simple grey one, and far too thin for the beginning of winter. Mary, dressed in red, is talking with great excitement. I watch my ghost in profile, see how it nods at her as if it has heard her story before. Then it says something in return and Mary loops her arm in its own. That is the moment they both turn and begin to walk away from the market.

My girls' faces show nothing of this: Kathy is too busy complaining. 'You said we could have pineapple.' My heart is beating hard. 'Let's play a game first, Kathy,' I say. 'Do you see the lady walking up ahead, with Mama's friend, Mary?' She shakes her head: she's bored with this. 'I want some pineapple,' she whines again. 'When you've finished your toffee apple and Mama has caught up with her friend, I promise. Let's play this game first. Let's follow them, just to see if we can catch them.

Come: I need you and Izzy both to watch them very carefully.'
Izzy is doubtful this is any kind of game, and Kathy only wants
another toffee apple, but I can't abandon my chase just yet.
I don't know what I intend by following these creatures – I
doubt it is really Mary I see, either – but I won't turn away.

My breathing is shallow as we stumble, the three of us,
too fast through mud and fallen leaves, away from the market
and down towards the river. 'It's a chase, you see, Kathy: we
must chase them!' I'm panting to keep up, but I needn't worry:
my girls have twice the energy I have, and now they're part
of it, they pull me along, chide their mama for her slowness.
It's like a dream: no matter how much I try to make my legs
move faster, I cannot, and the creatures ahead are slipping now
round this corner, now past some trees, now along this path.
We're soon away from the part of town I know best but I'm
used to strangeness by now. They trace the path by the river,
then stop at a carriage and I think I've lost them. But no: they
turn away. My ghost sneaks a look behind her to make sure
we're still following. It's intended then, this chase. The thought
chills me, but I continue after them just the same. I'll confront
them at the end, even if the end is what I am hunting down.

I ask for protection for my girls. *And deliver us from evil.*
These shape-shifters are conjured by magic but I won't give up
the chase if I'm to keep my girls safe. I'll deliver them from
evil: I will face these spirits down. But the day is darkening
quickly: I'll lose them in the November dusk. Or perhaps they
won't stop at all and my girls won't have the strength to go on.
But still we tramp over sodden fields and muddy bridges and
I carry Kathy on my back when she can't walk any further, and
tramp along more dirt tracks and over more fields. The landscape around us is bare of folk: the farming day is ended and
I realize they have taken us away from town for a purpose. I
think I hear pigs squealing in the distance but the hedgerows
are too high for me to see. I long for hills to give me a view,
but we are hemmed in now by great bushes and all I can hear
are Izzy's sighs and Kathy's gasps in my ear. We are alone in a

strange land, it seems to me now: I don't know this country's rhythms after all, for all the time I've lived here. This lush, thick, wet earth; these black hedgerows: babes in the wood, lured into danger, and I am mad indeed to be making such a journey.

Which is why I stop. They're still well ahead of us, flittering and flapping like giant birds, but I've taken my girls too far into this wet wilderness. And when we stop, they stop, too. I set Kathy down. 'Shh!' I say to them both. My breath mingles with the mist. 'But aren't you going to speak to them?' asks Izzy. The women stand ahead in profile, still talking. 'Why must we be quiet?' Suddenly, they turn into a gap in the hedgerow and disappear. 'Yes, yes,' I say, 'I will speak to them now.' We follow them to the same point and I see that the hedgerow gives way to a path, and that the path leads to a tiny church.

'Wait here with your sister,' I say to Izzy. 'Don't let go of her hand. And don't leave this spot.' She nods, frowning in the gloom, but I won't let her follow me. 'If anything alarms you, call out straightaway and I'll be with you at once. I will only be a moment.' And I dip down through the hedgerow and follow along the path to the church. My feet are damp and heavy now, my hems trail in the mud. The women ahead are visible again under a yellow autumn moon. I follow them round the side of the church to the cemetery behind. They stop by a grave, where they kneel down as if in prayer, and rest their heads against the gravestone.

My moment has come. I take a few more steps to hear their whispered words but I stumble on an overgrown rosebush, tangled across the path, and fall hard, crying out as the thorns stab my palm. When I struggle to my feet, I know even before I look that they have gone.

The chase is over. I've followed them as far as I'm meant to. There's nothing more for me to do but try to pick my way home somehow with my girls and make them forget this strange adventure. And yet, even though I've left them alone at the hedgerow, I don't fear for them any more. I walk along the path to the gravestone where the shape-shifters so recently sat. The stone is simple, with a short inscription: '*Mary Wollstonecraft, beloved wife and mother, 1759–1797.*'

I know Mary used to court the man she married at her mother's graveside. I know it was where they first spoke of their love for one another, and where they planned their future, running away together. It has meaning for her ghost, this place. But for me and mine? Mary's mother died giving birth to her: she thought she was alone in the world until she met Mary's father and fell in love. But why did my ghost wait here? I touch the damp headstone, but there's no answer.

My good girls wait patiently for me in the dark by the hedgerow. I return to them at last and we carry on further along the road, not back the way we came, and very soon a glow in the distance promises a village and the possibility, I hope, of shelter. 'Keep going, Kathy,' I say. 'Not long now.' But she stumbles and scrapes her knee and starts to cry. 'I can't walk any more. I want to go home!'

We're on the outer edges of the village now. 'Not much further, only a little more,' I say, but she refuses and nothing can budge her. 'I can't leave you here and we can't stay outside in the cold all night, please, Kathy. I can't carry you, you're too big now.' But Izzy is sitting down on the freezing ground and won't move, either. I'm close to tears: this is my fault, walking them so far. But we can't stay here or we will freeze to death. I look about, and there's a light at a good-sized house nearby. Children's voices come from it; a family lives there. 'Girls, do you see that light in the window? Do you think you can manage just to that house?'

They take some persuading but eventually get up and we limp, all three, in the direction of the dilapidated house. More childish screams, as if this is a mid-summer's day and not a cold night in November, and as we get closer, two pigs run squealing past us. 'I told you before, Edward!' a woman's voice rings out, loud but not coarse. They are a genteel family, for all

the dilapidation, I reassure myself, and we stumble up the rag-
gedy garden path. The front door is ajar, but I knock as loudly
as I can. Nobody comes; there is chaos inside. I knock again,
but I cannot be heard above the din. 'Is anyone at home?' I call
out and knock again. And then the door is opened, and my
surprise makes me step back, for whom do I see but my friend
John Conolly standing in front of me.

'Mrs Booth! What has happened? Is it David? Do you
need me?' he asks in a rush, as tiny, dirty faces appear around
his legs.

'Dr Conolly! I had no idea this was your home. I'm not
here on any errand for David – and he is well, thank you. But
the girls and I – we took a wrong turning. We were at market
earlier...'

'A wrong turning? All the way from Richmond?'

I look apologetic as he steps towards me, lifts my face to
the light from the door.

'You're not in any danger? You're not hurt?'

'I am well, really.'

I can see he doesn't believe me. He ushers me inside to sit
down, and children cluster round us. 'David must be worried
– it's too late to get any kind of message to him. You must stay
here with us tonight and I'll take you back tomorrow,' he says,
kindly. His house is shambolic but warm; Kathy has found
kittens under a chair and is playing with them, her scraped
knee forgotten already, and Izzy is examining a large doll with
a broken nose that one of Conolly's daughters has shown her.
He shouts above the din. 'My wife will find somewhere for
you, won't you, Harriet?' as a woman appears like magic by his
side.

'Is it always like this?' I ask, forgetting my manners. For
this, too, feels like a dream: the walk, the shape-shifters, the
grave, and now Conolly. I'm not sure any of us are real; did I
not say this was a strange land?

'Oh, I like them to obey their own natures,' he smiles and
pours me a drink. The liquid warms me and makes me drowsy.

'Rousseau, you know. "Childhood is the sleep of reason." There is plenty of time for them to be awake.'

The sleep of reason. And I realize how tired I am. 'It must be near midnight,' he says, taking my beaker and patting my hand. Where are my girls? I cannot see them but I'm not worried; childish noises in the distance relax me and I close my eyes.

'A blanket, Harriet, for Mrs Booth,' he says, and warm arms envelop me, pat me into the chair. 'Rest now: we will return you to David when you wake.'

And that is what I dream of, all the hours until morning.

7.

Holborn, November 1823

Two days after Isabella went missing, Alexander received a request from David Booth to come once more to Richmond. He hadn't thought to ask after her, having his hands full with Thomas, who was now showing signs of more extreme behaviour. Annie wouldn't go near him, too frightened he would hit her after he shouted and swore at her one afternoon, but she left food for him on trays outside his door. He'd heard objects smashing in the night when Thomas was pacing about, and more than once, the front door banging shut. When Alexander had got up to go after his brother, he found that nobody had seen him leave. He'd become an odd sort of spectre, whom nobody attended and nobody noticed, passing from one state into another, as if he were not more material than the wind. Alexander couldn't even be sure when Thomas had returned to the house: he'd only hear the locking of his bedroom door when he retired, or the fixing of a chair under the handle.

How was he to analyse a ghost? A man who was not just a shadow of his former self but who only ventured out at night and passed into the gloom unobserved? Thomas was an ever-elusive past who left only the stench of unwashed human flesh behind him to show he had once been there. Smells, sounds: nothing for Alexander to grasp, nothing for him to give substance to in case notes.

He couldn't admit defeat: not yet. Not Thomas as well as Isabella. She had since returned home, David Booth had written to tell him. She had spent the night nobody knew where, and his daughters were frightened and disturbed, he said. She had possibly put their lives in danger and this 'madness' couldn't go on. '*You must sign the request*,' he wrote. '*She must be put away as soon as possible.*' He asked for Alexander to attend them as soon as possible, but Alexander had been putting it off. Failure was chasing him and he couldn't shake it off. Only drink kept him from walking away and leaving it all behind.

That same mood of despair finally roused him from his chair the following day, though, dark and wet as it was. Another note from Booth urging his signature yet again both irritated and energized him: he would finish this matter at last. Then he'd pack his bags and return to Montrose: back to his career, his fiancée. Away from ugly dreams and the smell of failure. Away from Thomas, from Isabella, from them all. If he was meant to live out his life as an insignificant mind-doctor, growing fat with his sons and his wife and attending local dances with local dignitaries who were as insignificant as he was, then he'd have to settle for that. It was as good as he could hope to be.

I owe her nothing, he thought, as he hailed a carriage in the pouring rain and clambered inside, shaking his hat and his coat. Booth certainly picked the right day for putting away his wife; it was as miserable an action as the weather. But he'd make sure she was secured somewhere kind. Not Bethlem. There would be an upsetting scene, but her incarceration would cauterize his sense of failure. He was keen to hurt somebody, to pass on the pain.

His journey was halted many times; lashing rain churned up the streets into muddy byways that tipped and jolted the cab, almost upending it. He wasn't, then, in the best of moods when he stepped out at last and ran through the downpour to the familiar battered and chipped cottage door, pushing it open in his hurry to get out of the wet. But something was blocking it and when he shoved at it again, and called out, he heard a child's whimper in reply. 'Who is there?' he called out. 'Kathy? Is that you?' He caught sight of a tiny shoe, wedged in the doorway, and bent down to the ground. 'Little Kathy, it's me, Dr Balfour. Can you let me in? Are you left alone? Are you hurt?'

Another whimper greeted him but she did shift a little, enough for Alexander to twist his body through the gap. 'Where is your mama?' he asked her, as he made sure her tears weren't caused by any physical pain. She was too distressed to answer and he was about to lift her into his arms and carry her into the parlour when an animal cry erupted from the kitchen, accompanied by the crack of wood on stone.

The weak son of a weak man: his first instinct was the gather up the child – he wasn't so weak as to contemplate leaving her behind – and flee. He wanted no part of some intruder's violence. And he could have got away but then another howl, followed by a woman's scream, made him understand at last what was happening. No intruder made that noise.

He ran along the short hallway and wrenched open the kitchen door. Booth was facing him, his hair wild and face red, with a piece of rope fastened tight around his wife's neck. She was on her knees facing him, too, like a sacrifice, choking now with the pressure on her throat. Her husband was holding a broken chair in his other hand, raised high behind him, as if ready to strike her down with it. The strength of the insane was impossible for one sane man to defeat: Alexander knew that Booth, older and more infirm as he was, could easily throw him off in his present state.

'She has the Devil in her!' Booth roared, as Alexander held his hands up flat. 'I'll throttle the demon out of her! Don't try to stop me!' Isabella's fingers scrabbled uselessly at her neck before he yanked hard on the rope and her body slumped as she lost consciousness. Alexander knew he had to hurry, but this was slow work. 'Stay away or I will strike you!' Booth yelled as he stepped forward. Alexander could see the man was lost at that moment: spit flew from his lips and his grey hair was jagged and wild, as though he'd been hacking at it with a blunt knife. His eyes were blank of reason or sense.

'Let me deal with her,' Alexander said, his voice low and steady. 'I've come to cast out the demon. Let me be the one to do it.'

He shook his head, furiously. 'She is my wife! It's my duty, no one else's,' and he jerked the rope upwards again. Alexander raised his hands high, which distracted Booth for a moment and Isabella's eyelids fluttered open. She squeezed two fingers under the rope, easing the pressure on her neck, which bought Alexander just a little more time. He took another small step towards the man whose reason he had been admiring so recently. His doubt of Isabella might kill her, even as Booth's madness now permitted his theories, after all. But he had no time to think of this: there had been occasions in Alexander's life when he'd had to rely on instinct alone. He remembered Marie in that instant, though: he wouldn't be blamed for this.

'Put the chair down and let me cast out her demons.'

Booth's gaze alternated between Alexander and his wife, as if he couldn't decide which of them was the greater threat. 'You are David Booth,' Alexander spoke, quietly. 'David Booth: a man of reason. It is to your reason that I appeal. Hand her over to me.'

Booth raised the chair even higher above his head: Alexander steeled himself to rush at him if words proved to be of no use. Isabella's eyes had closed again: she was slipping away. For the longest seconds of Alexander's life, he stood motionless as though movement might trigger another murderous impulse in the man before him, before the blankness of Booth's eyes filled with a kind of pain he had rarely seen, and the chair clattered to the ground. Booth sank to his knees, his hand still clinging fast to the rope around Isabella's neck. At least she could breathe again: gasping and choking, she too collapsed on the floor. Alexander rushed to hold him fast, as he howled his misery and shame.

'What have I done? What have I done? Help me! God help me! I am a good man!' His shaking body made Alexander forget his own terror, and more than for any other human being perhaps, he felt pity for this brilliant man so lost to himself and weeping on the floor beside the wife he'd tried to destroy. And pity for himself: wasn't this man Alexander's own wicked compulsions of the last few years made real and murderous and mad? Why the mad terrified the sane so was easy to understand: they were merely themselves, in antithesis. As he held the sobbing man, tears started into his own eyes, and Alexander wept, too, for himself, for his brother, for all the damage and pain the human mind could inflict, and for the little he could do about it.

Some minutes passed before he judged it safe to release him and check on Isabella. He eased his arms from around Booth's chest and stood up. Isabella had crawled away and was sitting propped up against the wall, fumbling with the rope. Alexander helped her undo it. 'Kathy?' she croaked and he nodded, slipped out into the passageway to find the little girl still curled in a ball by the door, shivering and weeping. He carried her back into the kitchen and handed her to her mother.

Booth lay crouched on the floor in the foetal position, quiet now. Was goodness only the absence of evil? Had they only dialectical terms to think of it: sane and insane, powerful and powerless, good and evil, he wondered. This weeping man, his wife with the livid red gashes on her neck, the weeping child: simple oppositions didn't explain what had just taken place here. 'Don't be afraid,' Alexander said to Isabella, as he passed her some water and stroked Kathy's head. 'I won't let him hurt you again.' Her words came cracked and slow. 'I'm not afraid of him. But one day he will finish me. Or my girls.'

When she was ready, Isabella stood up and took Kathy with her, to fetch help. Alexander waited with Booth alone, ready to sign the papers he had been so ready to authorize for his wife. Booth didn't protest as he was eventually carried away; his reason had only partially returned and Alexander doubted he was fully aware of what was happening or where he was going. 'I'll visit him tomorrow and assess the extent of his delirium,' he told Isabella. 'If I judge him well enough to travel, I'll have him transferred to Montrose as soon as possible.'

If he'd told her that her husband would have to spend the rest of his life in Bethlem, Alexander doubted she'd have protested against it. So he was surprised and even shocked when she asked, 'But what about our plans? Can we still be together if he is there, too?' She was sitting in the parlour then, cradling Kathy on her knee and trying to tempt her with a little honey and bread. The dark, wet day had dampened into night: Izzy, mercifully, was at her grandfather's. Isabella couldn't eat, but every so often she would lick the spoon of honey; it would help her throat, he told her.

Alexander didn't want to argue with her just then. 'Let me attend to him over the next few days,' he said. 'Then we can decide what's best.' She looked to protest but Kathy stirred and distracted her. 'I doubted you, and I'm sorry for that,' he said, suddenly.

'Why did you doubt me?' she asked, puzzled. The wine they sipped was rough and cheap but it was all she had and he didn't want to leave her just yet, even though the taverns beckoned and he wanted to be alone, to think through the day's events and ponder what he should do next.

'I kept something from you,' he said at last, and told her about Booth's letter. 'I can see now: the kind of mania he suffers from that makes him lucid for periods, then behave the way he did today. I should have believed you but his brilliance dazzled me.'

'As it did me, once upon a time.' She shook her head then kissed Kathy's hair as the girl slept in her mother's arms. The parlour was warm and dim; Alexander felt sleepy, too, and wondered that the sight of this mother and child, saved from such recent violence, didn't touch him more than it did. Then

Isabella's face lit up strangely. 'You thought you had been making love to a mad woman, then? At least your theories are intact. You must be relieved about that,' she continued, in the same bright voice. The edge of hysteria: and who could blame her, he thought.

He slipped his arm about her shoulder: had any stranger glanced in on them, they might have taken them for the closest and most tender of families, a loving husband and father with his wife and child. 'I'm a man of science,' Alexander said. 'Forgive me if I'm occasionally less imaginative than I should be, less able to trust what I cannot see.'

She twisted out from under his arm. 'But you could see me,' she said. 'You saw all there was to see about me. It was your business to know me as a doctor and as a man. And yet you did not. You knew nothing, in spite of the hours I spent talking with you. You have learned nothing about me, have you?'

He couldn't answer her. He'd saved her life, what did it matter that he'd misjudged her for the briefest time? The demands of women – Marie, Philomena, Isabella – they exhausted him. 'You're tired: let me call on you tomorrow after I've visited David,' he sighed, his own tiredness plain. Isabella gazed into the dimness of the room as though he hadn't spoken.

'You'll really take him north?' she spoke flatly, finally.

'I won't decide yet,' Alexander said. 'I've not witnessed this kind of mania before but I know that usually such an episode is preceded by a build-up of strange actions and behaviours. Yesterday's incident seems to have come out of the blue. I saw him repeatedly and detected nothing to make me suspicious. I need to spend more time with him – that may not be possible here. I can't stay away so long from my employer…' But what about Thomas, now? Now that his theories could proceed after all, he had no more need of his brother. He sighed again and Isabella raised her hand to his cheek. It wasn't the conciliatory gesture he took it for, though.

'Why would you?' she asked in the same tone. Alexander didn't understand. 'You have spent, what? An hour or two at the most with him over the last four or five days. You think that is enough to see his "strange actions and behaviours", as you call them? You could have asked me about his behaviour at any time over the last few days, but you didn't. You haven't had any contact with me at all.'

Tears filled her eyes and gave him some relief: she was a lover pleading for more attention, merely. He knew how to deal with this. 'You know how busy I am, the pressures I face,' he said, and stayed her hand. 'But you're part of it all. You mustn't forget that. If occasionally it seems I don't pay enough attention to you, be assured, my dearest – I'm always mindful of you.'

'Perhaps I should inform Conolly.' Her normally pale cheeks flushed and she assumed a bold look. 'I'll send for him, get his opinion.'

'But he's against any kind of asylum. Why would you consult him?'

'Perhaps I'll still keep David at home. Let him be my patient: I'd have complete authority over him. Conolly did promise to help more.'

'After what he tried to do to you? He's not safe – you're doing this to spite me.' Alexander got up to go.

'Wait – don't leave me on cross words.' Isabella was thin enough for him to crush with one hand, or for a gust of wind to blow over. David Booth hadn't left her with much. 'I'm only anxious for escape from this, how it's to be managed...'

He removed her arm gently from his. 'We can't even begin to contemplate that now,' he said. 'I've too much to learn about your husband, if my case is to be made. I won't go back to Montrose without it – or without him.'

'But I can only look after David for so long. I need to know that the end is coming.' Harshness wasn't helping Alexander escape her any sooner so he softened, held her hand in his.

'Don't worry, Isabella. And please trust me. Let me see what can be arranged.'

That seemed to satisfy her for she let him leave and he hurried out of the cottage and into the lane. She was putting his work in danger: he couldn't allow Conolly to supersede him. Mind-doctoring was a competitive business, after all. *We all want greatness*, he reflected as he hailed a carriage from the street. Conolly, he knew, was no different.

8.

Richmond, November 1823

I watched them from my bedroom window the night they came to riot and throw us out. I think now my father must have known something was going to happen and been ready for them. There had been scuffles on the streets in Dundee over the jute. His was yet another unproductive factory. People we never thought about were losing work, families we didn't know were being thrown out of their homes. My father kept his worry to himself.

Until the night it hurled itself at our door, angry and calling for our blood. I was asleep in bed when I heard their shouts. I crept to the window and saw torch-lights jig about the garden as though it was carnival time, not a protest or a rout. Christy's feet shook the floorboards above, Robbie crashed through the hallway. Aggie's voice calling from somewhere downstairs. Margaret was newly married, and our mother dead: we had no thoughts beyond our own family. It was Aggie who came upstairs to hold our hands and tell us not to be afraid.

We gathered in my father's room and clustered by new brocade drapes delivered from London six months ago and made up in Dundee. There was nothing he could do, he shouted down from the window. It wasn't his fault, he told the mob standing in our garden. I thought of the trampled seedlings Christy had been tending, the cherry blossoms that looked like snowflakes in the torchlight. Markets had plunged all over the world, my father was saying. He had no ready money to pay people their wages but he would do what he could. The ringleader, I couldn't see, but I heard the disbelief and anger in his voice. What had my father kept back for himself, he wanted to know. How did he pay for the upkeep of his 'grand house'? When he said that, a cheer went up that shrivelled my belly. This was our home.

'Why shouldna we hauf the gran' hoose instead?' the foreman shouted. 'We're doin' the honest day's work and we're sufferin' for it.' More cheers, and the torches shook in the dark.

'Burn them oot!' one man shouted above the cheers. 'Tak whit's oors,' yelled another.

Christy's nails nipped the flesh of my hand. 'Don't go down to them,' she pleaded as my father pulled on his boots and his coat. 'They want to hurt you.'

'They think I'm talking down to them as it is,' he said. 'We need to look each other in the eye. It's the only way. Lock the door behind me and stay here, all of you.'

Robert wanted to go with him, but my father wouldn't let him. The front door slammed shut. From behind the curtains we watched our father step out of the dark to speak to the foreman. Light from the man's torch showed a hard face and fierce, but it was weary, too, and desperate. I could see the raggedness of his trousers in the torchlight, like stained, coarse paper compared to my father's thick, spotless ones; I saw the patches on his coat, without buttons or a collar, and too thin for this time of year. There were a few insults at my father's appearance but they stopped once he began talking to the foreman.

'They're hungry, an' they're feart,' Aggie whispered behind me. 'They want a hearin' that's aw. They'll no' harm him.' She was right: after some minutes of low discussion we couldn't make out, my father came back inside and the torches began to fade.

It was a warning, though, of what was to come: that we wouldn't have our home forever. That some people wanted what we had. And that one day soon we would have to give it to them.

* * *

That was the last time I felt my life was in danger. Now such a long time ago; a time before my husband almost succeeded in putting an end to me, as he's threatened to so many times. But I am far from feeling exhausted and wretched by it all as I should be. Or afraid. Mary's mother's gravestone is in the north of the city, nowhere near here. I couldn't have covered so many miles with my girls that day, and on foot. Yet we did. And what I saw that evening, what those beings showed me, was indeed her grave, not my imaginings.

Wasn't it?

That we'd really walked so far was confirmed as much by the stiffness in my legs and blisters on my feet, as it was by my girls' questions about our strange adventure, though. Yes, it was as real as we are.

Wasn't it?

A new sense of purpose and vigour dispel the haze and fill me instead. I touch my neck under the scarf, stroke the marks he made as if they signify the change in me. Something material, after all; Alexander would agree, he has no truck with ghosts. The soul and the imagination drove me on, he'd say. But is the immaterial really so powerful? If it is, then my will also has power. This purpose, this vigour: my will. That's what defeated him when he had the rope around my neck: my will. Not just Alexander's strength. I wouldn't leave my girls unprotected. I will never do that.

I spoon the porridge into their bowls this bright new wintry morning. Kathy seems to have forgotten what she saw; she says nothing and smiles at her sister, so I have to believe it. The cottage is peaceful again. 'What will we do today?' I ask them, try not to think what we will do without money until

Alexander can take us in. Alexander – could he have meant to take David with us to Montrose? Perhaps it will be possible… but my head is too full with the last few days. 'Shall we bake cakes?' But there is a knock at the door and I hear Conolly's voice. 'Mrs Booth!' I had forgotten I'd written when Alexander left last night.

'I am here, in the kitchen,' I call back as merrily as I can.

The shock on his face reminds me that I must carry more scars of the attack than I think. 'I'll never forgive myself…' he begins, after my girls let go of him and I shoo them upstairs with a biscuit each. 'He was much more dangerous than I ever thought.'

I shake my head, then wince as my neck pulls, and finger the burns. 'It doesn't hurt me now, really. Dr Balfour wants to take him north, but I think a move might disturb him more…?' I can't keep the hopeful tone out of my voice.

'Indeed, indeed,' Conolly frowns. 'Yes, he should stay here in London. You will remain nearby?'

Tears fill my eyes and he rushes forward, pulls a kerchief from his coat pocket. I want to laugh – of course it is covered with stains, just like the man himself, but I accept it just the same.

'I have to tell someone what I've done, what I need to do…' I begin, but we are interrupted by another knocking at the door, this more frantic than the last. And Alexander's voice is calling out, but not for me.

'Conolly, thank God you're here,' and he appears before us in the kitchen, red-faced and panting, his clothes askew and his coat flapping open so that my heart lurches for him, even though he barely gives me a glance. 'It's Thomas – he's gone missing. They told me at home that you were here…' Only now does he stop and stare at me as though I shouldn't be here.

'Who is Thomas?' I ask.

'My brother… Mrs Booth. He's been staying with me. He is… troubled in his mind.'

First my husband and now his brother. Do mind-doctors

attract all the mentally confused, I wonder. I'm about to ask why he's never mentioned this brother to me, but Conolly interrupts. He seems to know all about him, and I wonder how that can be possible, wonder what other things Alexander has been keeping from me.

'Do you have any idea where he might have gone?' Conolly asks, rising up and buttoning his coat. 'When did he go missing?'

'He was awake last night, I heard him pacing in his room. But I fell asleep... Annie, the housekeeper, left food for him this morning but he was gone, I have no idea where. So some time between one in the morning and six.'

'Five hours in this city...' Conolly shakes his head. Alexander slumps against the kitchen table. 'Plenty of time for him to get lost, or find a good place to hide. We have to get moving.'

'Let me come,' I say. 'Let me help.'

'You don't even know what he looks like.' Alexander frowns at me – why would he refuse my help like this?

'He's your brother, isn't he? Can he be so unlike you in appearance?'

I catch an odd look on Conolly's face as I address him; we're betraying our familiarity with one another just as he and Alexander did. Now *he* will be wondering what Alexander has not told him. 'You need all the bodies you can get. I am another pair of eyes,' I continue, quietly, and at this, Conolly agrees. 'My neighbour will look after the girls, let me hurry and ask her.'

Within a few minutes, the three of us are in the lane and pondering the best direction to take. It's still freezing but bright. 'If he has been out all night in these temperatures,' Alexander begins but Conolly hushes him.

'Is there a special place he liked to go?' I ask. 'When you were younger perhaps? A place where he would feel safe?' Alexander has taught me well; or perhaps I understand the troubled mind of a brother.

'He liked the river,' Alexander shrugs.

'Then let's begin there,' Conolly says.

'He'd only be there for one reason.'

'Let us not assume the worst yet. We cannot know his mind. We cannot predict his actions. Let us simply follow him, if we can.'

Conolly is reassuring in his authority but I know how authority can fail us: I have the marks to prove it. We make our way along the road quickly and watchfully; Alexander won't hail a carriage, too wary of missing his brother, even though this street is far from his home and would mean nothing to him. He and Conolly talk a little but I say nothing, run when I have to keep up with them, try and picture a brother of Alexander's, not in his right mind and alone. They begin to argue.

'I should never have taken him in,' Alexander is saying. 'That place was terrible but at least he was safe.'

'He couldn't be kept in like a prisoner,' Conolly's calm voice has an edge to it.

'You made her keep her husband at home and look what he did to her. You made me keep my brother at home and now look what has happened! Your ways are disastrous.'

'Stay calm, Alexander. We'll not find Thomas this way,' I say, but he ignores me.

'You think that home is the best place but home is where the trouble lies. I asked you to help me save my brother – I have lost him for good!'

Conolly says nothing but marches on. We've been walking for many hours now and are close to the part of the river now they used to haunt as boys, these troubled Balfour men, but it has changed since then, is not the playground it once was. The sun has long gone and the noise of the city streets is behind us. We're entering a part of the city I scarcely know; a part of the city where the poor and the friendless and the mad come to die. It is sparse and cold yet full of shadows and as we duck down under the bridge, I shiver, pull my thick shawl closer.

'We shouldn't have let you come with us,' Alexander mutters, as yet another roughly dressed man steps out of the evening gloom to jostle me and curse. He takes me by the arm to steady me. 'You're not strong enough for this. You'll hold us up,' but that last accusation is almost apologetic. I think I see tears in his eyes, and my heart swells.

'I've been through worse than this place can throw at me,' I reply, hoarsely. We hurry to keep up with Conolly's strides. 'I won't go home until we've found him.'

But now the river is busier where traders are packing up, and it's almost impossible to single out an individual soul who doesn't want to be found. 'Let us stop for a moment,' Conolly turns to us, panting and dishevelled. 'I know somewhere near here…' and he directs us both back from the riverbank and towards a tavern. 'Pull your shawl over your head,' he instructs me. 'And don't speak to anyone.'

But the brew we sip warms our bellies only for moments before a cry goes up a few hundred yards away. The body of a man has been found, someone shouts, and Alexander closes his eyes. 'Thomas,' he murmurs, and we know it is him.

9.

Holborn, November 1823

If his brother's death did anything for Alexander, then it made up his mind for him. Conolly and his 'home' theories were banished forever. Isabella, whom he'd doubted so long and come so close to rejecting, was reinstated in his affections and in his theories. No – more than reinstated. She occupied a place she had never occupied before. She had helped him find Thomas; she had taken him to her home when the shock of it brought him to his knees; she had nursed him and cared for him there through the night when he thought he'd lose his own mind. She had written to Browne to explain his further absence; she had taken care of everything.

He would write to Philomena and break off the engagement as soon as he could – he and Isabella would return to Montrose, and they would take David there, to be his patient. His presence would not prevent them from being together, he told her, and so it would be. He would look into the legal position, how they could bring their marriage to an end. He didn't care about scandal, or social position. All that mattered was that she, the most loyal of all the women he'd ever known, stayed by his side for the rest of his life.

It was three days since they'd found Thomas, drowned by the banks of the Thames. Three days of the worst regrets and the darkest misery. But now, on this fourth day, he felt different. He couldn't stay mourning inside forever, he told Annie, as he prepared to go out that morning. 'I have patients to see,' he said. He hadn't forgotten David Booth. He hadn't forgotten his work. It would save him as much as anything else. He pulled on his gloves, regarded his thin frame in the glass. The events of the last few days had told on him, if the dark circles under his eyes were anything to go by. But he was stronger now. He was ready.

* * *

Where Booth was housed was not one of the worst institutions, certainly not so bad as Bethlem. Alexander barely noticed the reek of urine in his nostrils when he stepped inside the building. He was shown only a grudging deference on his way to Booth's rooms but that didn't bother him, either.

Although Booth knew enough to use the chamberpot provided for him, it looked remarkably clean, and Alexander had his suspicions about the dark patch in the straw-covered corner of the floor, which pricked that womanly squeamishness in him once more. The mattress was stained and the walls hadn't been washed for some time. The request Alexander had made when Booth was first admitted for clean bed linen had clearly been ignored. Still, he could not be dismayed. Booth wouldn't be here long. He'd install him in a room with a view to the sea, and one close to his own, once Booth was at Montrose. Away from other patients. Keep him separate, analyse his mind in complete isolation. He had Isabella's testimony and she would give him her journal, too, she had promised. Now he would examine and isolate the source of her infection. Booth would be treated like a gentleman, he and Alexander would talk, he would confide in him. A special diet, of course, and only certain books. He would draw up an exercise plan, too.

The quickening of his breath, the tingling in his fingers, at his closeness to it: did he feel pity for Booth, trapped in this dismal room? Rescue wasn't Alexander's intention, not yet. And at least Booth was, at this moment, relatively safe: he examined him carefully, asked to see his hands, tapped his back gently, checked his hair and scalp, saw no signs of physical harm. They knew not to abuse him, although he'd refused food and they'd had to force some into him through a tube pushed down his throat. But Alexander's touch frightened Booth, who began to shake as he felt for his heartbeat. 'I have a good place for you,' Alexander reassured him. 'Away from here. It will not be long.'

Booth looked at him, uncomprehending. 'A continuous noise – my ear – no sleep,' he gasped. 'Do – what they will.'

His grey hair was damp, which made him look even older. The lines on his face had deepened in only a few days, it seemed, and he twitched and scratched at himself so severely that in a short time he'd begun to draw blood. His inhuman strength on the day of his attack on Isabella had deflated, leaving him withered and small, crouching on the end of his narrow bed. Alexander brought the single chair closer to him, pulled the rough blanket around his shoulders.

'I will prescribe a little opium to ease it. I have forbidden the use of any purges, so you needn't be afraid of those,' he added, gently. 'I'm doing my best to hurry your release from this place.' Still, Booth showed no interest in that possibility. 'Would you be more comfortable if you came north with me, to Montrose?' Alexander asked, thinking he might recall the name from their discussions, but again Booth said nothing. He decided to risk mentioning Isabella. Booth looked about him, as though she were responsible for the grey hangings, the dim light. Then he gazed down at his wrists, as though she had tied them herself and so made a prisoner of him.

'She only wishes you to be better,' Alexander said. 'I'm sure she can forgive you, in time.'

'She is a whore,' he shrugged, suddenly, as if it were a matter of fact. He took a deep breath. 'I have tried to save her, I even sent friends to help her. Good friends, wise men who believe in God, but it was no use. She wouldn't listen to them. She cannot be saved.'

Alexander was pleased that he was at least lucid enough now to speak in full sentences. 'She is your wife,' he said, eagerly. 'She loves you.'

'She is not my wife. She deprived me of my real wife,' Booth raised his voice, lifted his chin. Alexander feared the mania that was coming.

'Your real wife?' he said.

'Because of *her*, I lost Margaret. I lost my wife. Isabella tricked me into marrying her. And foisted her bastard children upon me.' He sighed, a thick, guttural explosion of acceptance of another's wrongdoing.

Alexander shook his head. 'No, no – you must know how she has cared for you since your marriage nine years ago,' he said. Booth remained placid yet, but Alexander was waiting for the change. 'Can you remember that day? Can you remember how you felt when you first glimpsed her on your wedding day?' Blinking like a man emerging from a dark tunnel into the light of day, Booth looked pityingly at Alexander and said, 'I courted her for many months.'

'She wouldn't have you at first, then?' Alexander relaxed. So he had broken through at last: reminding him of his past good behaviour, his past good life, just as moral management advocated. If only they had cleaned him up and dressed him smartly, if only his room was fresh and bright and airy, if only all things of refinement were nearby to bring his mind back from savagery and madness, they could maintain the illusion that they were simply two gentlemen indulging in private conversation on equal terms, he thought.

'Oh no,' said Booth, and this time he smiled. The vein in his temple stood up: Alexander had an urge to puncture it. 'I saw very quickly how she liked me, though, from the beginning.'

'That must have pleased you. You saw her love for you from the beginning. You see how you could always be sure of her.'

'Yes. But her mother had been very ill. Her family needed her. Eldest daughters are often the most needed, is that not so?'

'No,' Alexander said, gently and reached for his arm. 'Not Margaret. I mean Isabella, her sister. After Margaret died. Isabella loved you from the beginning. You remember?'

His breakthrough was nothing of the kind. Booth shook off his arm and shouted, hoarsely, 'She is a whore! There was no wedding day, we exchanged no vows! They would not let us: it was forbidden. She stole my wife away, was placed in my life by the Devil.'

He began shaking again and Alexander gripped his shoulders. 'She is Margaret's sister, and your lawful wife,' he insisted, quietly.

'Never! I am married to Margaret!'

Alexander could draw no other word of sense from him for the rest of his visit. He took as many notes as he could and promised to return in the morning with fresh food and bedding. The superintendent had too many charges to make Booth a special case, but he passed him some coins for extra water, to let him wash himself. The source of his madness was not in his epilepsy, of course, or in any childhood experience, but in his relationship with Isabella. Guilt over marrying his dead wife's sister had driven him mad. Their marriage was poisoned from the moment it began. The question was, could it be mended? Could he be cured?

Alexander could see now, the book he was to write. He left, not only thankful to be out in the open air, but inspired by his own genius. He had Isabella, and he had the case that would make his name. He found that he was shaking.

10.

Richmond, November 1823

I forget the letter until the kitchen is tidy. A break in the rain lets my girls out into the garden at last, and even though they will return covered in mud, I'm happy to let them go. So happy, with all the tragedy that has befallen us the last few days. But the ways ahead are clearer now, Alexander says. And yes, we will take David north with us, but we will be together, he has promised me, and I believe him. We are rushing: the day after tomorrow we will be gone, the four of us travelling north together, with David to follow.

Euphemia has managed to save some paper, after all, and even remembered the address I gave her. I settle down with my cup of tea, let my hair uncoil at the back of my neck and wind it over my scars. I'm pleased to read that she's well, that she continues with her writing, that she misses me and wonders when I'll be back. Her husband has given no sign of being ready to have her home yet and I frown at this part. But she's happy to wait, she says, for his goodness and kindness to forgive her. 'You are too good, Euphemia,' I mutter, as I turn the page:

> *And I do not want to miss the exciting events to come,*
> *Mrs Booth. We are to have a dance, here at the hospital! It*

is to mark a special occasion that we are forbidden to discuss,
but I cannot keep a secret from you. It seems that our direc-
tor, Dr Balfour, is just engaged to be married, to a very eli-
gible young lady from the town, a Miss Philomena Stewart.
I do not know of her, but the matron says that she is a very
pretty lady, and they are to be married in the spring. It was
announced at our morning assembly by the matron, who has
also ordered materials for us all to make our own dresses for
the celebrations. You will perhaps come back for the event?
I would not care to celebrate it without you, Mrs Booth, as
you were so kind to me.

Forgiveness: a slight thing, but elusive. Easily said: I forgive you.

It's not yet noon, but I've made up my mind. The girls are
still in the garden: a bright winter day now of brown and green,
but they're too young for romance. Will my girls see ghosts
one day, too? It's unlikely: they prefer the world of stones and
snails. 'Don't put it on my hand!' Izzy squeals. 'It feels horrible.'
Kathy mutters, 'I didn't mean to, I thought it was a stone,' and
inspects the underside of it carefully. When I look in my basket later, I'll find a small tiny snail tucked inside its shell, lying
beside the fruit. A gift: or a reminder of how easily one thing
is taken for another.

'You can take your dolls with you,' I say when I wrap them
up as Kathy waves her bundle of rags at me. 'But I don't like
Mrs Lowrie,' she protests. 'She smells funny.'

'Mrs Lowrie is very good to us,' I say, as we proceed along
the path, 'So please don't say things like that about her. It's not
kind.' My will is too strong even for my girls: even though she
welcomes my girls with a blast of the vinegar and liniment she
uses to treat her gout, I will force her goodness on them. 'I'll
be back before nightfall,' I say and thank her with some of the
apple pie I've baked this morning.

'They're good bairns,' she says, as I lay it on her kitchen
table. Her home is even smaller than mine; her red face and

Fife accent will never be softened by this town, for all the years she's spent here. How many of us are far from our native lands, calling on favours from neighbours instead of from our families? My resolve strengthens.

I kiss my sulky girls goodbye, take a deep breath and head down the bare path into the lane, taking care not to slip. I want to be quicker to wake up and stretch my stiff muscles, but the wet path is slimy underfoot and soon my wet skirts cling to my ankles. The road to market changes, becomes unfamiliar but I'm not afraid, not when I'm chasing after something. Clean clothes are neatly folded in my basket under the fresh bread, cheese and pears. A little money is in my pocket to save walking later. God may not be beside me but something good is accompanying me all the same, and I think of good women who have made this journey before me. Perhaps their ghosts keep me company. They're no less immaterial than a single God by my side.

I have to ask directions three times on my way and even then I still get lost, so it's late afternoon by the time I reach the front door. It's not the fearsome, bolted barrier I expect but more homely, as is the building itself. It could be a home, I think, then I enter and there's nothing homely here. The man who attends to guests like me is neither warm nor kind but he is efficient and once he's recorded my name and address, and established my relationship to the patient, he agrees to take me to him. An animal smell permeates the dim corridors where benches sit on straw unused, for the only poor souls I pass choose to huddle on the floor instead. I hear unearthly sounds, too, and am reminded, by the contrast, of Montrose's quiet industry. Doors slam and keys rattle as we proceed, echoing through the corridors. My sodden hems drag straw in their wake; damp seeps through my winter coat. To be confined in such a place! This is punishment, not care, and for a moment I doubt myself and wonder if Montrose is better after all, and if Alexander is right and I am wrong. If I keep him to myself, I am being selfish; if I let him go, I am being selfish, too.

At last we stop outside a plain wooden door with a grill at eye level and a large lock. Again, I think of Montrose. The key turns easily and the door swings open to a darkened room with a bed, a chair and a small window, up high. My guide lights a candle to let me see him better – my husband, curled in a faraway corner on the floor. His clothes are unsoiled and he doesn't look unhappy: he's fast asleep, strangely peaceful, curled up as he is. I approach slowly. The bed is as hard as the floor: I can see why he would prefer it and for a moment I almost smile.

'Mr Booth! Your wife is here for you.' The spell is broken and David opens his eyes. I'm sorry to do this to him. *When I wak'd I cried to dream again* but he's no Caliban, whatever he's done. 'David,' I whisper. 'Do you know me?' His face has aged in only a few days and white bristles on his chin and throat give his skin a vulnerable fuzz. He looks pleasantly confused, as though he has to pick between joys, and the confusion seems to suit him here. Then a smile disrupts his features.

'Margaret! Is it really you?'

The right answer is not always the wisest; the wrong answer not always the most foolish. Our moral choices are less clear than the church elders taught us, once.

'Yes,' I say, taking his hand. 'Yes, it's me. I've come to take you home.' His eyes water – from relief or just waking, I can't tell. 'My dearest husband,' I whisper, and take up his loose, too-light hand. 'Let Margaret take you home.'

* * *

I spied on them, once. It was their first visit after their honeymoon. Margaret gave nothing away: she was disappointingly the same as she had been before. No longer a sister but a wife, she still gave us orders about dinner and hangings and how we spent our days, and my father listened to her as closely as he had before, too. I told myself I was bored with talk of Florentine hills and painted villas, and went to the kitchen to see Aggie and Mona. But they didn't need me either, with so much to do for our guests. 'It's just Margaret,' I said, sulkily.

'Wait till it's yer turn, then ye'll see!' Aggie clicked her tongue as I got in her way, tipping up the pot of bramble jam. I had to leave then, and so I wandered down to my scary little brook, whispered to it as it gossiped back.

They were upstairs in Margaret's room: I saw them standing at the window. Margaret was pointing away from the garden, towards another, larger house in the distance. For some reason, David wouldn't follow her gaze and she pointed again, pulled at his arm, urging him to look. But he shook his head. Was it a house she wanted him to buy for her? She must have known he didn't have the funds. Was he disappointed with her material concerns? Has she only married him for a house of her own? I made up their dialogue in my head as I watched my sister wipe her eyes, then nod, and close the drapes. When I returned to the house, they were sitting in the same positions in the drawing room, as though they had never left it, and I could not ask them.

* * *

The hour is late evening and David is sleeping upstairs, as are my girls. They were excited to see him; can Kathy have forgotten it all so soon, I wonder. They showed only wariness of disturbing him, of hurting him as they helped me get him to his bed. My girls, so careful and so strong. He won't make them mad: we will make him well and keep him here with us. Our patient, not theirs; and not Alexander's. I'm expecting a knock on the door from him soon. He'll be angry to find David gone, and not to the destination he had in mind.

I sip my wine slowly. I have the usual list of dietary needs, times of exercise, play and reading in front of me. They didn't help me much before, but I have new weapons this time. I'm not who he thinks I am, and only now do I see how that will help me. I am Margaret, not Isabella. Isabella went visiting a phantom grave and she never came back.

11.

Holborn, November 1823

Alexander couldn't fathom at first what had happened to her since he last saw her. She was hostile as soon as she opened the door to him, as though he repulsed her. Everything about her was different: her pose, her way of talking to him, her way of looking at him. Where he expected obedience he got defiance; in place of adoration, only scepticism. Why? Was it her husband's brutality? He thought that after what Booth had tried to do, she would have turned to him with even more eagerness: that was what he expected when she opened the door to him. Not this sulkiness, not this quiet.

He had prepared everything so well. He'd had his trunks packed and a carriage ordered for the next day. A speedy departure would be best for them all. He'd slept little the night before, anticipating too many complications, but exhaustion had given him an edge.

The change in Isabella's manner was matched by the change in her appearance: she was very pale and thinner than ever. Her already small breasts had finally disappeared to nothing beneath her bodice, and the sleeves of her dress flapped at her wrists. Alexander decided to be gentle at first, until he knew what the matter was. 'We've put you through a great deal, David and I,' he said and kissed her on the cheek, even as she pulled away. He frowned at that. What games was she playing now? 'It makes me ill when I think of losing you,' he continued nevertheless, and put his arms around her tiny frame, so easily crushable.

He felt her weaken against him: this was the moment. He pushed her gently away and took something out of his coat pocket: a ring that belonged to a wealthy patient at Montrose. He rarely stooped to steal but the woman would never recover her sanity enough to ask for it, and even if she did, Alexander would blame the missing jewellery on her deluded state. 'It was my grandmother's.' His voice was pained, full of truth. 'Please keep it and think of me. My gift to you. Until we can be together properly.'

He had a second object for her, but that could wait. Isabella held up her hand. He thought he could see through it to the wall behind her, so transparent was her skin. 'Answer me something,' she said. 'That's all I want.'

'Anything,' he said. He suspected something like a challenge, and he was right.

'Do you love me?' she said, predictably enough, and so he answered like with like. Of course he loved her, he told her. He loved her as he had loved no other woman. His love was eternal, steadfast and true. And he meant it, however often he had said it before. Esme Fleming. Marie. Philomena Stewart. She stopped him with a kiss and he pushed the ring onto her finger. It was far too large. 'Keep it on a chain close to your heart,' he whispered. It was time: he put his hand in his pocket again, ready to take out the document that would signify in writing that she had handed her husband over to his care.

But she had a document of her own. She smoothed it out over the little parlour table. Alexander shrugged. 'What is that?'

'Read it.'

He didn't bother much with the first sheet: a letter from Euphemia. He couldn't understand at first why some young woman's gossip would interest him and then he realized it all. His engagement had been announced without his permission, and the date of his wedding given as a few months' hence.

Exposure was something Alexander might have sought from his patients but not of his own affairs. He knew what the wrong kind of exposure meant. 'It's talk, that's all. You women are all the same,' he said, impatiently, playing for time. 'You don't respect a man's privacy, his right to order his own affairs.' Women talked, and he used that talk for his work. But they were never supposed to talk about him.

'It would appear you are engaged to be married.' Isabella stated it, brittle yet needy at the same time, pleading as much as accusing. 'It will be a strange sort of life for us together, if you are married to someone else.'

'It's a misunderstanding, she's deluded in her affection for me...'

'Oh, is she a patient, perhaps? Like Euphemia?'

'I don't know what that little bitch has been telling you but nothing happened between us.'

'But you can't deny this engagement – it's been announced!'

He was caught and he knew it. It was disappearing in front of him: David, her journal, his book, their life together. Dear God, he thought, she'd be a misery in a few years' time for this; a bitter, cruel woman who deserved nothing from him. *A lucky escape.* 'It's not as it seems,' he began one last attempt, but her fist struck his cheek.

He caught her wrists, held her easily and she spat in his face. 'Who do you think you are?' he shouted. 'How dare you interfere in the work of genius?' She struggled to free her wrists but he pulled her down, forced her into the chair. 'Do you really believe I could want you? An over-educated bluestocking, always thinking of herself and without a penny to her name? Who would disgrace me with divorce? You thought I wanted that?'

Her eyes were huge and full, her body a sickening sack of bones and skin with chattering teeth and dirty hair. How could he ever have thought he loved her? He let go of her wrists. 'You really mean very little to me, beyond my work, and that will be done with or without you or your journal.' He ripped the letter into pieces and threw them at her. 'Some confetti for you. I hope your dreams were better than the reality.' She was weeping, repulsing him even more with her snivelling and gulping, her clutching at her chest. 'Do not contact me,' he said, quietly. 'Do not write.'

He left the cottage with her deranged, womanish pleadings in his ear. There was nothing to keep him here, not in this cottage, not in this city, not even at Montrose. The Continent was where he needed to be. Coming back was a mistake: all of it had been a huge mistake. But his work could continue, at least: Isabella had given him enough to carry on with his 'sympathy' theories – he would find another example of married influence, in Leiden perhaps, or at Groningen. He could still picture the books he would write, but this time his work would be different from what he had sought in Gheel. Not Crichton; not childhood. Sympathy and madness, instead. At least she had given him that much.

Did he regret his last words to her, now his heart had calmed at last, as he sat in the carriage all the way back to Holborn? No, he decided. Thomas was gone; Isabella was faithless; *science travelled alone*. This way was better; their parting was for the best. He imagined the softer, kinder words he would use when he wrote to Philomena Stewart, ending their engagement, and smiled at the thought of a third jilting. Well, he could hardly help that, could he?

He leaned back to picture his next appointment. He would blaze a new trail abroad, become the greatest of the mind-doctors. He would be new-fashioned yet again, just as he had thought himself at Montrose. *A different creature, indeed*. His breathing eased, restored his sense of self. He *was* his work, after all. No woman would ever change that.

His trunks were still packed and waiting for him. He only required a change of direction. South, not north. Alexander cheered at the prospect and nodded to himself in the dark of the carriage ride home. His future was assured: he could be confident of what he was, and what he would become. That he would be remembered.

12.

Richmond, November 1823

The right thing can also be the foolish thing. My reading hasn't made me clever, not with David nor with Alexander. I'll not consult another book or debate moral choices again. I'll keep silent, but that doesn't mean I'm impotent.

David calls, 'Margaret! Where are you?' and my girls smile at each other again as we sit in the kitchen: it's a game.

'I'll only be a moment,' I call back, and begin to prepare his tray.

'If Papa can call you Margaret, why can't we?' Izzy asks, and I trust her innocence, though Kathy is giggling.

'It's my middle name, I told you. Papa has decided he likes it better but it's only for him, not you.' *Forgive me for my lies; forgive me for taking you away from him.*

'I don't understand,' she persists. 'He never called you Margaret before.' I make her hand me the salt dish: David likes his porridge salty.

'Why can't we call you Margaret, too?' asks Kathy.

'It's only for Papa: now that's enough on the subject.'

'He thinks you're somebody else,' Izzy says and my heart sinks when Kathy pipes up, 'I want a new name! I want to be Jane!'

'Eliza!' shouts Izzy, and they argue over which names they prefer as I slip away upstairs to David with his breakfast.

'My dear wife,' he pulls me to him and kisses me on the cheek. 'I know I never thank you enough for all you do.' I sit on the bed beside him. 'But I want you to know how much I love you for it. How much I have always loved you.'

I had two loves; David has two loves. The power of the sane over the insane. A word from me and David will never enjoy the light of day, or the laughter of his girls. I can choose to be benevolent: it's only by my goodness that my husband lives here.

I wonder about destiny, and how to manage it. It would help, in years to come, if Christy is close at hand after all, I think. I wouldn't have David's upsets to deal with alone, then. And her nieces will grow up beside her.

Does that picture help me? When I remember my last meeting with Alexander, all those weeks ago? When he knocked and I opened the door, I couldn't see properly. He had a gift for me, he said: a ring, and it was very like one I'd seen before but I still can't recall where from. Then I placed the letter in front of him and made him read.

'It's not as it seems,' he said. 'I don't love her. I met her before I met you. I'll give her up, I'll walk away. She trapped me.' He scrabbled for more and I stood back as he got down on his knees. 'Forgive me – I couldn't tell you. I knew how it would look. But I love you, Isabella. We can still be together. Let me have David...'

That was what he wanted all along, of course. Not me: never me. He begged and pleaded, squeezed out tears. My dear boy, his dark red curls and pale eyes: how easy to give in and comfort him, believe his words. But I stayed strong for my girls. 'David is dangerous,' he carried on, couldn't stop. 'You can't manage him alone. What about my work – *our* work. You are a part of it. I need you – your words, at least let me have your journal, if you can't bear to be with me yourself...'

But I won't be alone, I told him. I have my girls. And I've burned my journal: no good can come from anything I've written, I said. My box had held my 'self' for so long, but I don't need to lock it away any more. I can *be* my 'self', perhaps for the very first time. And I took him by the arm and showed him, protesting, into the hallway. He said he didn't understand how I could be so cold to him, and I knew I couldn't tell him what I'd pictured all that time since reading Euphemia's letter. That one day, when we settle north and I pass through a certain town and catch sight of a certain stylish and respectable married couple walking arm-in-arm, their children at their feet, he a famous mind-doctor and she his admiring wife, I won't turn away from the sight, however much it pains me.

I couldn't tell him that my girls will help me rule here until that day. And that before it comes, I'll look up from tending my kitchen garden and squint in the sun to see my husband standing there beside me, a cup of water in his hand that he has brought out just for me, and hear the words, 'For you, Bella.'

I couldn't tell him that I know I am a gaoler as much as a protector. That I know protection will not always be enough and that the demon will visit David once again, that I will become his gaoler once again, too, and so it will go on until the madness wears him out and we travel north to be by my own kin for the last time.

I couldn't tell him that I am strong enough for all of it now. That I am Isabella Baxter Booth and I know myself better than any man can know me.

I couldn't tell him this, and so I opened the door.

Author's Note

Although Isabella Baxter Booth, her family and Mary Shelley are real people, Alexander Balfour is a figment of my imagination. Where possible, I have kept the dates of the lives of the former as close to historical fact as possible, but with minor characters and references I have taken a few liberties.

In 1875, a 'Dr Bulckens' was in charge at Gheel. I have changed his name slightly and reinvented him for Alexander Balfour's stay in 1823.

George Combe did not publish on phrenology until 1824, although he had founded the Phrenological Society in 1820.

John Conolly graduated from Edinburgh University in 1821, but did not come to reside in London until 1828.

William A.F. Browne was the director of the Montrose Royal Lunatic Asylum from 1834–38. His book *What Asylums Were, Are and Ought to Be* was published in 1837.

The Society for the Diffusion of Useful Knowledge, for which both David Booth and John Conolly wrote, was not founded until 1826.

Many biographies and historical works provided me with essential information, but I'm particularly indebted to Miranda Seymour's *Mary Shelley*; *The Selected Letters of Mary Wollstonecraft Shelley*, edited by Betty T. Bennett; Tom Devine's *The Scottish Nation 1700–2000*; and Maurice McCrae's *Physicians and Society: A History of the Royal College of Physicians of Edinburgh*.

Acknowledgements

I first began working on this book in 2006. It's been a long journey, and I'd like to thank Emma Tennant for the wonderful reference she gave me that helped me win a substantial award from Creative Scotland way back at the beginning. Those who have read over manuscripts in their various stages since then: I'd like to thank Ben Mason, Dexter Petley, Elisabeth Mahoney, J. David Simons and Moira McPartlin. Those who gave advice, made recommendations or had discussions with me about ideas: I'd like to thank Nick Brooks, Andrew John Hull, Russel D. McLean, Victoria Finnigan, Geert Lernout and Helen Fitzgerald. Those who helped bring this book to the public: I'd like to thank Kevin Pocklington, Sara Hunt and Craig Hillsley. And finally, to my mentor, advisor, sometime editor, bank manager and Mum, Irene McDowell, I'd like to dedicate this book, as it really wouldn't be here without her constant support and encouragement over the years.

Lesley McDowell is a literary critic for *The Independent on Sunday*, *The Herald*, and *The Scotsman*. Her first novel was *The Picnic* (2007). Her second book, *Between the Sheets: The Literary Liaisons of Nine 20th-Century Women Writers*, was shortlisted for the non-fiction prize in the 2011 Scottish Book Awards.

Bob McDevitt